Praise for the novels of Heather Gudenkauf

"Fully realized, wholly absorbing and almost painfully suspenseful… The journey is mesmerizing."
—*New York Times*

"Intelligent, thought-provoking… If there's such a thing as a 'thoughtful thriller,' this is it."
—**Sandra Brown, #1 *New York Times* bestselling author of *Out of Nowhere***

"Heather Gudenkauf is a master of suspense."
—**Liv Constantine, bestselling author of *The Last Mrs. Parrish***

"Heather Gudenkauf proves herself the master of the smart, suspenseful small-town thriller."
—**Gilly Macmillan, *New York Times* bestselling author of *What She Knew***

"*The Overnight Guest* is not only compelling, it's addictive."
—**Samantha Downing, bestselling author of *My Lovely Wife***

"Masterful and absolutely addicting… Tense, taut, and terrifying."
—***Kirkus Reviews***

"A tale so chillingly real, it could have come from the latest headlines."
—***Publishers Weekly*, starred review**

Also by Heather Gudenkauf

EVERY ONE IS WATCHING

HEATHER GUDENKAUF

PARK
ROW
BOOKS

PARK
ROW
BOOKS™

Recycling programs
for this product may
not exist in your area.

ISBN-13: 978-0-7783-1079-2

Everyone Is Watching

Park Row Books
22 Adelaide St. West, 41st Floor
Toronto, Ontario M5H 4E3, Canada
ParkRowBooks.com
BookClubbish.com

Printed in U.S.A.

In memory of my father,
Milton T. Schmida

PROLOGUE

MatthewSwimBikeRun was sitting on the sofa staring at what was unfolding on his laptop. *One Lucky Winner*, a reality show his coworkers were droning on and on about, was streaming. He had listened to them endlessly babble about the show for the past four days. From what he gathered, the contestants were competing for ten million dollars. Curious, he decided to tune in.

On-screen, a group of four people, dressed in the same white outfits like some kind of cult, were sitting on a fancy outdoor patio drinking wine. Another woman, dressed in a white high-necked halter top, appeared and seemed to be holding court. Riveting stuff. He glanced at the comment section on the right-hand side of his screen.

They are going too far.

You think this is real? Nothing on TV is real.

Have you even been watching? It is real! And someone is going to die if they aren't careful.

This got Matthew's attention. Someone could *die*? How? Why? What was this? *Squid Game?*

He set the laptop on the coffee table in front of him, leaned forward, elbows on his knees, and examined the contestants more closely. Based on the bruised, angry faces he saw on the screen, there was some kind of drama happening. One of the women had her face buried in her hands and one of the men, fist balled, banged on the table, causing the glasses of wine to jump. At the sudden sound, Matthew jumped too.

"Speak or shoot?" the woman in the white halter top asked calmly. "The choice is yours." The man didn't respond at first. Simply stared at the woman, the muscle in his jaw pulsing.

Wait a second, Matthew thought. He knew halter-top lady. Knew the host of the show, though he couldn't remember her name. They'd lived in the same building in New York for about a year. If he recalled, she was an intern on some big-time network show. *Wow*, he thought. *She ended up making it big. Impressive.*

That's when Matthew saw it. Sitting right in the center of the table, atop the white linen cloth, long-barreled and glinting in the candlelight.

Is that a gun? Matthew typed.

Just tuning in, huh? someone responded.

It was a gun. A Ruger with hardwood grips, and a seven-and-a-half-inch satin stainless steel barrel. This was a gag, right? Why was there a gun sitting in the middle of the table for anyone to grab?

Someone should call 911. This is getting out of control.

No! came the swift responses.

It's fine. It's just part of the game.

I don't think so...

She's handling that asshole perfectly.

Yeah, don't screw up the show by calling the police.

Matthew had to agree. He was hooked. Let's wait and see what happens, he added to the mix.

Is that a bruise on her neck? someone typed.

I think it's just a shadow, said another.

"Speak or shoot? The choice is yours," the woman in the halter top said.

The man reached for the gun. Lifted it from the table and, despite himself, Matthew gasped.

"I choose shoot," the man said, calmly getting to his feet and pressing the gun to his temple.

OMG! Don't do it!

Someone call the police.

Someone DO something!

Just stop! You don't think this is real, do you?

Of course it's real!

Matthew rolled his eyes. The thread devolved into profanity and name-calling. *Hilarious*, Matthew thought. All these bored armchair warriors threatening to kick each other's asses.

He had to agree with the naysayers. Everyone knew there was nothing real about reality television. He took a closer look at the man holding the gun against his head and his eyes widened. Then he recognized him. What were the chances that he knew *two* people on the show?

Isn't that… Matthew began typing but stopped when the man

on-screen lowered the gun from his head and extended his arm. Matthew saw himself staring down the barrel of the gun through his laptop screen. The man was aiming the gun directly at him.

Three explosions in quick succession filled the air and the livestream went black and silent. It was loaded. The gun was really loaded. Matthew covered his mouth with his hand, his heart knocking against his chest.

It was quiet. Too quiet.

Finally, comments began to appear.

What happened?

Did someone get shot?

The livestream flickered and lit up. It showed the veranda, but this time, from a different angle. All that could be seen was an up-ended chair lying on the stone floor. There was still no sound, no lady in the halter top, none of the other contestants could be seen.

What is that? someone typed.

Oh, Jesus.

Matthew stared, mouth agape, as a slow stream of red liquid crept across the white stone collecting in a crimson puddle.

I think it's blood.

Matthew agreed. It did look like blood. Once again, the livestream went dead.

The man had shot someone. But whom? And why? Matthew felt sick. He wanted to close his laptop but couldn't tear his eyes away from the screen, half hoping the livestream would return, half hoping it wouldn't. What the hell kind of game was *One Lucky Winner* and why was it worth killing for?

ONE

THE BEST FRIEND

Maire Hennessy squinted against the bright October sun as she drove down the quiet Iowa county road. The fields were filled with the stubbled remains of the fall harvest and stripped bare by heavy-billed grackles and beady-eyed blackbirds eating their fill before the cold weather set in. It made her a little sad. Winter would be coming soon, unrelenting and unforgiving.

That morning, she had packed up her girls and Kryngle, their four-year-old Shetland sheepdog, to drop them off at her former mother-in-law's home. Maire, who hadn't traveled more than a hundred miles away from Calico since she'd abruptly dropped out of college over twenty years earlier, was embarking on an adventure that could change the course of their lives forever. Ten-year-old Dani kicked the back of Maire's seat in time to the throbbing beat coming from her older sister Keely's earbuds. Keely, a twelve-year-old carbon copy of Maire, had the hood of her sweatshirt pulled up over her head, her red curls springing out around her sullen face, as she silently pretended to read her book.

Maire tapped her fingers nervously against the steering wheel. "You're going to be just fine," she said, turning onto the highway that would take her children to her ex-mother-in-law's home. Shar was a decent enough person. Except for the fact that she smoked like a chimney and gave birth to a shit of a son, Maire knew she would take good care of the girls while she was away.

"I don't want to go," Dani murmured. "I like my own bed. Grandma's house feels weird."

Both Dani and Keely dreaded the two weeks that they were going to stay with their grandmother, a bland, unexcitable woman with steel-gray hair and stooped shoulders. There would be no movie nights, no special outings, no grand adventures, but they would be well-cared for, safe. And that's all that Maire wanted.

"I thought you liked Grandma Hennessy," Maire said. "You'll make cookies and she's going to teach you both how to crochet. You'll have a great time."

"Why are you going to be gone for so long?" Dani asked, staring at Maire through the rearview mirror, her eyes filled with hurt. A wet cough rumbled through her chest and she buried her mouth in her elbow.

That familiar cloud of worry that materialized every time Dani had a coughing fit settled over Maire.

"It's only for two weeks and it's not that I don't want to see you," she said. "You know that. I would be with you every single day if I could. It's kind of a work thing and I can't pass up the opportunity."

"You work from home," Keely said, briefly pulling out an earbud.

Maire didn't mind lying to Shar but lying to her children was different. She had the chance of a lifetime and in a way, it *was* work related. Money was involved. Lots of it.

"It's like a contest," Maire explained. "And if I win, well, that would be nice. And even if I don't, a lot of people will learn about my Calico Rose jewelry and might want to sell it."

"Like Claire's in the mall?" Dani asked.

"Yes, Claire's, Target, who knows?" The lies slid so easily off her tongue now. Dani's kicks to the back of Maire's seat slowed as she mulled this over.

"I'm sorry," Maire said. "I know it's hard." Her voice broke on the last word. Hard wasn't anywhere close to how things had been for the last year. Terrifying, humiliating, devastating, soul-crushing were more like it.

Bobby had never been much of a husband or father, but his health insurance had been a lifeline for Dani. When he lost his job at a local grain elevator and then took off with the nineteen-year-old waitress from the Sunshine Café, gone was the health insurance and any hope of child support. When the first $3,000 notice for Dani's nebulizer treatments came in, Maire ran to the bathroom and vomited. It was impossible. Too much.

Between the implosion of her marriage, the impact it had on the kids, her bank account that was dangerously low, the unpaid medical bills, the jewelry she made for her Etsy shop, and the search for a job that provided decent health insurance, Maire was exhausted.

Things couldn't go on this way. "It will get better," she promised.

Maire glanced over at Keely and caught her accusatory glare. Out of all of them, the divorce hit Keely the hardest. Despite his drawbacks, Keely was a daddy's girl, and she was suffering in his absence.

The worry never ended. At the top of the list was Dani's health. Her cystic fibrosis was stable for the moment, but she was fragile. Her last infection required a two-week hospital stay, a PICC line with multiple antibiotic infusions, therapies, and nebulizer treatments. It was so much that Maire had to put together a binder for Shar filled with in-depth directions for Dani's care, and she hoped she wasn't making a huge mistake by leaving. A lung infection that may be mild for most children could be deadly for Dani. And poor Keely. Quiet, shy Keely was getting lost in the shuffle, becoming more removed, isolated from them. Another thing to worry about.

A month ago, when she got the email about the show, she almost deleted it. Maire had been online, scanning articles about the newest cystic fibrosis research, when she heard the ping. Grateful for an excuse to tear her eyes away from words like *Fibrinogen-like 2 proteins* and *cryogenic electron microscopy*, she tapped the email icon on her phone.

CONGRATULATIONS–YOU'VE BEEN NOMINATED, the subject line called out to her. She scanned the rest of the email. Trip of a lifetime, groundbreaking new reality show, ten million dollars. *Scam*, Maire thought and went back to reading about clinical trials and RNA therapy. But an hour later, she was still thinking about the ten million dollars. She opened the email again to read it more closely.

Congratulations, you've been nominated to take part in the groundbreaking new reality competition show *One Lucky Winner*! Set in the heart of wine country, you, along with the other contestants, will battle for ten million dollars through a series of challenges that will test you physically, mentally, and emotionally. Competitors will spend fourteen days at the exclusive Diletta Resort and Spa in beautiful Napa Valley. When not competing, spend your time in your lavishly appointed private cottage, swimming laps in the 130-foot pool, or head to the spa for our one-of-a-kind vinotherapy-based treatments—massages, wraps, and scrubs made from grapes grown in the Bella Luce vineyard. As a special treat, each contestant will receive a case of Bella Luce's world-famous cabernet sauvignon with an exclusively designed label just for you!

Maire snorted. It had to be a joke. A rip-off. She closed the email, even sent it to her trash folder, but an hour later, she pulled it up again. Ten million dollars. Maire was one month away from not being able to pay the mortgage on the house, from not being able to make the car payment, from not being able to put money in the kids' school lunch accounts, from not being able to pay for one dose of Dani's medication.

She should probably just sell the house, take the loss, start over, but this was her home, the kids' home. There was no way she was giving it up without a fight. She didn't need anywhere near ten million dollars to save the house, but that was what it was worth to her, and that kind of money would change her life, all their lives.

Who would have nominated her? And how did that actually work? *Hey, I know of someone who could use ten million dollars.* The entire thing had to be fake. The email was signed by someone named Fern Espa, whose title read Production Assistant, *One Lucky Winner.*

Anyone could send an email. Maire trashed the message again.

Then, over the next three days, the car started leaking oil, Kryngle ate a sock and had to have emergency surgery, and Dani's hospital bill came in. Her credit cards were maxed out and she'd given up on any help from her ex. Maire needed money, fast. Burying her humiliation, she called her parents and asked for a loan. It wasn't nearly enough.

Maire hung up and went to the garage, sitting in her leaky car so that the kids wouldn't hear her crying.

Maybe this was the email she was waiting for. The sign she needed to finally take control of her life. Maire wasn't a fool though. She did her due diligence. While sitting in the waiting room at the vet's office, she looked up *One Lucky Winner* and found a website and an IMDb entry—both short on details—but it clearly was a real show. She searched for the name Fern Espa and found a LinkedIn entry that looked legit. And the Diletta Resort looked amazing.

And now, under the guise of a work trip, here she was,

dropping her kids off at her former mother-in-law's house for two weeks, hopping on a plane to Napa to take part in some *Survivor*-type reality show for the off chance she might win ten million dollars. It was ridiculous, over the top, maybe even irresponsible, but it ignited a spark of hope that she hadn't felt in a long time.

"You'll be okay," Maire said to the kids as she turned onto the cracked concrete of Shar's street. Shar was waiting for them, standing on her rickety front porch, a cigarette dangling from her knobby fingers. With hail-pocked, dirty white aluminum siding and a crabgrass-choked yard in need of mowing, the home her ex-husband grew up in was grim and depressing. But Shar was a sweet woman who loved her grandchildren. Maire scanned the street. Every house was in the same state of disarray and neglect. A jolt of fear shot through her. If she didn't turn things around, they would end up living in a place like this, or worse.

Jesus, Maire thought. *I'm making a huge mistake.* She fought the urge to drive right on by. Instead, she gave the girls her bravest smile. "It's okay. We're all going to be okay."

Ten million dollars would make everything okay.

TWO

THE ASSISTANT

Fern Espa leaned against the wrought iron railing and looked down at the great hall below. The gleaming white marble floors winked up at her, the scent of furniture polish and flowers filled the air. Every marble statue was in its place, every piece of furniture dusted, every window washed.

Everything was perfect. Her boss expected nothing less. Well, almost everything was perfect. She tried not to look at the section of the great hall where towering scaffolding climbed to the cathedral-like ceiling. The hope was to have the repairs to the dome finished along with the restoration of the fresco, but despite her boss's ranting and raving, the planned restoration was nowhere near complete. Fern could have told her that there was no way a multimillion-dollar restoration could be completed in less than a year, but Catalina James could not be deterred. She screamed at contractors, threw more money at the problem, threatened litigation, all to no avail.

But still, the estate was gorgeous. The contestants would barely notice the cracked ceilings or the faded frescoes. The incomplete, unrenovated rooms were behind locked doors. It wouldn't do to have any of their guests get hurt because of rotting floorboards or crumbling stone walls. And, of course, all the unsightly spots would be kept out of the camera's field of vision.

The production crew moved efficiently through the space, checking cameras, microphones, and lighting. The director, Alfonso Solomon, was reading through his notes from Cat. He was a pro in the reality show business, having won an Emmy and a Golden Globe.

"Fern," Alfonso called out, peering out at her from behind his reading glasses. "Have you seen Cat? I have a few questions for her."

"Have you tried texting her?" Fern asked. Cat was close by but wanted to remain behind the scenes during production. It was one of Fern's many jobs to run interference.

"Yes, texting and calling," Alfonso said impatiently. "Can you tell her I need to speak with her?"

"Sure," Fern said breezily without slowing down. If given the chance, he would rattle off his list of demands and make sure Fern wrote down each and every one. She didn't have the time. Best if Cat talked to Alfonso herself. She moved to the kitchen. Good. The caterers were unpacking the food for the cocktail party. Everything was coming together.

From a distance, she heard her name being called. Cat had expressly told Fern that she needed her close. This was a big day. The biggest.

"Fern!" Cat shouted. She sounded slightly unhinged.

Fern sighed. She still needed to make sure that the drivers were at the airport, ready to pick up the guests when their flights arrived, and find out why the host of the show hadn't yet shown up. Her cell phone buzzed. A text from Cat.

Where is the Ruby Nights Red red lipstick? I need it!

Fern pushed back from the railing and felt a slight wobble of the iron. Fern would have to remind the guests not to lean against the railing and get it fixed as soon as possible. It wouldn't do to have someone fall thirty feet to the marble floor below.

Her phone buzzed again. Fern didn't quite understand why Cat was leaving her livestream to the last minute. She could have prerecorded it, but her followers were expecting her. For the last four years, each Monday and Thursday night, Cat went live on Instagram and waxed poetic on everything from the hottest fashions from Milan to the latest book or movie she consumed, all while she expertly applied her makeup. She hadn't missed one night, not even when her husband left her for good. Cat had soldiered on that evening, and Fern had been right along with her. Afterward, Cat had lost it, moving through the house throwing things and smashing bottles of wine against the marble floors.

Fern ended up taking a shard of glass to her upper cheek—she still had a faint scar. Cat felt terrible. Fern had nearly quit that time. Her therapist told her that under no circumstances should she tolerate such behavior. In theory, Fern agreed, but in the end, she forgave Cat. Fern could understand the anger. Cat had lost her husband. Fifteen years of marriage thrown away—for what? Cat never said, but Fern wondered if it might have been another woman. Whatever it had been, Cat was devastated.

But, as always, Fern was right there by her side, picking up the broken glass, pouring Cat a glass of bourbon, telling her that everything was going to be okay.

Fern moved to the large room that Cat used as a video recording studio and stood in the doorway. She watched as her boss, dressed in ivory linen pants and a matching sleeveless T-shirt, was getting ready to do a promo for *One Lucky Winner*. A white distressed end table was placed next to a king-size bed covered in layers of down comforters, cashmere blankets, and piles of pillows all in a crisp snowy hue that hurt Fern's eyes if she looked at them too long. Today, in preparation for the livestream, she had set a vase of white hydrangeas, their heavy heads as delicate as cotton candy, on the bedside table.

With effort, Fern wheeled the long marble-topped table across the white carpet to the spot marked with a duct-taped X. This is where Cat kept her laptop, microphone, and ring light. If she placed the front left wheels of the table on the X, the camera would catch the perfect angle of the bed, the table, and the flowers.

There was no way Catalina was going to let millions of viewers into her actual bedroom. That was just too intrusive, but her "Lovelies," as Catalina called them, liked thinking they had a peek into her private, luxurious, beautiful world. The bed in this room had never been slept in, probably didn't even have sheets covering the mattresses, the spines of the books on the bedside table had never been cracked.

The room also held a walk-in closet filled with her most expensive clothes, shoes, and accessories. Despite her sleek white-blond bob and her perfectly pressed wardrobe, Catalina James was not tidy. Her everyday closet was cluttered, the silk blouses hung askew, sweaters were wadded up on shelves, and her shoes heaped in mismatched jumbles on the floor. A weekly cleaning crew made sure that every other room in her home was camera ready.

Atop the marble table, Fern had neatly laid out all the items Cat would need to get ready for going live: brushes, concealer, bronzer, blush, eyeliner, and a dizzying number of other beauty products. Confident that everything was good to go, Fern made her way down the steps. There was so much to do before the guests arrived. Catalina liked everything to be perfect.

"Fern!" Catalina shrieked. "Where the fuck is my lipstick?"

It was five minutes until showtime. "Here, let me look," Fern said, easing open one of the craft table drawers. Fern learned over the years that remaining calm rubbed off on Cat. She pulled out a handful of tube-shaped lipsticks from one of the drawers. *Hot Red Mama, Red Door, Naughty Red*, but no *Ruby Nights Red*.

Fern scanned the floor. "Here," Fern said, bending down to retrieve the wayward tube.

Cat snatched the lipstick from Fern's hand. "Is Philippa here yet?" Philippa was the supermodel host of *One Lucky Winner*. With her six-foot lithe frame, long raven hair, and authentic Italian accent, Philippa was the beautiful face of the show.

Fern shook her head. "Not yet. I've tried to call and text but haven't heard back. She's probably stuck in traffic."

"Dammit," Cat said, sliding her phone into its stand, and adjusting the lighting and reflectors. "We need her here, now. How the fuck are we going to do the show without our host?"

"She'll get here," Fern assured her boss.

"She wouldn't pass up this opportunity. Unless..." Cat paused, letting the word hang.

"Oh, God," Fern said. "Is she partying again? I thought she gave that up for good. She promised."

In frustration, Cat slammed the drawer shut. "Let me think." Cat rubbed her forehead.

"She'll probably come running in at the last minute..." Fern said.

"No." Cat shook her head. "Philippa had her chance. If she shows up at the gate, do not let her in."

"Then who?" Fern asked. It would be nearly impossible to find someone to take Philippa's place on such short notice.

"What about Nevaeh?" Cat asked.

"She's in Paris doing that thing with Yamamoto," Fern explained.

"Chance Leopold, then," Cat said. "We'll go with a male host."

"Unfortunately, he's in rehab," Fern said, scrolling through her phone and searching for another idea.

Cat dropped onto a chaise longue, thought a moment, then

shook her head. "There's no one. I won't have time to bring anyone up to speed. We're screwed."

Fern chewed on her lip, waiting. Finally, Cat returned her gaze to Fern. "It has to be you," she said reluctantly. "You know the show, the contestants. It's not ideal, but it is what it is. Don't screw it up," she said before standing up and positioning herself in front of the camera.

Fern couldn't speak, couldn't believe she had heard Cat correctly. She wanted her, Fern, to be the host?

"Jesus, Fern," Cat said. "If you embarrass me, I swear to God…"

"I won't, I promise," Fern said, praying that it was true.

"I'll text Alfonso with the change," Cat said. "You'll still be able to handle all your usual duties, right?"

Fern nodded, though she wasn't sure how she was supposed to take care of all the behind-the-scenes logistics and fill the shoes of a supermodel in front of the camera. But she had to. This was her chance.

"And make sure you clear the set of all nonessential crew before the contestants arrive," Cat said, sliding a headband over her forehead to pull her platinum hair away from her face. "And for fuck's sake keep everyone away from me." She set a hard gaze on Fern. "If anyone asks, I'm not here."

"Got it," Fern said. Few people knew that Cat James was the driving force behind *One Lucky Winner* and Cat wanted to keep it that way. Nondisclosure agreements were signed, threats were made if anyone revealed Cat's involvement. Yes, she would do promos to build buzz around the show, but Cat didn't want anyone to know of her involvement until the final, jaw-dropping episode. Because of the secrecy of the project, Cat insisted on a closed set. There was too big of a chance of footage being leaked, so while there would be a crew, it would be scaled down, an elite few. This made sense to Fern. *One Lucky Winner* was entirely unique and the first game show of its kind to offer such a huge purse. Ten million dollars! It was staggering. And with the over-the-top challenges, people would be talking about them for years. They would be talking about her. Finally.

Cat sighed, examining her face on the screen. This was the part of the tutorial that Fern knew Cat hated the most: when people saw her stripped of makeup. Her pale skin, skimpy lashes, the purple shadows beneath her eyes, the tiny lines that marched along her lip line, the deeper ones that clotheslined her forehead, all on display for the world to see.

But this is what her audience wanted, to see the magnificent transformation from plain to pretty, from boring to bombshell. It cost Cat for others to see her at her most vulnerable, but it's what attracted her huge audience. Fern thought her boss was beautiful with or without makeup.

Cat waved her hand impatiently, nudging Fern aside, and Fern stutter-stepped backward, out of the frame of the camera.

Cat pressed the button to go live. "Good evening, Lovelies. It's Cat James and I'm so happy that you are here with me." Cat held up the crystal-encrusted tube. "Did you know that women have worn red lipstick for thousands of years? Cleopatra, Queen Victoria I, suffragettes, Marilyn, Audrey, Rihanna, Salma, Jennifer, Gaga. They all have mastered the art of the red lip. Well, tonight, we are going to do the same. Are you ready to become your most beautiful, most powerful you?" Cat lifted her chin and gave the camera a sly smile. "And we must discuss the most-talked-about new cultural phenomenon. Have you seen the promos? Are you feeling lucky?"

Fern left Cat to her livestream and made her way down the grand staircase, nodding numbly to the set director and her assistant, her heart thumping. This was her chance. Fern was now the face of *One Lucky Winner*. She could finally prove to Cat that she was much more than a trusty assistant.

Fern found herself in the doorway of the villa's library. It was a beautiful space—not her favorite room on the estate (that was the kitchen), but with its dark wood, floor-to-ceiling book-shelves, and hushed, old-world aura, it was in the top five. The room smelled like a mixture of lemon cleaner, a heady scent of wine, and red roses.

Fern tucked her thick black hair behind her ears and checked the slim silver watch on her wrist. It was nearing nine o'clock. The contestants would be arriving soon. All their months of hard work, *her* hard work behind the scenes, was paying off. *One Lucky Winner* was finally becoming a reality. But now this could be the project that could shoot Fern to the stratosphere, professionally speaking.

For the last six months, Fern had worked meticulously on all the details. She had been the one who liaised with the contestants, answering their questions, making their travel arrangements, making them feel like the stars of the show that they would soon be. She worked with the tech company who installed hundreds of cameras throughout the property, directed the landscapers, the maid service, the carpenters, and contractors, miraculously managing to bring the vision for *One Lucky Winner* to life.

Most of the time Cat was there hovering, watching, demanding, critiquing and, try as she might, Fern couldn't help but resent her boss. She owed Cat so much but when would that debt be paid? From the looks of it, never.

Ten years ago, Fern and Cat had worked at the same company. Cat was a director in the company and Fern was a lowly intern for the powerful CEO. The CEO was particularly handsy, devastating Fern, who, at twenty-two, had walked into her first job with stars in her eyes.

The CEO was handsome, charming, and had a way of making Fern feel like she was the only one in the room. Special. She shrugged off the way he treated most of her other coworkers with indifference, even scorn. They obviously weren't working hard enough, weren't dedicated enough. But Fern was. She poured her heart and soul into her obscenely low-paying job. At first, the hand on her lower back, the feathery touches across her breasts, seemed incidental. Just two colleagues standing close to one another, bent over the day's schedule.

Then, Fern started to find herself alone with the CEO in his office. Door shut. The accidental, innocent touches lingered, turned into something else. Fern wanted none of it. She knew better than to get involved with her boss. She thought he was impressive, brilliant at his job, but Fern would never sleep with him. It never crossed her mind. She avoided being in a room alone with him, but that proved to be impossible. When the boss called you into his office, you went.

Fern did her best to sidestep his advances, but she could see he was getting impatient. But whom could she tell? The woman who sat in the cubicle next to her? Could she tell Cat James, the glamorous director of social media for the company? No, Cat barely even knew Fern was alive and didn't acknowledge her unless it was with impatience or disdain. Fern had no one.

One afternoon, the CEO ordered Fern to his office. Fear filled Fern's body. Had she done something wrong? She wracked her brain, trying to think. She tried to be so careful, so thorough in her work. No, she had made no big mistakes. Nothing to warrant such a chilly summoning. He shut the door and Fern was sure she was going to be fired. For what, though? It was the sound of the turning lock that turned her stomach liquid.

She fought back, at least tried to, but the CEO was stronger than she was, had the element of surprise. Fern managed to get away from his grasp, running to the door and flipping the lock before being dragged backward and pushed up against a wall. Fern wanted to scream but couldn't. *Strange*, Fern thought, how life was going on as usual outside the office door. Meetings were being held, phone calls made, while in here, Fern was living a nightmare. Still, she struggled until the CEO grabbed something from his desk. A letter opener, sharp as a dagger, and held it to her neck.

"Enough fighting," he breathed in her ear. "Let's play." He slid the letter opener down her chest, over her stomach, and beneath her skirt. Fern felt the blade bite into the skin of her thigh, felt her underwear flutter to the ground.

Suddenly, Cat James was there.

She gave the CEO a tongue-lashing and threatened a lawsuit. The CEO laughed, telling her that no one would believe either one of them. Cat led a disheveled Fern from the office. Security was waiting for them as soon as they reached Fern's desk. They were both fired and led from the building. Cat told her not to worry—she had been fired when she was just starting out as a young journalist. Fired for trying to do the right thing. It was the way of the world and their plight to carry.

Cat told her that the CEO was right. No one would believe them. She said that bosses like the CEO were roaches. Nearly impossible to smash. But if Fern wanted to go to the authorities, she would back her up. Or, she could try to forget what happened and move on. Fern could come work for Cat because she was going to build something big. Something special. And she did.

Cat got back on her feet quickly and, using her social media expertise, became one of the most popular lifestyle influencers on YouTube, Instagram, and TikTok. She also bought this gorgeous estate and vineyard. As soon as she was able to, she brought Fern on as her personal assistant. The hours as her boss's assistant were long and extremely demanding, but most days Fern didn't care. If Cat hadn't stood up for her and then stood by her, she didn't know where she would be now.

Lately, Fern had been rethinking things. Cat's unrealistic expectations, the rotten pay, the denigrating comments, the brutal hours all bordering on abuse. Fern paced the library floor. How much more could one person humanly take? It was abusive and Fern knew she couldn't do this forever, but now the years of patience were paying off. Cat was finally letting Fern take the lead on something, even if it was by default.

Fern was ready. This was the moment she was waiting for. It was a big job. Huge.

Fern tried to tamp down her nerves. She couldn't get flustered now. She consulted her clipboard. The caterers were setting out the appetizers and desserts. And the wine. The wine would be flowing tonight.

They had put several bottles with the new labels that Cat had personally designed on ice. They were so different from the elegant grapevines that previously graced the bottles from Bella Luce. They were awful, really. The labels displayed the image of a frighteningly realistic painting that Fern recognized as that of three Greek goddesses. Three very angry goddesses, partially clad, with snakes for hair, converging on a terrified man and a woman with a dagger embedded in her chest. The only way Fern knew it was their wine was because *Bella Luce* was written in elegant script across the label. Fern hadn't bothered asking why her boss made the change. She always had her reasons.

Including the reason why Cat insisted on being a silent producer on the show. *I'll be a distraction*, Cat said. *I want all the attention on this brilliant concept I created. It's going to change reality television forever.*

Fern dared to ask her why this reality show only had five contestants. Cat readily explained it away. *Viewers will be more invested, will be glued to their screens to see what happens to their favorite character.*

Except they weren't characters. They were real people that Cat had carefully vetted. Fern flipped through the dossiers on her clipboard with the contestants' photos.

Audrey Abreo of Boston, Massachusetts. Twenty-nine years old, restaurateur, married, one child. Funny and larger than life, Aubrey's sharp tongue would keep everyone on their toes.

Samuel Rafferty of Atlanta, Georgia. Forty-two years old, Georgia district attorney, single, no children. Movie-star handsome and smart, Samuel was both buttoned up and gorgeous. If anything, the viewers would tune in just to see his six-pack abs.

Richard Crowley of Dripping Springs, Texas. Sixty-eight years old, former US senator, married, four children. Senator Crowley was of a certain age but appeared to be in decent shape. He was good-natured and gave off an "aw shucks, ma'am" vibe. Half the audience would love him for his politics, half would hate him.

Camille Tamerlane of San Francisco, California. Thirty-eight years old, psychiatrist, marriage counselor, and podcast host, divorced, no children. Camille was no more than a wisp of a thing but could command a room. At once analytical and empathetic, Camille would bring the mind games to *One Lucky Winner.*

Maire Hennessy of Calico, Iowa. Forty years old, artist, divorced, two children. Maire brought the Mom Factor to the show. She was relatable and, with an ill child, would definitely bring emotion to the show. She also looked like the human incarnation of a Disney princess with a mane of curly red hair, pale skin, and a smattering of freckles across her nose.

Yes, quite the mix. Each file contained the most compelling stories, even contained a few bones scattered about. Talk about must-see TV.

Her phone buzzed, alerting Fern to the fact that someone was at the gate. She took a deep breath. It was time to meet the contestants.

THREE

THE BEST FRIEND

When Maire landed in San Francisco, she spotted the driver who was going to take her to the hotel and spa. She had gotten a little thrill when she saw him standing at the baggage claim in his black suit and chauffeur's cap, holding a small sign that said *Hennessy* in block lettering. She enjoyed the feeling of eyes on her as she warmly greeted the driver. She felt like someone important, someone special. But once the driver, a hulking man with hooded, close-set eyes, took her bag and gruffly told her to follow him, Maire's excitement was replaced with unease.

Once in the SUV, she tried to shake away her worry and enjoy the scenery. They crossed the Golden Gate Bridge, the sparkling water of the bay below, and Maire was struck at just how beautiful it was. But the moment was fleeting. Something didn't feel right. She dug through her bag in search of her cell phone. Not seeing it, she used her flashlight key chain to shine a light into the depths of her purse, found it, and checked in with Dani and Keely. They said all was well but Maire was sure that she heard a wheeze in Dani's voice and her worry doubled.

The landscape flew by—windswept flatlands, rolling hills, golden vineyards shedding their summer green—but Maire couldn't enjoy it. She fought the urge to call the girls again. If only she could tell them about the show, that she could win millions of dollars. They would understand then, would be excited, but the rules of the game were explicit. Maire could not tell anyone the real reason she was going away or she would be disqualified. Once the game started, it would be different. They'd see her on-screen, see her competing, and would be so proud of her. Or mortified.

Soon the sun started easing its way down just as a thick fog rolled in, enveloping the car in a velvety cloud. The road in front of them disappeared but the driver didn't slow down. He blindly wound around curves in the mist-covered road.

Maire clutched the seat in front of her. "This doesn't seem right," she said. "I think you were supposed to turn back there." Alarm fluttered in her stomach. She was in the middle of nowhere with a strange man, in a place she wasn't familiar with. She'd probably end up dead, or kidnapped, or drinking a White Claw at a Motel 6 next to the interstate. This trip was too good to be true.

"Just going where I'm told," the driver said shortly, making a sharp left turn. "The estate is just a few miles down the road."

"But you're supposed to take me to the hotel," Maire said. Her hand inched over to the door handle, and she checked her cell phone, relieved to see there was still service. Ahead, a gate flanked by a tall stone wall materialized. The fog curled itself around the wrought iron bars, making it impossible to see what came next. She tried to quash the little voice that urged her to tell the driver to turn around.

Instead, Maire stayed silent as the driver came to a stop next to the gate intercom system, rolled down his window, and pushed the call button.

"Good evening," came a woman's voice. "Welcome to Bella Luce."

"Yes," the driver said, tilting the paper in his hand trying to make the best use of the weak light from the lanterns perched atop the stone wall. "I've got a Maire Hennessy here," he said gruffly.

"Welcome. Please drive forward," the voice said, and the iron gates creaked open.

The driver glided slowly through the gates. The long, winding drive was flanked by dozens of towering cork oaks with stout trunks and twisted limbs that loomed gracefully above them.

Maire stared hard through the front windshield in hopes of seeing what was to come. She didn't have to wait long. Lights, softened by the dense fog, revealed the outline of what looked like a small village. "What is this?" Maire asked. "It looks like something out of a movie."

The driver ignored her, keeping his eyes on the stone driveway in front of him.

"Oh, wow," Maire said, surprised to see that what she thought were several separate stone buildings was actually one residence with varying, red-tiled rooflines and, remarkably, a bell tower. One section of the estate appeared to be in ruins with exposed beams surrounded by piles of ragged stone.

Wide-mouthed, winged gargoyles peered suspiciously down at them as the driver came to a slow stop in front of the massive home. It was a gorgeous estate but also foreboding, aloof and cold like an ancient Tuscan fortress built to keep enemies and lowly serfs at a distance.

More than two dozen stone steps, flanked by a terraced lawn, led up to a set of grand wooden doors set into an arched entry. On either side of the doors were two black lanterns casting a ghostly light that spilled to the stone floor.

Maire looked out the window again and unease puddled in her chest. She looked down at her pilled cardigan and cargo pants. She wasn't dressed for any kind of meet and greet and had actually been looking forward to one night of rest before the competition began. Room service in her hotel room and watching *Love It or List It*. She wanted to check on the kids one more time.

The driver stepped from the car and opened Maire's door, the interior light popping on.

"You aren't really just going to leave me here, are you?" Maire asked.

The driver gave her a Cheshire cat grin, his teeth flashing bright in the dark. "Why? You looking for some company?"

Before she could react, he grasped her hand. His skin was cold and clammy, his fingers caressing her palm. Maire tried to shake her hand free, and the driver laughed meanly before releasing his grip. Maire stood frozen.

"Listen, lady," he said. "Just tell me, what do you want to do? Stay? Go? I don't care but I need to get back to the airport."

Maire didn't want to walk up to this strange house, but more than that, she didn't want to get back into the car with the driver. He tapped his watch. She could either enter this gorgeous estate and win ten million dollars or get back into the car with the creepy driver.

"I'll stay," Maire said, scrambling from the car. She looked up at the spectacle in front of her. Never in her life had she seen such a home. A curtain in one of the upper windows shifted, and Maire saw someone step back into the shadows.

She began the walk up the steep stairway to the house, her luggage bumping against each stone step. She hitched her purse over her shoulder and glanced nervously back at the driver, who was already turning to leave. Through the hazy glow that lit her ascent, Maire could see that the front yard was overgrown with a variety of gray and silver ground cover. She caught a whiff of something honey-like trying to break through the pungent scent of rosemary. Somewhere nearby, she heard the soft gurgle of a fountain.

At the top of the steps, Maire paused, released the grip on

her luggage, and stared up at the large house. She imagined it was beautiful in the daylight, but right now it was downright imposing, rising out of the shadows like some medieval villa.

On either side of the arched doorway were several open-air windows—no glass, no screens. She peered through one of the openings. What Maire thought was the front door was really the entrance to a courtyard. Maire searched for a doorbell but couldn't find one.

Feeling foolish, Maire pulled open the heavy wooden doors and stepped inside the courtyard. She was beneath the bell tower now. Who lived in a home with a bell tower? She followed the row of lanterns where dusty-winged moths threw themselves at the filaments, and moved down the colonnade with its arched columns, her footsteps tapping sharply on the stone pavers.

At the end of the path was another set of heavy wooden double doors, again reminding Maire of a stronghold. She wondered, with a flash of anxiety, if the doors were meant to keep people out or in. She thought of Keely and Dani and fumbled in her purse for her phone. She would call them just one more time.

The phone rang and rang. *Please answer,* she begged. Finally, she heard Shar's rough voice on the other side of the line. "Hello," she rasped.

"Shar, it's me. I know it's late, but can I talk to Dani again?" Maire asked apologetically. "I'm just worried about her."

"I understand," Shar said. "But she's doing just fine."

In the background came the sharp bark of coughing. Maire tensed. She would know that cough anywhere. "Dani's coughing? Why didn't you call?"

"I've got it covered, Maire," Shar said softly. "She's fine."

"You nebulized her? Took her temperature? Used the vest?" Maire asked. The vest was the high-frequency chest wall oscillation vest that Dani wore to vibrate loose the mucus in her lungs.

"Yes, yes, and yes," Shar said. "What she really needs right now is rest. I'll call you if anything changes. I promise."

More coughing. An endless stream of wheezing, gasping. Was it a *go to the hospital* cough? Maire couldn't tell. She needed to see Dani, feel her forehead, lay her hand against her chest.

In front of Maire the door began to open.

"I have to go," Maire said in a rush. "But call me if she gets any worse, please."

"I will," Shar said gently. "But we'll be fine. I promise." Then she was gone. Maire had no choice but to trust her. Trust Shar with her daughters, with Dani's life.

Maire blinked back tears as a young woman appeared in the doorway. She was dressed in a sheer blouse, high-waisted, wide-leg pants, and Converse sneakers, all in black. Her shoulder-length black hair was sleek and made edgy by severely cropped bangs. She wore no makeup, nor did she need to. She was naturally stunning with full lips and dark eyes behind chunky, black-framed glasses. A small V-shaped scar was etched into one sharp cheekbone.

"Hello," the woman said in her low, husky voice. "Welcome to Bella Luce. Ms. Hennessy, correct?"

"Yes," Maire said, trying to peer behind the woman and into an atrium. Inside was a fountain with a life-size statue of a beautiful woman holding a mask of a man with wild eyes and a twisted grimace. From the open cavern of the mask's mouth, water gushed. Maire was overcome with a current of dread and she had to force herself to look away from the statue.

"I'm Fern Espa, we spoke on the phone. Welcome." The woman offered a hand and Maire took it. Fern's grip was strong but slick with sweat. She was nervous, Maire thought, glad she wasn't the only one. "I'm the host of the show and that is Melpomene," Fern said, nodding at the fountain just beyond the window. "One of the nine muses. We call her Mel. Please come in."

"I'm sorry," Maire said, shaking her head. "I'm just a little confused. I was expecting to be taken to the resort. I'm not sure where I am or why."

"Our cocktail party is an extra treat for the contestants," Fern said, fiddling with an earpiece tucked in her ear. "We thought it would be nice for you to meet your fellow players before the competition begins. Now, please come in."

Hesitantly, Maire stepped through the front door onto terracotta set in a fishbone pattern. Her mind was still spinning. Wasn't Fern the production assistant whom she had been corresponding with? And now she was introducing herself as the host of the show?

"Imported from Italy," Fern said, mistaking Maire's quizzical expression as interest in the flooring. "Please excuse some of the mess. The owner is doing some restoration. The estate was built in the late 1800s and much of the home's bones come from the Lombardo region."

Maire nodded. The entryway was dimly lit from above by a crystal-and-iron chandelier hanging from a domed ceiling. On the right hung a full-length mirror in a gilded frame, where Maire caught her reflection. With her unruly red hair, oversize cardigan, wrinkled cargo pants, and shearling-lined moccasins, Maire looked as rumpled as she felt. Her shoulders sagged. She wasn't prepared for this.

Next to the mirror was a side table that held a crystal vase filled with a graceful mix of blush-pink roses, hydrangeas, and lisianthuses. On the opposite side was a round marble base with a sculpture of a woman holding a lyre.

"Calliope, another muse," Fern explained. "Now, I'm afraid this is the awkward moment when I have to ask you for your cell phone," Fern said, biting her lip.

Maire narrowed her eyes. "My phone? Why?"

"It's for security reasons," Fern said, pointing to a lockbox sitting atop a waist-high pillar.

"Security?" Maire repeated.

"For the show," Fern explained. "You cannot begin to know how many people would like to get a sneak peek into what's going on here. There could be spies anywhere. Part of the intrigue of the game is all the secrecy we have around it. Everyone on set has to relinquish their phones for the duration. It's in the contract."

Maire remembered seeing something about phones and confidentiality in the contract but figured that just meant that the players couldn't share pictures or videos. "But what if I need to contact my children?" Maire asked, panic threatening to take over. She hadn't gone a day without talking to her kids. "My daughter has a chronic health condition," Maire said. "I need to be able to check in with her and be reached if there's an emergency."

"I'm sorry," Fern said frowning, "but it's in the rules. I'm sure you understand that if key details are revealed, it would be devastating for the show. We can't risk that, but I promise if we get an emergency call, I'll let you know."

What if Dani's cough got worse? What if she was suffocating in her own mucus right now? Regret surged through Maire. Why was she doing this? What was worth being away from her children for two weeks? *Ten million dollars*, she reminded herself.

Her phone was the only remaining thread that connected her to Keely and Dani, but she reluctantly handed it to Fern, who dropped it through the box's narrow slot. Maire tried to push the girls from her thoughts. She needed to focus, put all her energy into winning the money.

Fern briskly led Maire through a great hall with more stone flooring and another curved ceiling. Against one wall was towering scaffolding. Maire craned her neck to get a better look at the burgundy leaves, baroque curls, and vines that adorned the dome.

"How big is this place?" Maire asked, her voice echoing

against the walls as they passed through the church-like space, with its stiff, ornate furniture and the exotic scent of orchids.

Fern didn't miss a stride as she ticked off the list on her fingers. "Seven bedrooms, a music room, eat-in kitchen, atrium, small chapel, dining room, formal living room (we call it the white room), a sunroom that serves as a more casual gathering area, theater room, indoor pool, outdoor infinity pool, and, of course, a wine cellar."

"And someone lives here?" Maire asked, marveling at the scope of it all.

Fern paused in front of a door inlaid with intricate carvings of flora and fauna. "Yes," she said, "though the owner wishes to remain anonymous at this point. And here is the library."

Fern twisted the knob of a door and pushed it open to reveal floor-to-ceiling shelves made with foreboding, dark walnut and filled with leather-bound books. The coffered ceiling matched the wooden shelves. Half the books could only be reached by a tall library ladder on wheels. And there were more flowers. In this room, the vases were filled with hundreds of ruffled, wine-colored buttercups, so dark they almost looked black in the dim room.

Maire's eyes landed on a stranger who stared back at her. He stood next to the ladder, wineglass in hand. He looked vaguely familiar. Perhaps in his seventies, he wore khaki pants and a red golf shirt, with a full head of sandy hair and a ruddy, lined face that once must have been handsome or boy-next-door cute. Maybe a former football player gone to seed. He lifted his glass toward her and smiled broadly.

"Would you like something to drink?" Fern asked.

Maire pulled her eyes from the man. "Whatever's open is fine with me," Maire said.

"How about a pinot? The grapes are grown right here," Fern explained.

Maire nodded. Fern moved to a table lined with wine bottles, selecting one and pouring a glass while Maire regarded a second table filled with platters of food. Though she was starving, the man hadn't filled his plate. She covertly studied his face. Where did she know him from?

"Will the others be arriving soon?" Maire asked. "How many of us will there be?"

"Five in all," Fern said, handing Maire a glass of pale liquid.

Maire was surprised. She had assumed there would be at least a dozen contestants. That seemed to be the average number of players in all the reality shows she had binged over the past month.

She nodded over Maire's shoulder. "We are just waiting on two more," she said, looking at her watch. "And they should be here any moment."

Two more? Didn't she mean three? She scanned the large room and her eyes fell on a tall man, well over six feet, with a close-cropped head of hair and a silver-flecked black goatee. His dark eyes settled on Maire and she nearly spilled her wine. How was this possible? It wasn't. There was no way.

It had been twenty years, but she knew this man. Knew him well. Maire's heart stopped and then started again, skittering raggedly. The last time they saw one another, they vowed never to see, write, email, or speak to one another again. It was too chancy, too much of a risk. And until this moment, they had kept that promise.

They stared at one another, and the years slipped away. A cold, starry night, a partially frozen lake, the crunch of metal, his strong arms holding her tight. Then they were running, running for their lives.

FOUR

THE CONFIDANTE

Pulling her Prada suitcase behind her, Camille Tamerlane followed Fern Espa across the glistening marbled hallways of the villa, still not quite believing she could be a mere two weeks away from ten million dollars.

The email she hadn't realized she had been waiting for had come a month earlier. Normally she would have deleted the message without even reading it, but the subject line snagged her attention. ARE YOU READY FOR THE ADVENTURE OF A LIFE-TIME? Why not? She clicked on the email.

A reality show, Napa Valley, ten million dollars. She laughed out loud. *Yeah, right,* she thought, but didn't stop reading. The name of the show was *One Lucky Winner* and, apparently, she'd been nominated by someone to be a contestant. Someone who described her as "a woman who has dedicated her life to helping others become their best selves."

A jolt of self-satisfaction coursed through her. She *was* San Francisco's premier psychiatrist and hosted a number one podcast called *Your Best Life with Camille.* Her schedule was packed and her array of clients included a congressperson, a former child star, a world-renowned cello player, and a professional baseball player. Not that she would ever stoop to name-dropping—Camille would never do that. It would be unethical. She wondered who had made the nomination and flipped through all the possibilities: one of her patients, a *Your Best Life with Camille* listener, Parker (her producer). It was most certainly not her ex-husband.

But it was the ten million dollars Camille was most interested in. She needed that money. And fast.

Admittedly, she had gotten greedy—the Victorian home office in one of the most exclusive neighborhoods in the Marina District, the cars, the artwork, the designer clothing, the no-fail investments that failed miserably. Camille's stomach burned at the thought of her maxed-out credit cards, her ex constantly knocking on the door for overdue spousal support, the whole mess with Travis Wingo, or Wingo as he liked to be called, a troubled former client.

At the end of the month, once she was declared *One Lucky Winner*, she would settle her debts and go back to being the sensible doctor that she was. Probably.

She quickly replied to the email and hit Submit, thinking she would never hear anything about the show again.

But a week later, Camille received another email notifying her that she was officially a contestant. All she needed to do was sign a release form and play the game. Why shouldn't she be the winner? She was in good shape and she was smart. She could read people. That was her superpower. She was an expert in noticing and reading body language. She could sit across from a client in complete silence, no one uttering a word for an entire session, and learn volumes.

This was why she was such an effective psychiatrist.

And now here she was, in this gorgeous villa, just minutes away from meeting her fellow competitors. She smoothed the front of her navy dress, ran her fingers through her dark hair, and tried to ignore the way her Louboutins pinched her toes. She wished she hadn't drunk all that champagne on the car ride over. First impressions mattered. But it was Dom Pérignon after all.

"I trust you had a good drive in," Fern said, leading her down a long, dim corridor.

"I did," Camille said, dragging her eyes away from what had to be hundreds of thousands of dollars' worth of artwork and examining Fern.

Fern's slight build, dark hair, lopsided smile, the square of her shoulders—all so familiar. But it was her voice… Had she heard that voice before? She had a brief phone call with Fern about the show, yes, but there was more. They moved down a shadowy corridor. Camille had definitely encountered Fern Espa before.

She tried to puzzle it out as she followed Fern but was distracted by the magnificence around her. Despite the metal poles and wooden planks used for scaffolding, it was as if she had stepped back in time into a moody and complexly textured Renaissance painting.

"The library," Fern said as she opened a door and stepped aside so Camille could enter.

Immediately, Camille's eyes found a barrel-chested man sporting khakis, brown cowboy boots and flashing a broad grin. Camille recognized him instantly. Senator Richard Crowley. Interesting. She had seen Crowley make the rounds on cable news and wasn't a fan.

Camille responded with a wan smile and turned her gaze to a woman with a wild mop of curly red hair and a sprinkle of freckles across her nose, standing next to an unlit fireplace. She paid no attention to Camille, but instead sipped a glass of wine while covertly watching a tall, dark-haired, handsome man standing at a table that held a wide array of appetizers displayed on silver platters.

The dark-haired man had a meticulously groomed goatee and the slim, muscular build of an athlete. He picked up a wafer-thin plate and placed a bacon-wrapped date atop it, then added a spoonful of what looked like fresh calamari salad. Camille's stomach roiled at the sight, though eating something might be the best thing for her. She needed something to soak up all the champagne she'd consumed on the drive.

Camille watched as the man retreated to a far corner of the room with his plate, casting his own glances at the redhead who sipped from a wineglass. The way the man and woman kept ping-ponging looks at one another, Camille had a feeling there might be more to that story. The woman patted the pocket of her oversize cardigan and an expression of pure misery crossed her face. So she was missing her phone just as much as Camille was. Giving up her phone was hard. Without it, she was cut off from her patients, along with the rest of the world. Camille felt naked without its weight.

"Just waiting on one more," Fern called out as she pressed a glass of wine into Camille's hand, then retreated to a corner of the room. She watched as Fern's face furrowed in consternation as she pressed two fingers to her ear. She was wearing an earpiece and talking to someone. Whatever was being said was not going well. Camille strained to hear but was too far away.

After a moment, Fern moved to the center of the room and tapped a wineglass with a spoon. "As you know, I'm Fern Espa, and I'm your host for *One Lucky Winner*—the first reality competition of its kind to offer the winner the incredible sum of ten million dollars. All you have to do is outmaneuver your fellow competitors."

A shiver of excitement zipped up Camille's back. All that money. It was almost too incredible to be true.

"Unfortunately, our final contestant has not yet arrived," Fern said, her voice cracking nervously, "but will be here soon. I'm going to step out for a moment and check on her status. In the meantime, please get to know one another." Fern hurriedly moved from the room, the library door closing behind her with a loud click.

Everyone remained quiet, eyeing each other until Senator Crowley stepped forward and smiled. "Well, I'm Richard Crowley, I'm from Texas."

"Senator Richard Crowley," Camille couldn't help but say. "Champion of traditional family values, small government, big guns, and states' rights."

While Camille found Richard Crowley to be one of the more polite, less rabid politicians out there today, he was also big on obfuscation, scant on substance, but for some reason, his constituents kept reelecting him every six years. Recently retired, there was buzz that Crowley might make a run at the White House.

"Former senator," Richard clarified. "And I can't believe I'm celebrating my retirement by taking part in a reality show." He gave a self-deprecating laugh.

Camille looked down at her wineglass, now empty. How had that happened? She moved to an espresso maker perched next to the wine bottles. She was done drinking alcohol for the night.

"And who might you be?" Richard asked, homing in on Camille in that silky way that she had heard him speak hundreds of times while watching the news. Senator Crowley was not a proponent of mental health services. It made her skin itch.

"I'm Dr. Camille Tamerlane," Camille said, setting her wineglass on the nearest surface.

"And what is it that you do, Dr. Tamerlane?" Senator Crowley asked, reaching out to shake her free hand. His grip was strong. Despite his weathered skin and advanced age, and the way his paunch pressed against his golf shirt, the senator was in pretty good physical shape. And behind that good old boy facade was a ruthless politician used to getting what he wanted.

"I'm a psychiatrist and therapist," she said, extracting her fingers from the senator's grip. "From just down the road in San Francisco."

"Wonderful," Crowley said. "It's good to know someone will be able to tend to our psychological needs while we're here." The senator laughed and glanced around to see who might be enjoying his joke.

Camille smiled patiently, then turned to the tall man with the goatee. "And your name? Please don't tell me you're a politician too."

"Well," he said, with a small laugh, "I guess it depends on who you talk to. I'm Samuel Rafferty and I'm just an attorney from Atlanta."

"Not just an attorney." The redhead spoke up in a soft voice. Samuel's head snapped toward the woman, his face unreadable.

"I saw the news in the airport," the woman said. "You were the prosecutor in the Ricky Lee Forrest murder case down in Georgia." She shook her head with a slight shudder. "He's a monster, he killed all those boys. You convicted him."

"The *jury* convicted Ricky Lee," Samuel clarified. "I simply presented the case."

"I saw how his brother tried to come after you," she said, taking a sip from her wineglass. "You were so calm, so controlled."

Was that an edge to her voice? Camille wondered.

"It's not hard when you have an armed bailiff standing by," Samuel said, setting his plate aside, his eyes narrowing. "Thank goodness for that."

"That was you?" Camille asked. "I saw that on the news too," she said. "I've always been fascinated by the criminal mind."

"Well, while I'm no psychiatrist, I can say that the motives for crime usually come down to three things." Samuel held a fist and then extended a finger as he made each point. "Vengeance, greed, and jealousy."

"What about fear?" Camille asked, taking a drink from a

tiny espresso cup. The hot liquid burned her throat, but she was grateful for the sobering sensation.

Samuel raised his eyebrows. "Sure. Fear can make someone do terrible things."

He was right. In Camille's experience, fear was quite the motivator.

From her spot in the shadows, the redhead cleared her throat. "Well, I'm no one. I mean compared to you all. My name is Maire. I'm just a mom from Calico, Iowa." She held out her hands as if to say *sorry, but this is all you get.* "Oh, I do own an Etsy shop where I sell jewelry. It's called Calico Rose."

An artist? At first blush, Camille hadn't pegged the woman as an artisan. Maybe a teacher or a nurse. That's what she got for making assumptions. "Is that one of your pieces? May I see?"

Maire fingered the delicate silver chain at her neck and nodded. Camille stepped forward and lifted the small pendant that held one tiny blue flower. "How sweet," Camille said, dragging out the word. She looked up into Maire's gray eyes. Camille knew she was being bitchy, but anything to get into her competitors' heads. "A forget-me-not?" she asked.

"Yes," Maire said, taking a small step backward so that Camille had to drop the chain. "I use lots of different flora and create custom pieces for customers."

"What would you suggest for me?" Camille asked.

Maire tilted her head and bit her lip, looking long and hard at Camille. "Lily of the valley, I think," Maire finally said. "You're a psychiatrist, right? It symbolizes discretion."

Camille nodded. "That makes sense. Although, lily of the valley is toxic, am I right?"

Maire shrugged. "Lots of beautiful things are."

Ouch, thought Camille. This might be her most formidable opponent in the game. Seemingly unassuming, docile, sweet, but not to be underestimated.

There was an awkward silence as Fern slipped back into

the room with a man. *The final contestant?* Camille wondered. If Fern looked flustered, the man accompanying her looked frazzled.

"Everyone," Fern said. "I'd like for you to meet the director of *One Lucky Winner*, Alfonso Solomon. Mr. Solomon is a world-renowned director, and I know we will all be in good hands with his vision and expertise."

Alfonso nodded and gave a harried little wave. "Nice to have you all here. My advice: Be yourselves and pretend the cameras aren't here. The crew will be as unobtrusive as possible. This show is about you and the competition. It will be intense, brutal even. I don't even need to tell you how high the stakes are with *One Lucky Winner*."

With that, Alfonso leaned over, whispered something in Fern's ear, then exited the room.

"Everything okay?" Camille asked when he was gone.

"It's fine," Fern said, but her tight expression said otherwise. "Just the usual beginning of production scramble. We are still waiting on our final contestant to arrive but expect her shortly. I trust you all had a chance to meet one another?"

"We have," Senator Crowley said, draining the last of his wine and setting his glass on a table. "But, Fern, I'm curious, how's this—" he swept his arms wide "—all going to work?"

Camille was curious as well. The information sent to her about the format of the competition was big on hype and short on details.

"I'm glad you asked, Senator," Fern said, robustly. "You've all seen the other reality competition series out there. Like those, our competition will have physical tasks, races, puzzle solving, teamwork, alliances, but *One Lucky Winner* is unlike *anything* anyone has seen before." She sounded so rehearsed, so affected, Camille thought. "We're used to getting our fix of reality TV in predictable doses—same night, same time—but at *One Lucky Winner*, we do things quite differently. All around the world, potential viewers are receiving cryptic messages and links inviting them to watch at a moment's notice. An alert will go out, compelling people to stop what they are doing and tune in live. When they do, and it can be at any time, day or night, they will not be able to look away." Fern paused to meet everyone's gaze before continuing.

"Throughout our time together, you will complete several challenges that will push you to the edge. During the challenges, your goal is to finish first. If you do, you win what we call a Super Clue, a tidbit of information that, once put together with all the other Super Clues, will help you solve the overreaching mystery of Bella Luce. Also, along the way you may find a Game Changer. A Game Changer can come in many forms, but each will come with very specific, very important directions. Along with the Game Changer there may be a *tool*—" Fern's voice lingered on the word "—that if you choose to use, has the potential to steer the game in your favor."

A zip of anticipation went through Camille. These Super Clues and Game Changers would be crucial to winning the money.

"The winners stay and the losers will be sent home," Fern continued. "Except—" she raised a finger "—if our viewers *vote* for you to stay. Your fate is in their hands. At the end of fourteen days, one lucky winner will be crowned and will walk away with ten million dollars." Fern's eyes shone with excitement.

Camille looked around at her fellow competitors. Samuel was nodding, the senator rubbed his hands together, and Maire worried at her forget-me-not on the chain. Everyone was focused intently on what Fern was saying. They were all as determined as she was to win that money.

Camille scanned the room. There, tucked into a shelf among all the books, was what she was looking for. A tiny red light. A camera. They were being livestreamed. The game had already begun.

She looked around for more telltale red lights. There was one in each of the corners of the coffered ceiling, and she spotted one in a vase of flowers. She figured there had to be more.

"Quick question," Camille said. "Where do we sleep? I thought we were going to stay at the Diletta."

"Yes," agreed the senator. "I was really looking forward to a vinotherapy session before we started."

"Ah, the Diletta." Fern nodded. "I know that was what you were expecting, but we needed to keep the location of the competition under wraps for as long as possible. In reality, the Diletta was a decoy so work could be done behind the scenes here. It's the perfect locale. I think you will find it very comfortable."

"I'm sure we will," Camille said. She didn't really care where they were staying. She was only fourteen days away from ten million dollars and then she could stay wherever she wished.

"Because this is a game," Fern said, "there are rules. Number One, no contact with the outside world. If for some reason you reach out to someone outside the estate, you will immediately pack your bags and be sent home. Number Two, if you leave the property, for any reason, you are out of the game. Number Three, if you enter a restricted section of the property, you will be sent home. Any questions?"

Camille mulled over the rules. She didn't like the fact that she would be out of contact with her patients, but the requirements seemed reasonable. She caught the look on Maire's face. She had kids. It must be excruciating not to be able to talk to them. *Don't get involved*, Camille reminded herself. She would not get emotionally entangled with these people. She had a job to do.

"Okay, then," Fern said. "There is one last thing I want to show you before you retire to your quarters for the night," she said. "Follow me."

A tingle of excitement slid through Camille. She had summed up her rivals and, honestly, they weren't all that impressive. Samuel was clearly the most physically fit of the bunch and obviously smart, but not as smart as Camille. The senator appeared capable, but she knew she could handle him. She could be ruthless when she wanted to be. And Maire, well, Camille wasn't quite sure yet. She had an edge to her that was simmering just below the surface. As for the fifth and final contestant, they had yet to arrive and were an unknown entity. In the end, only one of them would win and Camille, without a doubt, was going to make sure she was the last one standing.

FIVE

THE ASSISTANT

Fern looked out at the contestants, their faces lit up with anticipation. "I'm going to take you to what we like to call *The Vault*," Fern said.

"The Vault?" Samuel asked, raising his eyebrows. "Sounds ominous."

"Its main function is as a wine cellar," Fern explained. "It's a spectacular space, if I do say so myself, but for *One Lucky Winner*, we are repurposing it for something special." She began ushering the guests through the library door. Camille's heel buckled and she clutched Samuel's arm to steady herself, then stumbled, almost taking them both down.

Camille was a bit drunk but that was to be expected. Cat wanted to make sure the wine and spirits were flowing, in hopes of loosening tongues and putting everyone at ease. Thankfully, everyone had signed away any chance for liability claims.

The contract was boilerplate, a basic agreement that informed contestants that the production company had no liability for accidents related to the game. Fern was sure that Samuel, as an attorney, had read through the document carefully. He was sharp. She observed that he was the first contestant to notice all the cameras in the library. He said nothing about them to the group though. His ability to keep his mouth shut would serve him well during the game. If first impressions meant anything, Fern thought Samuel had the potential to go far in the competition and Camille would be a close second.

Cat was watching them on the bank of video screens in her locked office, periodically popping into Fern's earpiece to tell her she was slouching, or that she was talking in that weird, affected way she did when nervous. Cat was intent on remaining behind the scenes, out of the camera's eye and anonymous to the contestants and most of the crew, explaining to Fern that she wanted *One Lucky Winner* and the contestants to be the sole focus of the show. If the media got wind that she was involved, the chatter would turn to Cat and how she made her money getting likes on social media. She was so much more than that. No, she wanted to pull the strings from the shadows and watch the show become the hit it was destined to become. That was when she would make the big reveal—that Cat James was the mastermind behind *One Lucky Winner*.

A crackle of static filled Fern's ear. She wanted to pull the earpiece out and shove it in her pocket, but she knew that Cat did not like to be ignored.

"Someone's at the door, Fern," Cat said through the earpiece. "I can see them on the security camera. It must be the fifth contestant. Better go answer it."

Fern's heart skipped a beat. Strange, she hadn't received an alert on her phone. Finally. Audrey Abreo had arrived. She hesitated. But maybe it was Philippa, wanting her job back. If so, Fern would be out as host.

"What are you waiting for? Go," Cat said. Fern could hear the impatience in her voice. "We need to get this show started."

Anxiety squeezed at her chest. It couldn't be Philippa. Could it? How would she get through the gate?

Cat spoke again. "Answer the door, Fern. You don't want to keep them waiting."

"Ah, it looks like our last guest has finally arrived," Fern said, forcing a note of cheer into her voice. "Follow me," she said, leading the group to the front doors. Behind her, she heard the footfalls of the contestants trying to keep up with her as she moved briskly toward the main hall. They were just as curious to find out who would be joining them as she was.

Fern paused, settling her face into a calm, welcoming visage before pulling open the heavy door.

"Welcome to Bella Luce and *One Lucky Winner*," Fern said, blinded for a moment by the light from the lantern hanging above the door. All she could see was the silhouette of a man looming above her. A man? It was supposed to be Audrey Abreo or Philippa. Perhaps it was a driver with the luggage.

But then the smell hit her. A familiar cologne. Sandalwood and limes and lilies. Fern felt her throat click and a stab of nausea coursed through her.

"Hello," the man said. "Am I in the right place?" It was his voice, the same tone, the same timbre. Fern grabbed on to the door frame to steady herself.

The man stepped from the shadows. "I have to say," he began, "creepy Italian villa was not on my bingo card."

Fern couldn't speak. Her eyes were locked on his feet. He had always favored Gucci horsebit loafers and that hadn't changed, though these were scuffed at the toe. And that smell. *His* smell.

"I'm here for *One Lucky Winner*," the man said. "If I'm in the wrong place, tell me now because my driver is leaving."

Fern wanted to run, but she was aware of the cameras on her, tucked into corners and hiding within flower arrangements. Cat was surely watching right now on one of the dozen screens in her office. Had she brought him here? Was it a joke, some kind of sick test?

She could almost feel his manicured fingers pressed against her throat, his hot breath in her ear, and she shuddered. Fern forced her gaze upward. He was just as she remembered him. Shaggy blond hair, pale blue eyes behind trendy tortoiseshell glasses. He was older than when she last saw him, ten years older to be exact, and would probably still be considered handsome to most, though his forehead was clearly smoothed by Botox.

"Are you okay?" the man asked. Did he recognize her? She saw no glint of familiarity in his eyes, only concern. She wanted to scream, to slam the door in his face.

"What's going on?" Cat asked through her earpiece. Fern bit her cheek so hard she drew blood. What in God's name was he doing here?

"Welcome," Fern managed to say, surprised at the strength in her voice. "Please come in."

Fern held the door open, and the man breezed in, pulling his oversize luggage behind him. "Nice place," he said, glancing around the great hall appreciatively.

"If you don't mind," Fern interrupted, "may I see your confirmation email?"

The man stared at her and for a moment Fern thought he finally knew who she was and her legs went weak.

With an impatient sigh, the man pulled out his phone, flicked through his email, and held the screen up to her face.

There it was—the official email that she sent to all the contestants who made the cut. But Fern had never sent this email. Not to Ned Bennett.

"Excuse me for just a moment," Fern said, fighting the bile that climbed up her throat. "I'll be right back." It was all Fern could do not to break into a run, but she forced herself to take even, regular steps down the corridor until she came to a scarred wooden door. She looked back down the long hallway to see the five guests staring back at her. With shaking hands, Fern pulled the master key from her pocket, an old-fashioned skeleton key they used for the doors not updated with the new security system. She slipped it into the keyhole, opened the door, stepped inside, closed it behind her with a quiet snick, and slid to the dusty floor.

The room was once Cat's ex-husband's home office, but after the divorce, Cat took a sledgehammer to it. Now Fern was sitting in a half-renovated construction zone.

Ned Bennett. Ned Bennett was here. Fern covered her mouth to hold back the scream that was building in her throat. Why?

"Fern!" came Cat's voice through the earpiece. "Who the hell is that? I thought the final contestant was Audrey Abreo." Fern tried to think fast. Ned had the email that confirmed that he was a contestant. A driver picked him up at the airport and knew to bring him to the estate.

But Fern had been the one to contact all the contestants, including Audrey Abreo. So why was Ned Bennett here instead? For ten years, she had prayed that she would never have to see him again. It had to have been Cat who invited him. But why? Cat knew full well what Ned had done to Fern, had witnessed it firsthand. She hated Ned almost as much as Fern did.

"Fern," Cat screeched in her ear. "Who is the new contestant?"

Fern cleared her throat. "It's Ned Bennett."

"You invited Ned Bennett to my show?" Cat asked in disbelief. "What the hell? What happened to Audrey?"

"I don't know, but it wasn't me," Fern said in a rush. "I thought it was you."

There was silence on the other end.

"Cat?" Fern prompted.

When Cat finally spoke, her voice was shot through with steel. "What gives you the right to fuck with me, Fern? After everything I've done for you, are you really trying to destroy everything that I've built, everything I've worked for?"

Tears filled Fern's eyes. "No, I swear, it wasn't me. I wouldn't. What should we do?"

"We?" Cat asked sharply. "*We* aren't going to do anything. As usual, I'm going to have to fix everything. First of all, did Ned recognize you?"

"I don't think so," Fern said, wiping her eyes. She had to keep it together. As much as Cat liked to claim *One Lucky Winner* as her own, it was Fern's show too. Yes, Cat had the money, the contacts, the beautiful home, but it was Fern who had done all the work. "He doesn't know who I am. He doesn't remember me."

"Figures." Cat gave a derisive laugh. "Bastard. Okay. Get back out there and proceed as if everything is fine. Get through the rest of the night and I'll come up with something."

"Cat," Fern said, "I swear I didn't invite Ned. I hate him, he ruined my life."

"Who, then?" Cat snapped. "Because it sure as hell wasn't me. I gave you the final list of names and you were the one who contacted them, who made all the arrangements."

Fern had no response. Cat was right. There was no fathomable reason for Cat to invite Ned to be on the show. Fern ran through other possibilities. One of the dozens of contractors who worked to set up the show? No, they wouldn't have access to Fern's email account. Fedko and Trevor, who were their behind-the-scenes IT guys? They had set up all the cameras, set up the app that streamed the video to Fern's phone and to the bank of monitors in Cat's office. The director, Alfonso Solomon? But that made no sense either. Someone from Cat's past? Maybe her ex-husband?

"Now get your ass back out there and act like Ned Bennett is the fucking star of the show," Cat hissed. "I'll deal with you later."

Cat disappeared from her ear and Fern was met with blessed silence. Getting unsteadily to her feet, Fern brushed sawdust from her clothing and blinked away the last of her tears.

Resisting the urge to grab a claw hammer resting on a nearby table, Fern opened the door and walked down the corridor toward the waiting contestants. Toward the monster who had nearly raped her. If it weren't for Cat, he surely would have, maybe worse. She could do this. She had to.

SIX

THE BEST FRIEND

Maire watched as Fern returned. Her eyes were overly bright, and her nose was red. Wherever Fern had gone off to, she was still flustered. It made Maire wonder if Fern was in the bathroom taking a hit of something—cocaine? Adderall? She had no idea what the drug of choice was these days.

Maire couldn't help noticing Fern's starstruck reaction to the newest contestant. Not that she could blame her. Maire was stunned herself. Everyone who was obsessed with true crime television knew Ned Bennett, the creator and executive producer of the hit *Cold, Hard Truth*. It was one of the more salacious true crime news shows and had been on the air for years. The show was chock-full of reenactments, bloody crime scene photos, jailhouse interrogation videos, and tearful interviews with victims' family and friends.

Ned dropped his iPhone into the lockbox and scanned the great hall appreciatively. He was dressed in jeans and a leather jacket that probably cost more than her entire wardrobe.

"Loved your show," the senator said, clapping Ned on his back and offering his hand. "Please tell me you have something new for us soon."

"I've got a few things in the works," Ned said, shaking the senator's hand. "I hope to share more soon."

Maire dared a glance at Samuel, who stood off to the side, eyes narrowed.

How could it be a coincidence that Samuel showed up here? It was impossible, wasn't it? Every nerve beneath her skin shimmered with fear. She just needed to play the game, win the money, and go home to her girls. But still, she needed to find the right moment to pull Samuel aside so they could get their stories straight.

Maire watched as Camille greeted and chatted effortlessly with Ned Bennett. Maire had hoped she would find an ally in another female participant. But no. She had heard the subtle condescension in Camille's voice when she asked Maire about her jewelry line. Camille was sly, but Maire had known women like this her entire life. She could handle her. Maire was getting impatient. She really didn't care about getting to know her competitors. She just wanted to play the game. She wanted to win.

Ned turned his attention to Samuel. "You're that lawyer who just about got attacked in the courtroom in Atlanta. They're playing that clip over and over online. 'Fuck you, fuck you,'" Ned said in mock fierceness, mimicking the convicted man's younger brother. "Wild," Ned said, with a little laugh. "Man, that would have played great on *Cold, Hard Truth*.

"And you," Ned said, pointing at Fern, "you look familiar to me. Have we met?"

Fern looked startled for a moment and then quickly recovered. "I'm afraid not," Fern said brusquely. "Now come along this way," Fern said, looking at her watch, "it's getting late. Follow me. I really want you all to see this."

Maire fell in line behind the others as Fern led them down a long, dim corridor lined with antiquated oil paintings of dourfaced men and buxom women.

Fern flicked on a light and it was with relief that Maire

stepped into a brightly lit state-of-the-art kitchen with a commercial refrigerator, a multiunit range, and a dizzying array of
appliances. The modern kitchen clashed with the old-world
Tuscan vibe of the rest of the house.

Fern moved to the far end of the room, pressed her hands
against a wall, and a panel popped open.

"This way," Fern said, stepping aside and revealing a dark
passage.

"You want us to go down there?" Camille frowned. "Where
does it lead?"

"What Italian villa wouldn't be complete without a wine
cellar?" Fern asked with forced cheerfulness. She reached into
the chasm and a dull light appeared. "Please, this way."

Hesitantly, Maire stepped forward. "Just down that way,"
Fern directed. "Don't worry, I'll be right behind you."

Maire stepped through the passageway and immediately the
temperature dropped. With one hand, she pulled her cardigan
close, and with the other she pressed her fingers against the
rough and damp wall. She peered down, but whatever was at
the bottom of the steps was lost in the dark. She heard the echo
of water dripping. A lonely, hollow sound.

"Watch your step," Fern warned.

Maire felt the air collapse in her lungs. There was no banister to hold on to and the steps were steeply pitched and so
narrow that she had to turn nearly sideways to navigate them.
She slowly picked her way down and at the halfway point she
stumbled. From behind, she felt a steadying hand and without
turning around knew it was Samuel.

Maire hated that he still had that effect on her. Back in college he hadn't even been her boyfriend, could never have been
her boyfriend, but that didn't stop her from melting from his
touch.

Samuel had been her roommate's boyfriend. They were
inseparable, practically engaged, but try as she might, Maire

couldn't stop herself from fantasizing about what it would be like to have his hands wrapped around her waist, his lips pressed against her neck. Maire shook away the memories and stepped away from him.

Once safely at the bottom of the steps, Maire turned and shot Samuel a dirty look. He wasn't going to screw this up for her. What happened occurred a lifetime ago. Maire was a different person now. And most importantly, she was a mother and everything she did, every move she made, was for her children.

Fern took her place at the front of the group and took them through a narrow stone passageway dimly lit by a series of bronze sconces. "All the lighting was imported from Italy and actually once held real candles. They have been restored and retrofitted," Fern explained.

Something skittered across Maire's foot, and she bit back a cry. She refused to get spooked by a rodent and let the others see any fear.

"One more door," Fern said, yanking on the round pull handle of an arched wooden door. "Please, go in, I'll get the light," she said.

Maire hesitated, then stepped over the threshold into a wall of darkness, her arms stretched out in front of her blindly. A light appeared and Maire found that they were in another corridor with one iron door.

"I want to show you where the most expensive wines are kept, follow me," Fern invited, and, making a wide berth around Ned Bennett, she punched a series of numbers into her phone. A green light appeared on the keypad affixed to the door and it popped open with a pneumatic hiss. "The special collection includes a 1787 Chateau Lafite and a 1907 Heidsieck that survived a World War I torpedo attack by a German submarine."

"Is this The Vault?" Maire asked.

"Well, this is where we keep the most expensive wines locked away," Fern said as she pulled open the door. "But it's not what we are going to use as The Vault for the show. I'll show you that in just a moment."

Everyone gathered into a tight knot to peer inside. The light behind them was barely bright enough to puncture the dark, windowless space.

"Come in, come in," Fern invited and the others stepped inside one by one. With the poor lighting, it was impossible to tell just how big the room was, but the dark seemed endless. Maire could hear the sound of a fan whirring. She looked up. An air vent with an elaborately scrolled iron cover puffed cool air across her skin. The stone walls were pitted and the floor slanted. Maire pulled her cardigan more tightly around her, imagining what might be crouched against the dusty corners. Fern used her cell phone to scan the rest of the space. It was larger than Maire first thought. There were shelves of wine, pallets of water, and jumbo-sized containers of snack mixes against one wall, and behind a metal cage were more shelves of wine. In a far corner sat a box filled with a jumble of odds and ends.

"The room is obviously part of the original home and the conditions are perfect for wine storage," Fern said. "But we won't be using this room during the show. We're set up through here. Let me show you."

Fern ushered them from the wine cellar, and, leaving it open, led the group down the hallway and through another door.

Maire heard Camille gasp. In the center of the domed ceiling was a twenty-four-arm Venetian chandelier with hand-blown chocolate-colored glass. Its light cast snake-like shadows across the floor.

"That's a sixty-thousand-dollar chandelier," Maire heard Camille whisper.

Maire didn't know where to look first. Most of the room was lined with mahogany shelves holding hundreds of jewel-colored wine bottles. Mounted into a recessed wall was a black-and-white painting of the skull of an antlered animal surrounded by a thorny nest. Its eyes were empty hollows. Behind a full bar hung a large, gilded mirror marred by a spidery crack. Maire looked into the mirror and her distorted reflection stared back. "The mirror is original to the home," Fern explained. "Over a hundred years old."

"Impressive," Camille said.

Maire watched as Camille moved languidly through the space, her fingers skimming the wine bottles. She was so self-assured, so comfortable. Something that Maire rarely felt herself. "So this is a fully operational winery?" Camille asked.

"It is," Fern said, reaching for a bottle of wine. "This merlot is produced here and can be found in a number of the valley's most popular restaurants and boutiques. You must try it." She began pouring the wine into five long-stemmed glasses lined up atop the bar.

Ned Bennett sidled up next to Fern and reached for a glass. He stood so close that his chest grazed Fern's back. "Nice," he said in a low, gravelly voice. Fern startled, and the bottle slipped from her fingers. It crashed to the stone floor, sending a shower of glass and red wine into the air and across Ned's and Fern's shoes.

Fern cried out as everyone jumped back to avoid the splash.

Maire looked around for something to help sop up the mess.

"No, please leave it," Fern said, taking in the small puddle of wine with dismay and looking as if she might cry. "I'll get it later. Let's move down here." The group shifted to the far end of the bar and with a shaky voice Fern asked, "Now, who would like to sample the merlot?" Both Samuel and Camille declined but Ned accepted. "Maire?" Fern asked, hopefully.

Maire accepted the delicate glass. She took a sip and murmured her approval, though honestly, all wine tasted the same to her.

"Now, let me show you The Vault." Fern opened the door

just behind the bar to reveal a small room designed to look like a bank vault with shiny metal walls, built-in lockboxes, and stacks of what Maire was sure were fake bars of gold. Inside, the only furniture was a table and chair. Atop the table was a laptop.

"Each of you will use this space as a sort of confessional," Fern explained. "Throughout your time here, you will come into this room known as The Vault, and record the answers to a series of questions using this laptop. This is the place where you can reflect and contemplate on why you are here, what you hope to achieve, all while relaxing with a glass of wine. We only ask that you are completely, brutally honest. We want viewers to connect with you, feel your emotions, experience the highs and lows right along with you, because the streaming audience could save you."

Fern paused dramatically to let the information soak in. "Each day, snippets of your time in The Vault will be aired, giving the audience a chance to vote for the contestant who strikes a chord with them. The contestant with the least number of votes will go home. So, when it's your turn, make sure to be vulnerable, honest, and, most importantly, be yourselves. One of you has been randomly chosen to enter The Vault first. When it's your turn, you'll sit at the table and follow the instructions on the laptop. It's easy. Tonight, you'll each have fifteen minutes in The Vault and then head upstairs."

"So who's first?" the senator asked. Through the flickering light of the candles, he looked as tired as she felt, Maire thought. It had been a long day for all of them.

"It just so happens, Senator Crowley, you are the lucky one," Fern said with a smile. "But before you go inside, I have a little something for each of you."

Fern ducked behind the bar and started lining up gift bags spilling over with shimmering gold tissue paper. One by one, Fern began handing them out. Maire saw her rip the tag from the last bag before handing it to Ned.

Maire waited an awkward beat until the others began pluck-ing out the tissue paper and peering inside. Then she looked in-side her own. It held a bottle of wine and other odds and ends.

"This is lovely," Camille said, setting her bag aside. "So very thoughtful of you, Fern."

"No, no, take everything out," Fern urged.

Maire reached inside and pulled out each item one by one. A bottle of Bella Luce cabernet, a bag of merlot-infused coffee, a Laguiole corkscrew, and a set of colorful wine chilling stones. As expected, there was plenty of oohing and aahing over the contents.

"What's with this logo?" the senator asked, holding up his bottle.

Maire took a step toward the table and peered over the sena-tor's shoulder to get a better look. The *One Lucky Winner* logo was on the label. It really was quite grotesque. The angry god-desses with snakes for hair converging on the tortured-looking man and woman. The design was so disturbing, dark and feral. There was one word, printed in bold, blood red ink: *Imbroglione*.

"I know who they are," Camille said. "They're the Fu-ries. Goddesses from Roman mythology. They fit in with the whole Italian theme that's going on here." She waved her hand around vaguely.

"What does this mean? *Imbroglione?*" the senator asked. "I'm a little rusty with my Italian."

Maire looked down at the wine bottle in the senator's hands. So strange. *Imbroglione* stared back up at her. It did look Italian, but what did it mean?

Ned spoke up. "I don't know Italian either, but it sure looks like someone is calling me a degenerate." He turned his bottle around so the others could see. *Degenerare*. "What do yours say?"

"Mine says, *Sfasciafamiglie*," Camille said, stumbling over the word. "Something about family maybe? What about yours, Samuel?" she asked.

"Traditore?" Samuel said, raising his eyebrows.

"Mine is *Uccisore*," Maire said with a shrug. "No idea."

"Well, it's getting late," Fern said, consulting her watch. "Senator Crowley, why don't you step inside The Vault, and you can record your piece. We'll wait out here until you are finished and then the others can have their turn."

Fern waited until everyone had stepped away from the door and the senator had taken a seat in front of the computer before gently shutting The Vault's door.

"Wait," Maire said, worry knotting her brow. "Is he locked in? Can he get out?"

"Yes, yes, don't worry," Fern assured her. "He can get out at any time."

"Has anyone else noticed that there is like no one here?" Ned asked. "I mean, when do we meet the rest of the crew?"

Maire had been wondering the same thing. "Most of you already met our director, Alfonso. He's waiting for you upstairs with the camera crew ready to film an introduction to the show. Since it's not one of the challenges, it won't be aired live but will be used in the opening credits as a way to present each of you to the audience," Fern explained.

Maire looked down at her pilled leggings. This was not how she wanted the world to see her for the first time.

"And remember, you can expect to be filmed all day, every day, but there are two places where you are assured privacy. Your sleeping quarters and the bathrooms. There will be no cameras in those spots, but everywhere else, at *all* times, expect a camera, expect someone to be watching. Viewers can tune in twenty-four/seven whenever they'd like at OneLuckyWinner.com."

Maire shifted uncomfortably and scanned the ceiling in search of more telltale red lights. "So people can see us right now?" She thought of her kids and what they would think if they stumbled on the website. Maire had thought the show would be taped, that she would have time to explain to Keely and Dani about the competition.

"Not just yet," Fern said, "but once the first challenge begins, we'll air the opening sequence and then the entire world will be watching live from there on out."

"Except in the bedrooms and bathrooms, right?" Camille asked. Maire wanted to be assured of this too.

"Yes, but try not to think about the cameras," Fern advised. "Before you know it, you'll forget all about them. It will be like they aren't even there. Now, please drink your wine, relax, and then I'll take you up to your room."

Fern got the senator settled into The Vault while Maire took a seat at one of the high-top tables and busied herself with looking at the contents of her gift bag in hopes that no one would sit next to her. It seemed to work because everyone gave her a wide berth. She was worried about Dani. Would Shar read the thick binder of instructions that she left with her and know what to do? And now Samuel dropped from out of nowhere like a bomb.

She pulled her wine bottle with the curious label from the bag and stared down at the pale-skinned Furies with a reckoning in their eyes. *Uccisore.* Maire rolled the word over her tongue. What did it mean? If she won the ten million dollars— *no*, she thought, *when* she won the ten million dollars—she would take the girls to Italy. They could go to Umbria, C.S. Lewis's inspiration for Narnia, or to a mask-making workshop in Venice.

Dani would get better, Keely would weather the storm that was middle school, and they would go to Italy. She would tell her story to the viewers of *One Lucky Winner.* Make them understand why they should save her, keep her on the show. How she needed to win for her girls, needed that money so that Dani could live to see her next birthday and beyond. She would be an open book. Bare her soul. Tell them everything. Well, almost everything. There was one thing that no one in the world knew. No one, except for Samuel Rafferty. That was a secret she would take to her grave. She would make sure that he did too.

SEVEN

THE ASSISTANT

After each contestant had their chance to record their vault segments and Alfonso recorded them for the show's intro, Fern had finally gotten them off to bed. They weren't happy about having to share one large room, but they were so tired that most of them didn't put up too much of a fuss. Except for Ned. He insisted on his own room, that he couldn't possibly sleep in the same space as the others. Fern tried to explain that it was part of the game, but Ned didn't care. Finally, she just had to walk away.

Being in the same room as Ned made her stomach roil and the entire time she was dealing with his constant questions and demands, Cat was barking in her earpiece, berating her.

"I've got it covered," Fern kept saying as she rushed down the cellar steps, finally ripping the earpiece from her head in frustration. She hated being down here alone. Despite the renovations that Cat and her ex-husband had done to the space, to Fern it was still cold, dark, and claustrophobic.

At the bottom of the stairs, she regarded the carnage of broken glass and splattered red wine. In her defense, Fern had been shocked by Ned Bennett's sudden appearance and when he brushed up against her, she was thrust back ten years to that traumatic encounter in a New York high-rise and corner office with a view of Central Park.

Fern could tell that the contestants sensed her unease around Ned. How could they not? Camille, in psychiatrist mode, had even pulled her aside to ask if she was okay. Fern assured her that she was.

She grabbed a towel and a garbage can from behind the bar. What a mess, Fern thought, eyeing the puddle of red wine and trail of broken glass that fanned out across the floor. With tears of exhaustion, she bent down and began picking up the shards of glass.

She still couldn't wrap her head around the fact that she and Ned Bennett were under the same roof, but who had invited him here? Was it someone who had a grudge against her? And why? Every move Fern made was dictated by Cat and everyone in their orbit knew that.

Fern had spent the last ten years dedicated to Cat and as irritated and frustrated as her boss could be with her, Fern knew that Cat wouldn't jeopardize the show by bringing in Ned.

But if the vendetta wasn't against Fern, then it had to be against Cat. God knew she had made her share of enemies over the years. She was a smart, shrewd businesswoman who crushed rivals left and right without a second thought. But why bring Ned Bennett to *One Lucky Winner*? He was sleazy, scary, unpredictable.

Fern lowered herself to her knees, the stone floor biting into her skin. She mopped at the red liquid, knowing that each droplet was wasted money. Fern glanced up at the security camera poised above the bar. Cat was probably watching her right now, pissed that she had taken out her earpiece.

Cat would take this out of her paycheck for sure. Above, she heard the echo of footsteps and closed her eyes. Cat was coming. This was the last thing she needed. It was bad enough being screamed at through an earpiece, but getting screamed at in person was an entirely different shade of humiliation. She stood and tossed the sodden rag aside into the small sink behind the bar.

The footsteps grew louder. She would just have to do what she always did when Cat was upset with her: look contrite, apologize, and work even harder. Hosting *One Lucky Winner* was Fern's big chance, maybe her last one, to make a name for herself.

"Jesus Christ," Cat said, as she clattered down the final few steps into the bar area. She was still dressed in her white silk outfit but had added a white cardigan. "That was a five-hundred-dollar bottle of wine," she said, hands on her hips.

"I'm sorry," Fern began, but Cat wasn't done.

"You can't even hold on to a fucking wine bottle and you expect me to believe you're capable of hosting the show?"

"It was Ned Bennett," Fern said in a small voice. "His being here threw me for a loop."

"What exactly did you think you would accomplish by bringing him here?" Cat asked, shifting her arms across her chest.

"I didn't, I wouldn't," Fern stammered. "I've spent the last ten years trying to get that day out of my mind and I can't. I'll never forget his face and he didn't even recognize me."

Cat gave her a hard look and laughed, a hoarse bark that held no humor. "You think that Ned Bennett cared who you were? You were just one of many stupid, naive girls who were dumb enough to go into his office alone and let him shut the door."

Fern could almost feel the way Ned had pressed his fingers to her throat, his hot, wet breath in her ear. The way he lifted her skirt with his sterling silver letter opener, its sharp blade biting into her thigh.

"I'm not stupid," Fern shot back, angrily. "It wasn't my fault.

He would have raped me." She blinked back tears. She refused to cry in front of Cat, who had zero patience for tears.

"Probably," Cat said matter-of-factly. "But I stopped him, didn't I? I protected you, took you away from there. And now I've been stuck with you ever since, cleaning up your messes." She pointed to a few stray shards of glass Fern had missed. "This is exactly why I should have handled all the arrangements. I knew you'd screw it up. If you didn't invite him, there must have been a leak."

"I'll send him home. Tell him there was some kind of mistake," Fern said, reaching down to gather up the last of the glass, snagging a finger on one jagged shard. Bright red blood oozed from the wound. She tightened her fingers into a fist, feeling blood puddle into her palm.

"That's the last thing we should do," Cat said sharply. "You know Ned. He's a baby and a publicity whore. He'd milk this for everything it's worth and drag the show down in the process. No," Cat said with finality. "Ned stays. We're just going to have to make the best of it. Besides, he's famous and is a good draw for the show. Hopefully he won't remember you."

Fern stood there, mouth agape. Cat didn't care how Ned's sudden appearance affected her. All she cared about was the show and ratings. Maybe Fern should just quit. Leave right now. Leave Cat with no host, no errand girl, no servant to do her bidding. What would Cat do then?

One Lucky Winner would fail, fall apart. Cat's dream of having a hit reality show would collapse, the investors would pull out, and Cat would be humiliated. The vision of her boss being skewered online and in the press sounded pretty good. *I quit* would be the two most powerful words she could utter right now.

"I'm sorry," Fern mumbled instead, the cut on her finger throbbing. She'd probably need stitches. But whom was she kidding? If *One Lucky Winner* imploded, it wouldn't be Cat who took the fall, the one to be blacklisted, disgraced. It would be Fern. Wasn't it always the underling who suffered? Fern would never work again. "I won't let him get to me again. I just don't understand why he's here."

"That makes two of us," Cat said. "But I'll figure it out. And I swear to God, Fern, if I find out you were behind this, I am going to kill you."

"I didn't…" Fern began, but Cat held up a perfectly manicured finger to shush her.

"Now I'm going to have to make some calls and somehow get a new host on such short notice. We'll probably have to delay production by a day," Cat said furiously.

"No," Fern said, the word catching roughly. "I can do it. I promise."

"That's the thing, Fern," Cat said, moving to brush past her. "I don't think you can."

"Wait," Fern said, snagging Cat's arm. "Give me a chance, I'll prove it to you. Just one chance."

Cat tried to shake off Fern's grasp, but Fern held tight. Cat's eyes flashed angrily as she stared Fern down. Sheepishly, Fern released Cat's arm, leaving blood behind from the cut on her finger. "I'm sorry," she whispered.

Cat looked down at her ruined sweater with disdain, then shrugged out of it, tossing it atop the bar.

Cat stepped past her and, with Fern close behind, hurried into the corridor.

"And you left the wine cellar door open? Really?" Cat asked aloud, stepping into the cellar.

Fern followed her inside, desperate to explain. Above them, a skittering sound came from the ceiling vent. Squirrels or mice. Fern shivered. Despite its cache of expensive wine, it was nothing but a dim, damp cave.

"What I don't think you understand, Fern," Cat said, her voice dripping with faux patience, "is that you are an assistant.

And that is all you will ever be, all that you will ever be capable of being."

Fern's breath lodged in her throat. How could someone be so dismissive, so cruel? Fern had been grateful to Cat for walking into Ned's office that day, for derailing whatever was going to happen next, but hadn't Fern paid her back the best way she could? She worked upward of twelve hours a day, seven days a week. She didn't date, didn't have friends. Her entire world was Cat.

No. Things couldn't end this way. Slowly, Fern moved from the cellar, leaving Cat behind and pausing just outside the door to look at her mentor. Fern had always hoped that one day she would prove her worth to Cat, that maybe, just maybe, she would see her as a colleague, maybe even a partner. That obviously was never going to happen.

"I can't believe I spent so much time, so many years trying to make you into something..." Cat said, looking Fern up and down, "better than this. What a fucking waste of space," she finished dismissively.

So there it was. Cat couldn't have made how she truly felt about Fern clearer. She was nothing but a hopeless disappointment, something to be cast aside like garbage. A cold anger formed a fist in her chest. It wasn't right, the way that Cat treated her. It needed to stop. Now.

"You're wrong," Fern said, her voice tremulous. "I'm the one who spent hours calling contractors and the caterers. I'm the one who made all the travel arrangements for the contestants and the crew." Her voice gathered strength. "I made sure that every single detail was perfect and I did it all for you. All to make you happy."

Cat crossed her arms across her chest and looked at Fern expectantly. "Are you finished?" she asked.

A soft sound of disbelief slipped from Fern's mouth. Cat hadn't listened to a word she said. She never had. Fern's hard work, her loyalty meant nothing to Cat. Ten years she had worked herself to the bone for this woman and for what? No more. Fern was done.

Fern gave the heavy wine cellar door a shove and watched with satisfaction as she saw Cat's face shift from irritation to disbelief. "Hey," Cat cried, dropping the bottle of wine she held, and lunged for the door.

It was too late. The door slammed with a metallic clang, trapping Cat inside. Fern pressed her ear against the cold steel. All was quiet except the sound of her own heavy breathing. The wine cellar was secure. It had been built solidly with thick stone walls and the armored door to protect Cat's precious wine. Thick enough to absorb even the loudest cries.

Fern slowly backed away from the door, not believing what she had just done. In a panic, Fern thought of Cat's phone. Her eyes landed on the bar and saw Cat's cardigan smeared with the blood. She snatched up the sweater and with relief felt its heaviness. She slid her hand into the pocket and there it was: the phone, Cat's only lifeline to the outside world. Except, Fern remembered, the security cameras.

The camera into the wine cellar was different from the ones set up for *One Lucky Winner*. Because Cat didn't want millions of strangers knowing about her expensive wines, only Fern and Cat had access to see inside. Unless someone could hack the system, no one else would know that Cat was locked up.

Using Cat's phone, Fern scrolled to the video security app and toggled to the cellar's camera. There was Cat, pounding on the door. "God dammit, Fern," Cat cried. "Let me out of here now!"

Fern hesitated. If she unlocked the door and let Cat out now maybe this would all blow over. But no, Fern wasn't done yet. She still had so much to prove to Cat. Fern turned off the camera, ending Cat's stream of expletives, then scurried up the stone steps. The old wine cellar was solid, made of stone, soundproof. There was no way the contestants would be able to hear Cat through the stone walls or the iron door. The game could go on. She wouldn't leave Cat in there for long, she told herself. Just long enough to prove that she could handle the show, handle the contestants, handle Ned Bennett. Cat would forgive Fern for this transgression, she had to. Either that or Cat would kill her.

EIGHT

THE SENATOR

The Vault

"So. I'm Richard Crowley. Husband, father, veteran, former senator from Texas. And why am I here on *One Lucky Winner*? The short answer is ten million dollars. I mean, who doesn't want ten million dollars? That's big bucks for anyone. My sixties may be just about in my rearview mirror, but I'm strong, smart, and like to win.

"I've spent the last fifty years of my life in public service. Serving my community, my church, my constituents, my country, and, most importantly, my family. My family is everything to me. Without them, I'd just be a poor kid from central Texas. I married my wife, Genevieve, when we were both just eighteen. We'd been together since we were twelve, thirteen years old. The second I saw her, I was done for. I knew I was going to spend the rest of my life with that girl. We'll be married fifty years next month, so I'd say we're well on our way.

"We have four amazing boys who now all have families of their own. And let me tell you, there's nothing better than being a grandpa. I hope I've instilled in my sons the importance of family because I've done everything possible to be a good husband and father.

"What am I going to do with the money? First of all, I'm going to buy Genevieve the biggest damn diamond ring I can find. She never got a proper one the first time around. Of course Gen said it didn't matter, but it's always bothered me. So this time, I'm doing it right. A big shiny diamond in one of those fancy blue boxes.

"As for the rest of the money, I don't need it. I have everything I could ever need back home so I'm donating what's left over to charities that support our veterans. As some of the audience knows, I come from a long line of soldiers who have served their country. My grandfather, my father, my brothers, and I all served in the military. We all came home, but my brother Robert returned with significant injuries, both psychological and physical. He never fully recovered. If I win the ten million, every bit of it will go to organizations that provide health care, education, employment, and even homes to our veterans. It's the least I can do.

"First, I have to outlast the competition. My biggest threat? Hard to say so early in the game. We haven't even had a challenge yet, but if I must choose, I'd say the lawyer, Samuel. I think he's going to be the one to watch. He's in pretty good shape and obviously smart. But what he doesn't have is my experience, my ability to connect with people, to listen, to lead. Those skills will serve me well.

"The weakest link? In my opinion, it's the psychiatrist. But I've underestimated the wrong person before. We'll just have to see how things play out. It's an honor to be here and I'm going to give it my all."

AuntieEllen31—Yes, to taking care of our vets! You've got my vote

FriesPiesandBlueskies—Ewww! He's the worst.

JJstansMartha—Agreed! And any politician who says they can't afford their wife a diamond ring is LYING! And probably lying about a whole lot more.

FlyingMonkey—Yes, because looking after the woman and men who protect our country is such a bad idea 😕

PatriotGames95—Senator Crowley is a true American. Don't worry, we've got your back.

NINE

THE CONFIDANTE

The cherubs on the fresco above Camille's bed were staring down at her. It was unsettling. She turned off her bedside lamp, flipped over on the bed, and buried her head beneath her pillow to try to block out the senator's snoring.

Surely the estate had enough bedrooms for each of them, so why were they sharing? It had to be for the drama. Five strangers vying for ten million dollars in one overly heated space would be sure to cause tempers to flare.

She shifted on the bed again and fought the urge to pull off her camisole and pajama shorts. It had to be eighty degrees in the room. Did this place not have air-conditioning? Her head was spinning with everything she had come to Napa to try to forget about for a while. Her shrinking bank account and her patients, current and past, kept creeping into her thoughts, making it impossible to relax.

Steady your breathing, Camille told herself, just like she told her clients when they were in the middle of a panic attack. *In and out, in and out.* Her body was slick with sweat. Was hot air coming out of the goddamn vents? She had to bring her A game tomorrow. She wanted everyone to see the calm, professional doctor that she had worked so hard to become. And she wanted that ten million dollars. *In and out, in and out.* Her body relaxed, her breathing slowed, and soon she was at the precipice between wakefulness and blessed sleep.

Suddenly a high-pitched wailing hit her ears, and she was violently yanked back to the present. Scrambling from the bed, Camille tripped, her legs tangled in the sheets. She hit the floor with a thud. An alarm. Was there a fire? The room was pitch-black and she was unfamiliar with her surroundings. She didn't know which way to turn.

Terror clawed at her throat. Fern had led them up several staircases and through circuitous corridors to get them to their bedroom, and Camille was sure she wouldn't know how to find her way out. She couldn't think with the shrieking of the alarm pounding painfully in her ears. She felt around for the bedside lamp and when her fingers found it, nothing happened. The power was out.

She heard the others calling out, desperate fragments between the alarm's wails, but couldn't understand what they were saying. She blindly moved along the plaster wall. Where was the damn door? Someone bumped into her and then moved past.

Camille sniffed the air. Was that smoke she smelled? Her entire body was slick with sweat. Was that why it was so hot in their room? Could there be a fire just on the other side of the door?

There was a thunderous pounding and shouts of "Get out, get out! Hurry!" *It must be a fire.* She tried to move toward the sound of the pounding, but the shrill cry of the alarm muddled everything. Ahead of her there was a crack in the dark, not much, just a shift in the shadows.

"This way," came a cry. Someone had found the door. Camille continued to feel her way along the wall, expecting to notice a rise in temperature, but it remained cool to the touch. Finally, her fingers felt air. She was at the exit.

With relief, she stepped into the black hallway before slamming into what felt like a brick wall. The senator. The siren-like screeching continued, adding to Camille's confusion. Stunned, she stumbled and someone from behind steadied her.

"I got you," came a loud voice. It was Samuel. "Are you okay?"

Camille nodded, at once grateful and resentful of the strong hands at her hips. "Fine," she said.

"This way," came a woman's voice, and Camille turned to see a small prick of light puncturing the dark. Camille followed the light along with the other three shadowy figures beside her.

"Careful!" the woman shouted and through the dim point of light, Camille saw Maire. "We're at the steps."

"Do we have everyone?" came another man's voice. "Shout out your names."

One by one, they called out. *Maire, Camille, Richard, Samuel, Ned.*

"What about Fern?" Camille asked.

"We have to get out," came the senator's voice, recognizable by his Texan accent. "Let's get you all out and I'll come back for anyone left behind. Now, let's go," he ordered.

Camille used both hands to hold on to the banister and carefully made her way down the stairs, led by Maire's light. They gave up talking. Trying to hear over the caterwaul of the alarm only slowed them down. As they descended the staircase, Camille felt the air cool. They were away from danger now. They just needed to get outside.

Camille had no idea where they were within the massive house. She could only trust Maire and the little dot of light she held up like a beacon in front of them. She didn't like the feeling—having to rely on anyone else—though she preached to her patients how important it was to be able to trust in others.

"Here," Maire shouted. "I found it!" After an agonizing moment, a door finally swung open, and the group tripped outside, breathing heavily. A pale, full moon lit the sky.

With the door to the estate closed behind them, the relentless squawk of the fire alarm had dulled. It appeared they were at the back of the building, tucked beneath a portico. Camille collapsed onto a stone bench and lowered her head to her knees, trying to catch her breath.

"Did anyone smell smoke?" the senator asked.

"No smoke, but the room was an inferno," Samuel said, wiping sweat from his forehead. He was dressed in shorts and a T-shirt, reminding Camille that she was barely clothed, but she was too shaken up to care.

"Yeah, that was scary," Ned agreed. "I wonder where the fire started." Ned, like Camille, was barefoot. He wore boxers and was bare-chested, his pale skin glowing beneath the incandescent moon.

"Let's go around this way," Maire suggested. She wore the same outfit she had on earlier that evening and had the wherewithal to slip on a pair of shoes. "Hopefully Fern is around here somewhere," Maire continued. "We need to call 911."

"Wow, would you look at that," the senator said, and they all turned.

"Is that a pond?" Samuel asked.

"It looks more like a lake," Maire answered.

Just off in the distance, tucked at the bottom of the property, was a body of water, the light from the moon dancing on its smooth surface. This estate truly had everything, Camille thought.

"Hello!" came a voice, pulling Camille's attention from the shimmering lake. A light popped on. It was Fern, holding a lantern, standing in the shadow of a canopy of cork trees next to the house. "Come this way." She waved them toward her.

"What happened?" Camille asked. "Was there a fire?" Everyone began talking at once, asking questions.

"Is the fire department coming?" Maire asked.

Fern held up her hands. "Everyone is safe. Let's head this way." Fern gestured behind her, though it was too dark to see through the trees. "Follow me."

Why was Fern so calm? If the house was on fire, wouldn't she be frantic? Then she realized that Fern wasn't dressed in her pajamas like they were. She wasn't even wearing the outfit she had on earlier in the evening. She wore a floor-length gray satin tuxedo dress with a deep neckline and her hair was swept up in a knot. This was not what one wore when running from a fire.

Camille tailed the group as Fern led them down a long walkway, the stones cold beneath her bare feet. Beyond the cork trees was a great expanse of lawn illuminated by dozens of lanterns.

Fern stopped next to a table that held an urn, a rolled-up piece of paper tied with a ribbon, a large basket, and, to Camille's shock, a gun. "Please gather around," Fern said, setting the lantern on the table and turning to face them.

Behind her were five life-size marble statues of white wood nymphs, naked, holding flowers in one hand and beckoning with the other. Behind the statues was what looked like a wall that rose ten feet into the air.

"What's happening?" Camille demanded. "Is there a fire? A gas leak? What?"

Fern smiled. The lanterns cast ghostly shadows across her now perfectly made-up face.

"Thankfully, there is no emergency," Fern said, and Camille let out a breath of relief. But why were they out here? "*One Lucky Winner* has officially begun. Welcome to your first challenge."

That's when Camille noticed Alfonso Solomon and two men with cameras standing off to the side. Camille shook her head in shock. The fire alarm was one big ploy to get them out of their beds and outside.

"You have to be fucking kidding me," Ned said in astonishment.

"No way." Samuel ran a hand over his scalp. "You can't be serious." Camille couldn't help noticing his lean, muscular physique and knew that his athleticism would make him hard to beat.

"At *One Lucky Winner*, we are always *dead* serious," Fern continued. "After all, ten million dollars is on the line. Listen up because a lot is riding on this first challenge. Behind me, you'll see a hedge maze."

Camille squinted through the dark. What she first thought was a wall was actually a hedge, trimmed perfectly, smoothed into a flat surface.

"First, you will run through the hedge maze. There are several entrances, one behind each statue, but there is only one way out. Make a wrong turn and you'll hit a dead end."

"Wait," Camille called out, the cool October air extinguishing any of the earlier heat she felt. "I'm not dressed for running. I don't even have any shoes on."

Fern lifted her shoulders and then let them drop as if to say *oh, well.* "One thing you must learn very quickly in this competition is that you must be prepared for anything, at any time. Tonight is no exception. Now, would you like to hear what you are playing for?"

A murmur of assent rose from the group. Even Camille found herself nodding and saying yes, though she felt anything but ready. Not one bit.

"The person who makes it through the maze first will win a Super Clue." Fern bent over and picked up a blue lapis urn.

"Inside this urn is a clue that will be crucial in cracking a puzzle that can only be solved by winning challenges, connecting with your competitors, and putting all the pieces together."

Camille was good at puzzles. She could solve the *New York Times* crossword puzzle in record time—she just needed to get the urn before anyone else.

"First we need to mic you up." Fern held up a tiny black microphone. "We don't want our viewers to miss one exciting moment." An intern appeared from the shadows and began clipping the small mic to each of them. "These are top of the line, wireless, and waterproof," she announced. "Keep them on at all times during the challenges."

Fern held up a finger. "But that's not all. Throughout the maze, keep your eyes open for any object that might be a Game Changer. They can impact the entire trajectory of the competition."

Camille shivered, goose bumps erupting across her bare skin. She was suddenly self-conscious. Her camisole plunged down in the front and her silk pajama shorts did nothing to ward off the chill. Beside her, Maire shrugged out of her cardigan and held it out to Camille without a word. Camille hesitated, suspicious of the selfless gesture, but then nodded her thanks and slipped it on.

Camille looked around at the group. Everyone was already in game mode, their faces intent, muscles poised to act. She tried to do the same. "Wait," she called out. "What are the rules?"

Fern once again gave an inscrutable smile. "The rules are, there are no rules. Just get through the maze, gather any Game Changers you find, and the first one out wins the Super Clue. Oh, and one more thing. Since ten million dollars is on the line, you might find that these will come in handy." Fern reached behind the table and pulled out a stack of what at first glance looked like flashlights.

"These Renegade Tasers can help you get an edge over your competitors. Someone reaching for the same Game Changer? A little zap will stop them in their tracks."

"Did you say Taser?" Samuel interrupted. "You're giving us Tasers?" he asked in disbelief.

"So we can just shoot each other with them?" Camille asked skeptically. "That sounds dangerous."

"No worries," Fern said, holding up one of the devices with a flourish. "They are set at the lowest shock level and are completely safe. But remember you only get one chance from a distance of up to fifteen feet. Use your shot wisely."

Camille looked around at the others. They all looked as ill at ease as she felt.

"Any other questions?" Fern asked. Camille looked around, expecting someone to balk at the idea of using a weapon to ward off a competitor, but no one spoke.

"Okay, then," Fern said, handing everyone a Taser and giving them a brief tutorial on how to use them.

Camille tested the weight of it in her hand. It was the size of a cell phone and much lighter than she thought it would be. Maybe half a pound. Camille stole a glance at the others. Maire was staring down at the weapon uncomfortably while the senator already had his clipped to his pajama bottoms. Ned pointed his Taser into the darkness, squinting as if keying in on unseen prey.

"Are you sure this is safe?" Samuel asked, turning the Taser over in his hand, careful not to touch the trigger.

"Perfectly safe," Fern said. "The shock is minimal and will just slow you down. There's nothing to worry about." She lifted the gun from the table next to her. *A starter's pistol*, Camille thought. *To start the race.*

Camille looked over at Samuel and they exchanged glances. He looked as reticent as she felt.

"Okay, then," Fern said. "Are you ready to get started?"

Camille wasn't ready but the others had already taken a runner's stance, feet staggered, knees bent.

"On your marks," Fern called out, raising the starter's pistol. "Get set, go!" A crack filled the air and Camille ran into the black mouth of the maze.

TEN

THE BEST FRIEND

Maire skirted past one of the marble maidens and into the maze. Once inside, complete darkness descended, the ten-foot walls blocking any moonlight.

With hesitant steps, Maire moved forward, Taser in hand, fearful of crashing into a prickly wall of evergreen. All she could hear was the rasp of her own breath and the buzz of mosquitoes overhead. The sweet, woodsy smell of yew was overpowering. Thirty feet in, Maire hit a fork. She could turn left, right, or continue straight. She veered left and immediately hit a dead end. Backtracking, Maire stumbled and snagged her cheek on a craggy branch, drawing blood.

This was all so unbelievable. Yesterday morning she was kissing her children goodbye and dropping them off at her ex-mother-in-law's house, and now she was running blindly through a hedge maze holding a Taser in her hand.

She needed to move faster but it was impossible, it was too dark. Maire knew she had an advantage in what she was wearing. When the fire alarm sounded, Maire leaped from the bed, tried to turn on a light with no luck. She slipped into her shoes, grabbing her cardigan to put on over her T-shirt. As an afterthought, she fumbled for her purse in search of her key chain that did double duty as a flashlight. It ended up being their only glimmer of light as they clambered for safety.

Maire kicked herself for giving her sweater to Camille, but she felt sorry for the poor woman dressed only in a slinky camisole and matching shorts. If she had to do it again, she would have kept the cardigan. She had shown weakness, a very bad idea. She needed every advantage to ensure winning the ten million dollars. It wouldn't happen again.

Maire made turn after turn, ticking off the number of right turns on her right hand and the number of left turns on her left, but still she felt hopelessly lost. "Dammit," she muttered when she encountered another dead end. This wasn't working. How could she find her way when she couldn't see anything? Then she remembered what she had stashed in her back pocket. What had Fern said? There were no rules, just get through the maze first, and to do this Maire needed to be able to see.

Maire fumbled in her pocket for the key chain light.

She swapped the Taser for the key chain, pressed the on button, and a weak light glowed around her. Not much, but enough to be able to move more quickly through the maze. And if she could outrun the other players, she wouldn't have to tase anyone.

Now that she had a better sense of her surroundings, Maire was even more impressed by the maze. The yew walls were dense and impossible to see through. The pathways were narrow with hairpin turns. A wave of claustrophobia crashed into her. What if she couldn't find her way out? She'd lose, there'd be no money. She would be crushed beneath her debt. She wouldn't be able to keep the house. Dani wouldn't get the medicine she needed. The thought was enough to spur her into action.

Maire held the light in front of her like a talisman and pushed forward. Left, then right, then another dead end. She backtracked and took a left and the narrow path opened into a wide octagon with a stone bench resting in the center. *The middle of the maze*, Maire thought. Now she needed to decide which way to go. She heard the rumble of steps. The others were coming. She would go right, but before she stepped out of the opening, something caught her eye below the bench. A small slim rectangular box topped with a red bow. One of the Game Changers. Did she dare slow down to grab it? *Yes*, she told herself, *every little bit helps*.

"Hey, she's using that fucking light," Ned Bennett called out, gaining on her.

Hurriedly, Maire bent down, sliding her hand beneath the bench. Suddenly, she was knocked off her feet from behind, her chin cracking on the top of the bench. *What the hell?* Maire thought, tasting blood. It was Ned Bennett, his hand closing around the clue. Her clue.

"Son of a bitch," she cried out, massaging her chin. She thought about tasing him, but by the time she got to her feet, he was long gone. She could feel the others behind her. They knew she had a light and if they followed her, she was their best bet out of there. She swept past Ned, who was fumbling to hold on to the Taser and the box. It felt like she had been running forever, though it couldn't have been more than fifteen minutes. Above her, the buzz of insects grew louder and something swept by her ear. It felt too big for a mosquito or a moth. She shuddered and picked up her pace.

She had already lost the Game Changer; she wasn't going to let anyone get past her.

As Maire was approaching a sharp turn, the foliage in front of her began to shake and rustle.

What the hell? She envisioned some nocturnal, toothy creature with claws and red eyes. Beyond the wall there was a grunt, more shaking of leaves. Maire held the light up to get a better look. Three rows over, the head and torso of a man appeared above her at the top of the hedge. It was Samuel, struggling to pull himself up. With one great heave, he launched himself atop the hedge and lay there for a moment, breathing heavily. Samuel, the bastard, had climbed the hedge to get a better vantage point, to see where the exit was.

No rules, Maire thought.

She watched as he slowly pushed himself up onto his knees and surveyed the area around him, grimacing at the bite of branches against his bare knees.

"What's he doing?" came Ned's voice from behind her. "Hey, that's not fair!"

What was he doing? Was Samuel planning on walking atop the hedges to find the exit? No, there was no way the boxwoods would hold him. But Maire couldn't waste time worrying about Samuel, she just had to keep moving.

In front and above her, Maire watched as Samuel lowered himself over the side of the hedge and dropped to the path below. He was now two rows ahead.

Had he seen the way through the maze from his perch atop the hedge? "Dammit," Maire said. Of all people, Samuel figured it out. He found the exit. She might lose this game, but she sure as hell wasn't going to lose to Samuel Rafferty. She had already lost too much because of him. In all fairness, he probably thought the same thing about her.

Again, Samuel's head appeared atop the boxwoods. He was climbing over another row. Through the gloom, more shadows dipped and rose. Drones. There were drones overhead capturing their every movement on camera.

Maire wanted, with all her might, to grab the branches of the hedge and shake it so hard that Samuel would lose his balance and crash to the ground. The renewed anger she felt toward him surprised her. She thought she had put it all behind her. Not forgotten—she could never forget—but hidden away. Now, flashes from that night years before were all she could see. The mangled car, the splattered blood, the black sky with a million stars, the frozen lake a smooth plate of glass in front of them.

Was the path just to her left, the one that Samuel was now on, the way out? Maire considered climbing over the hedge and joining Samuel on that route. But no. Something made her choose this one. Maire made a left and then a right.

"Give it up, Maire," Samuel called from over the hedge. "You've got a dead end coming up. You can't win."

"Over my dead body," Maire shot back. She took another right.

Maire knew he was lying. There was no dead end up ahead. Instead, there was light. A beautiful, warm light illuminating an opening in the maze where Fern stood next to a table with the lapis-colored urn. From somewhere within the depths of the maze came a loud cry. Someone had been tased. From her left, Samuel suddenly appeared at her side.

Maire started sprinting but Samuel pulled ahead. He had the lead, but Maire knew it wouldn't last long. She wanted this more. Needed it more. Behind her, she could hear the footfalls of the other contestants. They wanted it too. Maire willed her legs to move faster, her arms to pump harder. She was almost there but so was Samuel.

She dug into her pocket for the Taser. She hadn't wanted to use it, but there was no other way. She had never used a Taser before, never shot any kind of weapon, but this could be her only chance. Maire couldn't miss. She stopped running, raised the Taser with shaking hands, and aimed for Samuel's legs. She didn't want to hurt him, just slow him down. Holding her breath, Maire squeezed the trigger.

Threadlike leads shot from the Taser, along with a shower of confetti. The leads did not strike Samuel in the legs, but instead, with a crackle of electricity, they hit him squarely between the shoulder blades.

Maire watched in disbelief as Samuel briefly froze, his muscles contracting. He let out an anguished cry, dropped to the ground, and began writhing in the dirt. She thought it was just supposed to give him a little zap, give her a chance to get past him. What had she done? This was much more than a little jolt.

Maire felt a shove from behind and fell to her knees. Looking up, she saw the senator running toward the exit. How did he get past the others? Startled into action, Maire staggered to her feet and started running. The senator had a few yards on her, but Maire was younger, stronger, faster. She tried not to look down at Samuel as she skirted past him. He was still contorting on the ground and Maire pushed down a pang of regret.

She hadn't wanted to hurt anyone, but this is what they signed up for, right?

The senator was just a few feet from the exit. With a guttural cry, Maire launched herself through the maze's exit and reached for the urn, her fingers grazing its smooth surface. She scooped it up, holding it against her midsection, protecting it like a running back protects a football before tumbling to the ground. Next to her, the senator hit the dirt with a thud, his hands also reaching for the urn, but she held tight. There was no way she was going to let it go. It was hers. She won.

Maire lay on the ground for several moments, trying to catch her breath, keeping her arms tight around the urn. She was vaguely aware of the senator getting slowly to his feet. Every inch of Maire's body screamed in pain. Her lungs burned, her leg muscles were spasming, and she wondered if she cracked a rib when she landed on the ground atop the urn.

Above her came Fern's voice. "Ladies and gentlemen, *that* is how you become one lucky winner! Congratulations, Maire. How are you feeling?"

Wincing, Maire got to her feet, still clutching the urn close just in case someone tried to wrest it away from her. "Good, I feel good," she managed to say between gasps.

"What did you think when Samuel climbed on top of the hedgerow? Did you think it was all over for you?" Fern asked.

Maire glanced to the right to find a camera in her face. She resisted the urge to shove it aside. Two more camera operators hung back, aiming their lenses on the other contestants. And there were probably dozens of cameras hidden along the maze, catching every single moment of the race. She wondered what Dani and Keely would say when they saw her tase a man. Would they be proud of her or ashamed?

Breathing heavily, Maire looked up at Fern. "When I saw Samuel on top of the hedge, I thought, this is a man who will do anything to win, no matter the cost, so I'm going to have to think fast, run fast, and get there first."

"And you utilized the Taser," Fern said. "Did you have any reservations about that?"

Maire did have reservations. Samuel still had not come out of the maze and she was afraid he could be really hurt, but she couldn't worry about that, not now. "No, I'm a mom with a mission," Maire said, standing upright, still breathing hard. "And that is going to be tough to beat every single time. I did what I had to do."

"Well said," Fern said brightly. "You'll want to crack open the urn and read the clue where prying eyes can't see, unless you want to share your clue with one of the other players. Because *One Lucky Winner* isn't only about winning physical challenges, it is also about whether or not you create and maintain alliances. How does that saying go—keep your enemies closer?"

Maire looked around at the crestfallen group around her. The senator was breathing as hard as she was, and Ned and Camille had finally emerged from the maze. Ned had a long gash along his cheek, and Camille looked small and frail, enveloped within Maire's cardigan. Samuel was still missing.

Had she hurt him? Really hurt him? Maire turned and rushed back into the maze. There he was, lying on his stomach, his head buried beneath his arms. "Samuel?" she cried, dropping to her knees. "Are you okay?"

Samuel lowered his arms and turned his face toward her. "Jesus, Maire," he said weakly, "the least you could have done was warn me. That hurt like a son of a bitch."

Maire let out a breath of relief and sat back on her heels. She hadn't killed him. "If I had known the Taser was that powerful, I wouldn't have used it."

With a groan, Samuel pushed himself up to a sitting position and sat next to her. He shook his head and gave Maire a half smile. "We both know that's a lie," he said.

He was right. She still would have done it all over again. "Need help getting up?" she asked.

"Nah," Samuel said. "Go on ahead. I'm just going to get my sea legs back and then I'll come out."

"You sure?" Maire asked, not feeling right about leaving him behind.

"Yeah, I'm sure," he said testily. "Just tell everyone I need a few minutes." Maire got to her feet and started toward the maze's exit. "Hey, Maire," Samuel called after her and she turned. "It's good to know you'd come back for me."

Maire had no response to this. She understood what Samuel was getting at. His words weren't meant to be a compliment. They were an accusation.

She stepped from the maze to find Fern and the others waiting for her. "So how about it, Maire?" Fern asked. "Are you going to share your clue with the others?"

Maire had always been the nice one. The one to go with the flow, to let others lead her and guide her, and she always listened. And where had it gotten her? No, she was tired of being the nice one. She was here to win ten million dollars and to do it, she'd have to do it alone.

"No, Fern," Maire said, still trying to catch her breath. "I think I'm keeping this for myself."

ELEVEN

MarketingMama sat on her bed, iPad propped up on her lap, her phone and a margarita in hand as she waited. She just received the alert on her phone that *One Lucky Winner* was about to come on. There was so much secrecy and intrigue around the show that TikTok was exploding with theories. The contestants were going to be celebrities or maybe nobodies who were desperate for money. Some said it was all hype and the show was just another typical reality show where downtrodden losers were vying for their fifteen minutes of fame. No one really knew and if they said they did, they were lying.

MarketingMama was dying to find out if the show lived up to all the buzz. As a marketing exec for an online ice-cream vendor, The Inside Scoop, which shipped premium pints of ice cream all over the United States, she was always on the hunt for ways to position the company. Finding the hot trends was key. Buyers could personalize the ice-cream flavors and cartons—perfect for birthdays, get-well-soon and congratulatory gifts, and so much more. If the show was as big as everyone said it was and she could get The Inside Scoop ad space on the show, it would be huge for the brand.

The hashtag #oneluckywinner was trending and some of her favorite celebs were sure to be live tweeting the premiere episode. She could just picture Tom Hanks ordering some Mango Margo-Rita ice cream for Rita Wilson's birthday. Or maybe Taylor Swift would order cases of Midnights Chocolate Chunk for her crew.

The premise was definitely unique. Five strangers, ten million dollars, and an unpredictable livestream. Instead of tuning in at a set date and time, viewers waited for an alert as to when the livestream was starting, then they watched. No one knew if there was going to be one livestream a night, two, or maybe even zero.

The kids were already in bed and MarketingMama and her husband waited. Minutes then hours passed, along with two more margaritas. Finally her husband gave up and wandered off to bed. She dozed, then woke with a start. Maybe there wouldn't be an alert tonight.

Finally, at 1:00 a.m. her phone pinged with the alert. Blearily, MarketingMama poked the link and dramatic music filled her ears while an aerial view of a Tuscan-looking estate filled her screen. The opening sequence showed snapshots of each of the contestants. The stunning brunette was referred to as the Confidante, the man with a goatee was the Boyfriend, the redhead was the Best Friend, and the oldest competitor was the Senator. She nearly fell off the couch when she saw the final image of the man wearing hip glasses and a devastating smile. Ned Bennett. The Executive.

A cold sweat erupted across her skin and any of the lingering effects of the tequila vanished.

She knew Ned Bennett, though she wished she had never laid eyes on him. She'd interned for him years ago at *Cold, Hard Truth*, long before she was married and had kids. She was so young, so naive. At first, she had been flattered by Ned's attention, basking in the warmth of his thousand-watt smile. But beneath the charming veneer he was a nightmare.

One day she had walked into Ned's office and thirty minutes later she had stumbled out, disheveled and in shock. She spent the rest of the day in the restroom, hidden in a stall, crying. The next day, she returned to work only to find that her key card no longer worked. She had been fired.

Heart pounding, MarketingMama watched as a chyron scrolled across her screen. Vote to make sure your favorite challenger stays. To save the Boyfriend text 01 to 21534... To save the Senator text 05 to 21534.

Before she knew it the competition was over, and the Best Friend had emerged from the hedge maze triumphantly. The comment section on the live feed exploded.

She totally cheated! Why should she be able to have a light while everyone was running in the dark?

Too bad, so sad. The rules are there are no rules.

Oof, that poor woman in her underwear! Hasn't she seen Big Brother? Cameras are everywhere, all the time.

Did you see the Boyfriend? He was fucking climbing on top of the maze like Spider-Man. If he's looking for a girlfriend, I'm available.

Did you see the way she nailed him with that Taser? That was badass.

They're hot for each other. Did you see the way they kept looking at each other before the race started?

No way! It's the Confidante and the Boyfriend.

I hope the Boyfriend is okay? Last I saw him he was still on the ground.

Tasers hurt like hell.

The Senator used the Taser too. He is a badass. #savethesenator

The Senator is a douchebag. I'm voting for the Boyfriend.

Is this it? A maze? I mean, I thought people would be jumping out of airplanes or scaling a mountain for ten million. #EasyMoney

MarketingMama's fingers itched to type the words, When I was nineteen years old, I was raped by Ned Bennett and discarded like trash.

But she didn't. Couldn't. She hadn't even told her husband what had happened back then. She hadn't told anyone. Not yet. But why couldn't she now? Why should this man be able to meander through life without facing a single consequence for his actions? And now he might win ten million dollars.

MarketingMama pulled her eyes away from the comments. The Best Friend was standing next to the hedge maze, her curly hair wild and tangled with bits of evergreen.

"I can't believe I won," she said into the camera. She held up the blue urn. "Apparently, a Super Clue is inside." She reached in the urn and came out with a weathered piece of paper. She unfolded it and stared down at it for a long moment and shrugged. "It looks like some kind of family tree."

She turned the paper to the camera. It *was* a family tree. An intricate one, with branches whose limbs were labeled with names or at least parts of names. MarketingMama caught an Irene and a Roscoe and a Lilibeth. She also noticed that there were gaping holes in the paper. One in the middle and one near the bottom.

The armchair detectives in the comment section were already theorizing. The family tree was that of some famous person and the puzzle was figuring out who it was. Others argued that it was the dates that mattered. One person told everyone to shut up, it was too early to know.

The video switched to the Executive, who was sitting on a stone bench outside the estate. MarketingMama held her breath. "Totally blindsided," the Executive said with a tight grimace, his face suspiciously smooth. Even the sound of his voice sent a ripple of revulsion through her.

"This game is fucked-up," the Executive said. "I can't believe that old cowboy tased me. It hurt like hell." He turned so that his bare back faced the camera. There was an angry red welt where one of the barbs struck him.

"I'm really going to have to up my game. There's no way a soccer mom from Iowa is going to beat me. I mean, come on." He ran a hand through his sandy hair. "If these people want to fight dirty, I can fight dirty. Bring it on."

MarketingMama tried to steady her shaking hands. She knew this better than anyone.

"I did find one of these." The Executive held up the small metal box. "One of the Game Changers. Hopefully this will help me put the redhead back in her place."

The Executive plucked the red bow from atop the box and tossed it aside, looking around to make sure none of the other contestants were nearby. He flipped open the lid and pulled out a folded slip of paper before setting the box on the bench next to him.

"Huh," he said, staring hard at the contents. "This was unexpected." He tilted the box to the camera.

Inside was a slim, black metallic object. MarketingMama had no idea what it was until the Executive pulled it from the box, pressed a button and a sleek, silver blade shot out. She reared back at the sight of the sharply curved, glinting steel. A knife.

The Executive picked up the piece of paper next to him and began reading, his forehead creased in concentration. After a moment he looked up at the camera and held up the knife. "Well, this certainly makes things more interesting, doesn't it?" he said with a grin.

MarketingMama's stomach dropped.

TWELVE

THE BEST FRIEND

Then

Maire stood at the edge of the bluff and peeked down at the frozen mirror that was Tanglefoot Lake. Above, the light from a million stars poked through a black sky. The effect was dizzying and Maire scurried back to keep from tumbling over the craggy precipice and into the lake below.

Maire accepted a flask from Lina and braced herself before taking a swig of cheap whiskey. She fought the urge to gag as the caustic liquid seared her throat and lungs, landing hotly in her stomach. But it did the trick. Within seconds, she was no longer shivering, and her limbs were pleasantly warm, if a bit rubbery. That was fine with Maire. She didn't want to be here anyway.

She preferred to be back in her dorm room working on her newest painting. Anywhere but hidden behind a cluster of towering pine trees nearly freezing to death on a secluded bluff that overlooked Tanglefoot Lake. Her roommate, Lina, whom Maire adored, made her come. She wouldn't take no for an answer. "Come on," she urged. "Classes start again in two days. Please." She gave Maire her best lower-lip pout.

Maire had a hard time saying no to beautiful Lina with her

silky dark hair, quirky sense of humor, and bell-like laugh. Lina was all fun. She never seemed to study and talked constantly. For the first four months they were dormmates, Lina harped at Maire to set her books and art projects aside to come out and have a good time until Maire finally relented.

It wasn't that Maire was against having fun—she loved fun—but just didn't love sitting around doing nothing but drinking in the freezing cold.

Maire's goal was to get out of Iowa completely, to eventually get into the School of the Art Institute of Chicago and make a real living from her creations. She wanted to put her hometown of Calico in her rearview mirror forever. Lina, on the other hand, didn't seem to have any particular goals and was determined to party her way through their four years at Tanglefoot University. Maire could resist, most of the time. But here she was. Again.

She stared at the group of six, five of whom were her friends, around the bonfire that hissed and crackled in the frigid air. The temperature had dropped dramatically over the past few hours, the rare, short-lived early January warm snap gone. Maire had met the six of them her freshman year and they were a ragtag group brought together more by convenience than anything else.

Figgy—no one knew her real name—was chatting up Damon, a junior on the hockey team who had a tongue as sharp as his slap shot. Figgy was Maire's roommate the year before. A drama major, she seemed like the perfect match for Maire. Both had come from small Midwest towns, were creative and dedicated to their art. They bonded while navigating a new campus and trying to find their niche. For the first eight months of their freshman year, they were inseparable.

Then Maire came across one of Figgy's psychology class papers and was surprised to find it was the exact paper Maire had turned in the semester before. The only difference was that Figgy's name was typed across the top.

Maire confronted Figgy and even offered to help her write her own paper. At the very least, she hoped Figgy would apologize. No such luck. Figgy didn't apologize. Ever. Instead, she laughed it off, saying it was no big deal. Maire threatened to go to the professor if Figgy submitted the paper. She didn't want to get caught up in a plagiarism scandal, or worse, didn't want to get expelled.

Figgy ended up turning in another stolen paper, got caught, and ultimately failed the class. Maire thought she was lucky not to get tossed out of school. Figgy accused Maire of turning her in. Not true. But suddenly a nasty rumor that Maire was sleeping with a married professor made the rounds. More than one person told Maire that Figgy was the source. Maire packed up and crashed on Lina's couch for the remainder of the semester.

"I'm sorry," Lina whispered in her ear. "I didn't know she was going to be here. Damon brought her." Maire shrugged as if Figgy's presence didn't bother her in the least. But it did.

Wes and Wade, twin brothers whom Maire had met in Freshman Rhetoric, were also at the bonfire. They were easygoing and always up to some mischief. Maire couldn't help but shake her head as she watched the two toss firecrackers into the bonfire and laugh drunkenly over the mini explosions.

Then there was Samuel, a political science major whom Maire had met through Lina. He was smart, tall, and handsome. He was also presently dating Lina, so Maire knew he was off-limits. She couldn't help but envy her best friend a little bit. In addition to being cute and off-the-charts smart, Samuel was genuinely nice.

"Jesus, Maire," Damon said, using a stick to bat around a pine cone like a hockey puck, "could you look more miserable?"

"Not miserable," Maire said lightly, "just cold. It's freezing."

"And is that paint in your hair?" Figgy asked, squinting to get a better look.

Reflexively, Maire's mittened fingers flew to her hair, most of which was stuffed beneath a stocking cap. Damon laughed.

She wasn't going to let Figgy get to her tonight. And why was Damon even with her? He knew what she was like. He knew what Figgy had done to her. Unless maybe he actually believed the lie.

And how did Figgy manage to look so perfectly put together despite the brutal cold? Her blond hair was artfully arranged beneath her cashmere hat, her skin flawless while Maire's was already red and wind-burned.

"If it doesn't involve a camera or watercolors, Maire isn't interested. Right, Maire?" Lina said, leaning into Samuel. Maire tried to tamp down the flare of jealousy that sizzled through her when Lina's fingers slid into the back pockets of Samuel's jeans.

"I'm sorry," Maire said, taking another swig from the flask. "Just not a fan of heights. Looking over the bluff threw me off."

"Don't worry, we'd save you," Lina said, affectionately. "And come on, relax for one night. Forget about school and your darkroom."

"Be nice," Samuel said congenially. "It's good that Maire knows what she wants to do with her life."

"You mean unlike me?" Lina said, looking up at Samuel, her forehead creased with hurt. "You know it's okay to not know what you want to do with your life when you're twenty years old."

"You know I didn't mean it like that," Samuel said with a sigh.

"Why did you even invite her if she's going to just sit there like a sad sack?" Damon asked, smacking the pine cone toward the fire but hitting Maire in the chest instead. It didn't hurt but she was starting to get pissed. What had Figgy been telling him about Maire?

"Because if it weren't for me," Lina said, "Maire wouldn't

come out of the darkroom. And, she's my best friend, aren't you, Maire?"

"Yeah, so was I for a while," Figgy said. "I'd watch out if I were you, Lina. Maire likes her boyfriends already spoken for." Figgy cast a knowing look at Samuel.

"You know that isn't what happened," Maire said sharply. She didn't want to rehash ancient history with Figgy, but she was getting tired of just sitting back and taking her abuse. She moved away from the group, her head swimming from the alcohol, and promptly slipped on an icy spot, landing dangerously close to the bluff's drop-off.

"Careful, Maire," Figgy called out. "We'd hate to see you go over the side."

Face burning, Maire got to her feet just in time to see Damon and the twins exchange mischievous glances and, before she knew it, they were upon her. The twins grabbed her legs while Damon grabbed her arms and carried her to the edge of the bluff.

Maire screamed in protest, trying to wiggle free. They held tight, their fingers digging into her wrists and ankles. In unison, they swung her like a pendulum back and forth. Below her, Maire could see the hardpack snow atop the bluff shift to the lake, a sharp drop two hundred feet below.

What if they lost their grip on her? Fear formed a hard lump in her throat and Maire could no longer make a sound.

"Heave, ho," Figgy cried and Maire could hear Lina's unmistakable laugh in the background. Even Lina had turned on her to join in on the fun.

"Hey, stop it," Samuel said, snagging Maire by the waist and stopping the momentum. Damon and the twins dropped her unceremoniously to the hard ground below and the air was forced from her lungs, leaving her momentarily stunned. "Stop being assholes," Samuel said, helping Maire to her feet. "You okay?" he asked.

Tears stung Maire's eyes, but she nodded. Was she being that bad? She wasn't being particularly chatty, but it wasn't like she was trying to sabotage the night. She was here, wasn't she?

No, it was Figgy. If Figgy wasn't here, no one would be acting this way.

"I'm fine," Maire said, picking up the flask that had fallen from her pocket. "I'm going for a walk."

"Maire," Lina said, drawing out her name like she was talking to a small, unreasonable child. "We're just teasing. Don't go, it's too cold."

"No, let her go," Figgy said. "It'll be more fun."

"I'm fine," Maire said. "I'm just going to look at the lake. I'll be back in a while."

"Don't fall in," Damon called after her. The twins exploded with grating laughs.

Maire wiped away the tears before they could freeze against her cheeks and carefully picked her way along an icy path through trees until the crackle of the bonfire and the derisive laughter faded away. Why had she even bothered to come? Because of Lina. She'd do anything for Lina, and what had her so-called best friend done? Laughed and teased right along with the rest of them. Resentment sizzled through her.

She *was* fun, Maire told herself as she moved along the sinuous trail that she figured would take her to the lake. Damon and the twins weren't really going to throw her over the edge and normally she would have laughed right along with them until they set her down. And yes, she spent most of her time working on her projects and studying, but wasn't that what college was for? She went out with friends occasionally, though she had to be cajoled. And she usually ended up having fun. But seeing Figgy after all these months of successfully avoiding her was what ruined the night. Figgy hated her and Maire honestly couldn't understand why.

Maire had been to Tanglefoot Lake several times before,

but never at night during January. Funny how seasons could change the landscape so completely. A few months earlier, she had tried to capture the cacophony of jewel-colored leaves that hung like a canopy overhead in a painting. Now all the maples, oaks, and quaking aspens were stripped and lonely. But still, it was peaceful here in the dark, surrounded by towering pine trees that looked velvety soft in the weak light from the stars. Next time she'd come out here by herself with her camera.

Maire, who had thought to dress sensibly in her warmest winter coat, boots, white hat, and matching mittens, found herself breathing heavily and sweating beneath all the layers. She pulled off her mittens and stuffed them into her pockets and found the flask. She took another long drink. The trail should have opened up to the lake by now.

Apprehension growing, Maire examined the trail in front of her more closely. Was this even a path or was it a game trail made by deer or maybe even a coyote? A rustle in the shadows caused her to stop short. She cocked her ear toward the sound and a shiver of fear ran through her. She hadn't thought about wild animals. She turned to look in the direction she had come from. Should she go back to the bonfire? To the others? Somehow they seemed less appealing than facing a bobcat.

"Hey," came a soft voice and Maire jumped. She peered into the dark as a figure came toward her. Tall, imposing.

"Who is it?" Maire asked, poised to run.

"It's Samuel. You okay?" he asked.

"You scared me," Maire said testily, not wanting him to know how badly he had startled her. "I'm fine," she added and began walking again, trying to force herself not to weave back and forth. The whiskey had hit her harder than she thought it would.

"Where are you going?" Samuel asked, falling into step behind her on the narrow trail.

"I told you, to the lake," Maire said.

"Well, you're not going to get there going this way," Samuel said with a chuckle.

"I'll get there eventually," Maire murmured.

"They're being assholes," Samuel said. "You just have to ignore them."

"Easy for you to say. Shit," Maire said glumly. The column of pine trees ended.

They had come to a road.

"Yeah," Samuel said, "that is not the lake." They looked out at the pavement, an icy ribbon in the starlight.

"It is not." Maire let out a puff of air. "You know, I do know how to have fun. People say I'm a lot of fun."

"I don't doubt it," Samuel said, trying not to crack a smile. "But to be fair, there's not a lot of fun to be had in Iowa in the middle of winter."

"That's where you are wrong," Maire said lightly. "We know how to have fun in all seasons. You just need to know where to look for it."

"Well, it isn't back there," Samuel said, hooking a thumb toward the bluff.

"No, it is not," Maire said. "How'd you end up here?" she asked. "Where are you from again?"

"A little bit of everywhere," Samuel said. "My family moved around a lot. My dad was in the military. I got a scholarship to play lacrosse—" he shrugged "—and here I am."

"Well, we're happy to have you," Maire said and inwardly kicked herself. She was so lame.

Samuel smiled like he didn't think she was lame. "And I was joking earlier. I do like it here. Everyone is really nice."

Maire gave him a skeptical look. "There are a few exceptions, I guess," he added. They both laughed. "Well, we should probably get back," Samuel said, reluctantly. "No lake here."

Maire didn't want to go back, not yet. She just wanted to stay right here, no matter how cold.

"Or," Maire began slyly. The whiskey was still thrumming through her body, making her loose-limbed, reckless. "We could have some fun."

THIRTEEN

THE ASSISTANT

Fern led the contestants from the hedge maze and back toward the house, still confused by the near disaster with the Tasers. Cat had assured Fern that the custom-made Tasers were set at a low voltage and that clearly hadn't been the case. Both Samuel and Ned had gone down hard but Samuel got it worse. Both prongs had struck Samuel squarely in the back, gripping into his skin and completely immobilizing him. Fern was worried that they were going to have to call an ambulance, but thankfully after a few minutes he was able to get up.

"Hey," came an angry voice from behind. Samuel. Fern kept walking, pretending she hadn't heard him. She understood his confusion, his frustration, but she had no answers. She had so much to do before tomorrow's challenge.

"Wait up," he called. "Hold on a second," he said, blocking her path and causing Fern to stop short. "What the hell was that?" he asked, his voice laced with barely contained anger. "You said the Tasers were set at a low level. You said it was safe. I'm healthy, my body could handle being shocked. But what would have happened if the senator was the one to be tased? He's seventy years old. The shock could have stopped his heart!" Samuel was shouting now.

Fern looked around. The camera operators and the drones were gone, but she knew there were cameras hidden throughout the estate. The show needed drama, but not when it was directed toward her.

"But you're fine, right?" Fern asked, steadying her voice. "Ned is fine and so is the senator. Everyone is fine. The Tasers were completely safe."

Samuel didn't move, not appeased.

"Come on," Fern said, "it's after two, why don't we get back to the house so everyone can get some sleep?"

"Does this look like they were safe?" Samuel asked, turning his back to her and pulling up his shirt.

Fern winced at the welts. *Never admit you're wrong*, that's what Cat always said.

Fern gave Samuel a sympathetic smile. "Would you like some ice? Some Tylenol? And it's your turn to go into The Vault."

"I'm not going into The Vault," Samuel said with a disgusted snort. "I'm going to bed." He shot a murderous glare at Fern and limped away.

Fern couldn't really blame him and wondered if the settings on the Tasers were an oversight or if it was a manufacturing error. Or maybe they were purposely sabotaged. It made Fern wonder what other surprises *One Lucky Winner* had for them all.

The trek to the villa and up the grand staircase was made in stony silence. Fern waited until the bedroom door shut before rushing down the steps toward the beating heart of the estate.

Fern made her way through the great room, past the white room and the theater room. Using her key card, Fern let herself into Cat's office. During the day, it was spacious, light, and airy, with large windows and white marble floors. Now it was dark and shadow filled, and much too quiet. Fern hurriedly found the light switch. Her boss's desk was situated in the center of the room. It was a work of art in and of itself, with white marble hewn into a modern triangle that defied gravity. Atop it was a laptop and a landline telephone. Fern looked in the corners of the room for the telltale red light of a camera. There were none.

Fern knew that Cat didn't have cameras in her office; too many private conversations went on in here. But still, she was paranoid. Fern had special permission to enter Cat's office but now she felt like a criminal. She was a criminal.

Fern pulled out the buttery-soft Italian leather desk chair and gingerly sat down. This was what it would be like to have an office of her own, not relegated to a small desk in the corridor. Someday, she told herself.

She had held it together all night but just barely. The reality of what she had done came crashing over her like a wave. She had hijacked *One Lucky Winner* by locking her boss in the wine cellar. Would she be warm enough? The temperature of the wine cellar was consistent in order to keep the wine at the ideal temperature, so it wouldn't go below fifty-five degrees. That was cold. Could people get hypothermia at fifty-five degrees? She didn't know.

Her chest constricted and she couldn't catch her breath. Cat was going to kill her, if she managed to make it out of the cellar alive. Fern lowered her head between her knees, trying to keep from hyperventilating. She was going to get fired and then hauled off to prison. Unless, Fern thought, *One Lucky Winner* was a runaway success.

She righted herself and pulled out her phone. Her stomach flipped with excitement. Close to a million people had watched the first episode on YouTube. She flipped to X, then Instagram, then TikTok. #oneluckywinner was the top-trending hashtag on all three platforms.

Remarkable, since the show hadn't started until the middle of the night. She prayed that the numbers would keep growing.

No matter how successful the show was, Fern was pretty sure her life was over. Fern gave a rueful laugh. The past ten years she had been Cat's prisoner—not in the literal sense, but a prisoner, nonetheless. How many days had Fern gone without eating or drinking because Cat *had* to have something done right then and there? How many sleepless nights had she spent hunting down Cat's latest obsessions, such as the macarons she'd had the last time she was in Paris but *couldn't remember the name of the patisserie*, or the exclusive Trinket fall makeup line that was impossible to get?

One wall of the office consisted of glass windows that looked out on the lake, now black as ink in the predawn dark. Another wall held a bank of a dozen screens. Each monitored a different location on the estate. The library, the corridors, kitchen, the courtyard, grand hallway, the pool, the atrium, and the wine cellar. Fern could sit in here and keep an eye on all aspects of the game.

She also had the same access to the video cameras from her phone as well as the power to turn them off if need be. It wasn't lost upon Fern that the challenges were streamed live and that anything could happen, but Cat made it clear to shut the feed down if it was completely unavoidable—which Fern took to mean never.

She flipped on the monitor that showed the inside of the wine cellar. Cat was pacing, hands clenched, face twisted in anger.

Fern turned on the intercom. "Cat," she began tentatively. Cat froze, her back to the camera. "The show is a hit. We already have a million views. And you should see how many commercial spots we've sold. It's going really well."

Cat slowly turned, her eyes pinned on the camera's lens. Even though Fern knew that Cat couldn't really see her, she felt as if she were looking directly into her eyes. The blood curdled in her veins. Cat dragged an old wooden box right below the camera. She climbed atop it and stared into the lens. "Fern," Cat began calmly. "Get me the fuck out of here."

Fern almost faltered, almost made a beeline for the wine cellar. But no, Fern needed to make a decision and not look back. Cat could handle one or two days in the cellar, just long enough for Fern to convince her that *One Lucky Winner* was the newest phenomenon, all thanks to her. Fern would show Cat all the celebrities who had tweeted about the show and maybe, just maybe, she'd forgive her. It wasn't likely.

"Soon," Fern said through the intercom. "I will soon. I promise." She then flipped off the camera, knowing that Cat was going to go ballistic. No one ever crossed Cat. Certainly not Fern. She fought the urge to open Cat's laptop. It would be so easy. What Cat didn't know was that Fern knew every single one of her passwords. She could access every email, every file, every voicemail. Cat's entire life was on this laptop. Maybe Fern could use it to her advantage. *Stay focused*, Fern told herself. *Stay professional. Do your job and everything will work out fine.* She turned her attention to the other monitors, but everything looked quiet. The corridor that ran in front of the contestants' room was still. She needed to figure out what to do about Ned Bennett. He couldn't stay here, could not be the winner of ten million dollars. She had to find a way to get him off the show without tipping her hand.

Fern thought of the hours she spent writing out all the Super Clues and placing them inside the urns and all the time she spent stashing the Game Changers around the estate. It gave her an idea. It wouldn't take long for the contestants to figure out that Ned was ruthless, that he was the one they needed to eliminate from the game. Fern would just help them along a little bit.

She opened Cat's laptop after all. But instead of digging through the files, she began to type, then printed the note, which was short and to the point. She reached into Cat's desk and pulled out a small orange bottle, twisted the cap, and dropped one small white pill into the palm of her hand. Fern sat there for a long moment trying to decide what to do. What she was doing was illegal, unethical, could be dangerous. But she needed Ned Bennett gone.

Fern slid the paper and the pill into an envelope. She lit a red wax stick, letting the hot wax drip onto the envelope, then pressed the *One Lucky Winner* sealing stamp to the small puddle.

She got to her feet and went to the closet. Inside were all the items needed for the show's challenges, including stacks of *One Lucky Winner* T-shirts, sweatshirts, and warm-up gear. She selected a set for each contestant and carefully slid the envelope between the folds of one of the T-shirts.

With the stack of clothing in hand, Fern exited the closet, closed the door behind her, and surveyed Cat's office. Everything was in its place. She needed to grab a few hours of sleep and then get ready for the day. It was going to be a long one.

FOURTEEN

THE BEST FRIEND

Maire awoke to a soft white light streaming through the window, her muscles protesting in pain as she stretched beneath the Egyptian cotton sheets. Maire was vaguely aware of someone entering the room and setting something next to her bed. Sleepily, she looked around the room. Three of the beds were empty and a fourth held a rounded heap beneath a pile of covers. Samuel.

In the light of day, it was a beautiful room with its terra-cotta floors and walls painted a warm honeycomb gold. A large fireplace with a flue big enough to climb up anchored the entire space. But the unpleasant scent of other people's bodies permeated the room.

Maire slid quietly from the bed, trying not to wake Samuel, and crossed the room to inspect a series of framed black-and-white photographs that lined one wall. They included images of shadowy tunnels and unique architectural elements. The contrast of light and dark in the photos was exceptional. She missed photography and painting. Maybe someday she would try again. She paused, leaning in closer for a better look. It took a moment for her to realize what she was looking at. They weren't just columns and walls made of stone, they were skulls. Rows and rows of skulls. The photos were of the catacombs. Maire turned from the wall, her stomach queasy.

Sitting atop her bedside table was a stack of bright pink clothing. Two T-shirts, warm-up pants and matching jacket, athletic shorts, and a sweatshirt, all with the weird logo of the women with the snaky hair and the words *One Lucky Winner*. She grabbed the clothing and tiptoed to the bathroom, shutting and locking the door behind her.

Maire set the clothes on the marble vanity and gingerly began to take off her clothes, her muscles protesting with each movement. She pulled a short-sleeved pink tee over her head, stepped into the warm-up pants and hitched them up over eggplant-purple bruises, and slid her arms through the bright pink warm-up jacket emblazoned with the *One Lucky Winner* emblem.

She stared at her reflection in the gilded mirror above the marble sink. Her curls were a riotous mess but there wasn't much she could do about that but try to corral them with a ponytail holder. She slipped an elastic band from her wrist, and it slipped from her fingers and to the floor. With a groan, Maire bent over and heard the crinkle of paper. Curious, she stood up and reached into her pocket, pulling out a small envelope.

Maire slid a finger beneath the blood red wax that sealed the envelope and pulled out a fine linen note card and a small, hexagon-shaped white pill.

Last night was just a taste of what is to come. By now you must realize that there will be many obstacles in your way. As the winner of the Maze Challenge, you have earned a very special Game Changer. This tiny pill could help you on your way to ten million dollars. When to use it? You pick the time, the place, and the recipient. How far will you go for ten million dollars? Only you can answer the question.

Maire stared down at the pill. What was in it? Her mind raced through the possibilities: a diuretic, a laxative, a sleeping pill. And was she really supposed to slip it into someone's food or drink? That was illegal. The show wasn't seriously encouraging her to drug her opponents, was it?

Maire gave a little shake of her head. She couldn't do it. Wouldn't do it. She'd learned her lesson years ago that playing with fate could have disastrous results. She moved to drop the pill in the toilet, to flush away the temptation, but stopped.

Maybe she'd keep the pill. Just for now. Just in case.

Maire stepped from the bathroom. Samuel was now sitting on his bed. He was shirtless and his entire torso looked as if he had done nine rounds with a rabid raccoon. His sculpted chest was lined with angry red scratches from where he had climbed up the ten-foot hedge. Deep scrapes striated his legs and arms. He stood, turned his back to her, and pulled on a kelly green T-shirt, but not before Maire saw the two burn marks where the Taser probes had struck him.

"That looks like it hurts," she said, despite her vow to not engage with him.

"Like a son of a bitch," he said, turning to face Maire. "Thanks to you." He looked her up and down. "Pink," he said. "Huh. I thought you always said you hated wearing pink, that it clashed with your hair."

"I do," Maire said, flushing. "But I really don't have a choice, do I? This was the stack of clothes next to my bed."

"How are you?" Samuel asked. Maire knew he wasn't asking about the scratches and bruises that covered her own body. She looked around the room in search of cameras.

"Don't worry," he said. "I've already looked. The room is clean."

Maire peered down into the lampshade next to her bed and then ran her finger along the gilded edge of a painting that depicted an Italian countryside. She moved back to her bed, trying to think of a place to hide the envelope and the pill.

"No, really, I already looked everywhere. There are no cameras," he assured her.

Maire crossed her arms in front of her chest, two decades of fear and shame billowing up inside her. "How do you think I am?" she asked, finally answering his question. When Samuel didn't answer, Maire went on, "You, on the other hand, look like you've done just fine. A college degree, a big-shot prosecutor. I bet you have a nice home, a decent salary. Am I right?"

Samuel looked over his shoulder, checking to see that the bedroom door was shut. "I am not fine," he said in a low voice. "Haven't been fine, don't think I'll ever be. Thanks to you."

Maire sat on the edge of her bed, pulling a pillow atop her lap. "You think I'm fine? I think of that night every single day. I dropped out of college, went home, and married a jerk. The only good things that came out of it were my two girls."

"Well, that's something," Samuel said, stretching his arms tentatively above his head. "I've never been married, don't have any kids."

"And you blame me for that too?" Maire scoffed. Samuel looked like he wanted to say yes, but instead he turned and went to the window. Maire took the opportunity to slide the envelope and pill into her pillowcase. She would decide what to do with them later.

"We have to talk about this," Samuel said, staring out over the estate.

Maire suddenly went light-headed, off-balance. Funny how two people could share one singularly horrible, life-changing night together and then never speak of it again, slouching off to their respective lives like it never happened.

"Yes, we do," Maire agreed. "But it's almost nine. Everyone will wonder where we are."

"It'll just take a minute," Samuel countered. "We have to decide what to do, what to say."

"I can't do this right now," Maire said, getting to her feet and moving toward the door. She reached for the doorknob, but Samuel blocked her exit. He was standing too close to her. Too many old memories, old feelings hit her all at once.

She had to focus on today's challenge. If she lost, there was a chance she would go home. She couldn't let that happen. "We'll find somewhere else later on. If we stay in here too long, they are going to think we know each other," she said.

"Maybe they'll just think we are going to work together to solve the clues."

"Even worse," Maire said, her voice rising. "We do need to talk, I know, but not here. Someone watching will make the connection between us. We'll be recognized. It will bring up questions, people will start digging."

"So what's your solution?" Samuel asked in exasperation.

"I don't know," Maire said helplessly. "But I really, really need this money."

Samuel looked as if he wanted to ask her why she was so desperate. Instead, he said, "I think we have three options. One, we just own up to it right now. Say, *Wow, what a weird coincidence. We went to college together years ago.*"

Maire was already shaking her head.

Samuel went on, "Number two, we pretend we don't recognize each other. It's been twenty years; we didn't know each other that well, just socially. You have a different last name, I've put on a few pounds, I have a goatee. It's not impossible to think we didn't make the connection, at least not right away."

"What's the third choice?" Maire asked, eager to get downstairs.

"We quit," Samuel said simply. "We come up with an excuse, an injury, something. And we drop out."

Maire bit on her lip, considering. She wasn't quitting. That was out of the question. She checked her watch. It was almost nine. They had to go, or the others would become suspicious.

"Okay," she finally said. "I think for now we pretend we don't know each other and then act surprised if it's brought up.

We did barely know one another," she said, as if trying to convince herself. "Now, go."

Again, Samuel hesitated, and for a moment the years fell away and a boyishness settled across his face. He always had such a gentleness to him. Except for that night. They both had become people they didn't recognize. "How are you, really?" he asked.

Besides wishing he had never come to look for her that night? she wanted to ask. Instead, she whispered, "Please let me go. Please."

Samuel shook his head as if disappointed and then stepped aside.

With relief, Maire opened the bedroom door and was grateful to find the hallway deserted. She stepped into the corridor and walked quickly toward the staircase.

"Good morning!" came a booming voice from behind her. "It's Maire, right?" Maire turned. It was the senator, dressed in a red *One Lucky Winner* T-shirt and shorts.

"Yes, it is," Maire said, trying to keep her voice light, friendly. "Good morning to you. How'd you sleep?"

"Fine, fine." He waved away her question. "Congrats again on winning last night. Any chance that you'd be willing to share what your Super Clue was?"

"Thanks, but I don't think so," Maire murmured, acutely aware that everything they were saying was being recorded and filmed. Moving down the corridor, she saw the blinking light of two cameras.

"How about a Game Changer? Did you find one?" the senator asked as they came to the grand staircase.

Maire thought of the tiny white pill hidden in her pillowcase, but she sure wasn't going to tell the senator. Instead, she gave him an enigmatic smile.

"I get it," the senator said contritely. "No pressure. But in the spirit of full disclosure, I haven't found one yet, but that TV guy did. Couldn't figure out what it was, but guess we'll find out. Why don't you see if you can get more out of him? We're going to have to up our game today. I may not be much at these physical challenges, but I'm smart." The senator tapped his temple. "I could be a real asset if it comes to solving puzzles and the like, just keep that in mind."

It was all Maire could do to keep from running back to the bedroom and slamming the door. Instead, she forced a smile to her face. "I will. Thank you for that."

At the bottom of the stairs, the other contestants were standing around a table filled with pastries, bowls of fruit, and coffee. Camille was wearing yellow, sipping on a latte, and Ned was dressed in electric orange, peeling a banana. A camera operator was set up a respectful distance away, but impossible not to notice. Maire turned only to find the lens of another camera fixed squarely on her. She murmured her hellos and busied herself with pouring a coffee.

A moment later, Samuel came down the stairs, greeting everyone, but he didn't make eye contact with Maire.

"So, well done on your big win last night, Maire," Ned said with a tone that was anything but congratulatory. "You and the senator really showed us you came to play. You both had no problem sending five thousand volts of electricity through us to get ahead."

Maire couldn't help laughing. "It's just part of the game," she said lightly. "You'd do the same. And you kind of did when you knocked me over to get to the Game Changer first."

"So maybe you're up for a little exchange of information?" Ned raised his eyebrows. "A little tit for tat?" he asked, his smile turning wolfish.

Maire shook her head with disgust and turned away when a young woman stepped into the room, clipboard in hand.

"Good morning, everyone," the woman said. "I'm Caitlyn, Alfonso's intern. I see you found your official *One Lucky Win-*

ner gear. You all look fabulous. Let's get you mic'd up. Fern and Alfonso are waiting for you outside."

The intern led them through the courtyard, and the cameras followed them as they moved. The sky was pearly white and hazy. Next to Maire, Camille shivered, though the morning was pleasant. In the daylight, the magnificence and scope of the estate was on full display. In front of them was the long driveway flanked by bowing cork trees with crooked limbs that eventually led to the iron gates where they gained entrance the night before. The estate sat on a hill and in the valley below were acres and acres of lush green vineyards that disappeared into a morning mist that hadn't yet lifted. To the right was the path that led to the hedge maze.

"It's just down this way," the intern said, and the group followed her down the front steps and toward a cobblestone path that curved around the estate and to the south. This path was lined with camellia trees that bloomed in white and then gave way to towering sycamores.

"What do you think the next challenge will be?" Camille asked, finally breaking the silence.

"Hopefully it won't include Tasers or a hedge maze," Ned quipped and there were chuckles. Maire didn't want to engage. She didn't want to get to know these people, didn't want to think of them as people. She kept her head down, eyes focused on the path in front of her. The cobblestone continued to wind and meander.

Maire began to wonder if they took the wrong path. She was getting antsy. What would happen if they were late to the challenge? Would they still be able to participate? Would they be penalized? Disqualified?

"Look," Ned said. "I think we're getting close."

"This is where I leave you," the intern said with a smile. "Fern is waiting for you right through there. Good luck today." Then she was gone.

Maire heard the gurgle of a fountain and up ahead the path opened to a wide stretch of land that once must have been covered in grapevines but had been transformed into something entirely different.

Ned gave a low whistle and then said, "Welcome to hell, ladies and gentlemen. Shall we see what the devil lady has in store for us today?"

"Jesus," Maire breathed, taking it all in. If she thought the maze challenge was grueling, the one laid out in front of her looked downright deadly.

"Your days are numbered, Red," Ned whispered in Maire's ear, sending a shiver of revulsion down her back.

Ned Bennett was nothing to her. None of these people were, not even Samuel. Especially Samuel. No, Maire wasn't going anywhere anytime soon. She had two little girls who were depending on her, and she wasn't leaving here empty-handed.

Ned Bennett obviously didn't know her. He didn't know Maire's determination or desperation. She straightened her shoulders and walked away from him without a word. Maire would do whatever it took to win. Lie, cheat, steal. After all, she'd done worse things before.

FIFTEEN

THE CONFIDANTE

Then

Dr. Camille Tamerlane checked her watch. It was ten past four and her last patient of the day, Chelsea Weatherly, was late. Camille was afraid this was going to happen. The red light on her phone flashed and she waited for Geraldine, her receptionist, to answer it from her desk in the reception area.

Camille moved to the window and peeked around the curtain. Across the street was Chelsea's estranged husband, Doug. He was why Chelsea hadn't shown up for her session. He was dressed in an expensive Italian suit and had his phone pressed against his ear. Camille glanced back at the flashing phone. That was probably him calling with more taunts, more demands to stop interfering in his marriage. Poor Chelsea, she had been trying to get the nerve up to leave Doug for over a year. With a sigh, Camille picked up the receiver.

"Dr. Tamerlane's office," she said, bracing herself for another tirade.

"Hello?" came a soft, tentative voice.

Camille closed her eyes. This caller was just as problematic. "Wingo," Camille said, trying to keep her voice even and professional, "I told you not to contact me, you are not a client of mine. I don't know how to make myself clearer."

"I'm sorry," Wingo said, miserably. "I was hoping you could see me, one more time, for just a few minutes. I have the money now. I can pay."

"Wingo," Camille said, her patience fraying. "It's not about the money. It's about your inappropriate behavior. It's about the flowers and the gifts." There was a tap on her office door and Camille looked up. It was Geraldine, her receptionist.

"Please," he said. "I promise…"

"No, Wingo. I have to go now," Camille said and hung up.

"Everything okay?" Geraldine asked, worriedly. That was so like Geraldine to always want to look after Camille. With her tightly permed gray hair, and colorful pantsuits, Geraldine was smart, efficient, and grandmotherly. A perfect combination for a receptionist.

"Yeah, it's fine," Camille said, waving away her concern. "Except that Doug Weatherly is standing outside again. We're going to have to figure out how to schedule Chelsea's appointments without Doug finding out. I'm worried about her."

"He must be hacking into her phone or email, or something," Geraldine said, shaking her head. "I'll see what I can do."

"Thank you," Camille said. "And since Chelsea is a no-show, I think I'm going to head to the recording studio a little earlier today so Parker and I can prep for the show."

"Before you go, a woman is in the waiting room. She sounds desperate," Geraldine said, apologetically.

Camille almost told Geraldine to send the woman on her way, telling her that she wasn't taking on any new clients. Which was entirely true. She was tired, her schedule was full, the podcast had taken on a life of its own.

"She said she'll pay cash," Geraldine added.

This tidbit caused Camille to pause.

Cash was good. It was a rarity, but not unheard of. Some of

her clients wanted assurance of their privacy no matter the cost. It meant no official paperwork, no submission to health insurance. And no taxes, which meant more money for the things she wanted. All fine with Camille.

"Okay," Camille said finally. "Send her in."

A moment later the woman entered the room reluctantly and hesitantly looked around. She was small in stature with thick black hair beneath a slouchy black hat. She wore black leggings, Chuck Taylors, a white T-shirt, jean jacket, and she had a large yellow handbag hooked over her shoulder.

The woman's face was hidden behind dark sunglasses. This wasn't unusual either. Patients often wore sunglasses to conceal teary, red-rimmed eyes. They were a barrier that Camille tolerated for a few sessions. After the third appointment, she would ask the patient to remove the glasses so they could get down to the real work.

"I'm Dr. Tamerlane. Welcome," she said, holding out a hand. The woman reciprocated with a grip that was soft, tentative. "Please come in and take a seat."

The woman looked toward the door as if she wanted to bolt. Instead she sat, perching precariously on the edge of the seat, placing her bag on the floor next to her and tucking her hands between her knees.

Camille wheeled her desk chair over so that she was sitting directly in front of the woman. She left her notebook at her desk, having found it put new clients at ease to know she wasn't writing down what they told her.

"I'm sorry, I'm afraid I didn't catch your name," Camille said, mirroring the woman's body language.

"It's Nan," the woman said in a soft voice, pushing the sunglasses up on the bridge of her nose. "Adams."

"As in Nancy?" Camille asked.

"No, just Nan," she answered, staring down at her Converse.

"It's a pleasure to meet you, Nan. Thank you for coming

in today," Camille said warmly. "I know it can be awkward meeting with a therapist for the first time. This first meeting will be a bit different than a regular session. I'll ask you some questions that will help me understand what you may be experiencing and feeling. And you can feel free to ask me questions too." Camille gave Nan a gentle smile. "I'll share my initial thoughts and observations and then we'll talk about a plan to help you feel better. What do you think?"

Nan let out a long, shuddery breath. "Sounds good."

"Wonderful," Camille said, pushing her glasses atop her head. "Let's start by talking about why you wanted to see me today. My receptionist said you felt it was quite urgent."

Nan twisted a hammered silver ring on her index finger but didn't speak. Camille let the silence hang there, not wanting to rush the woman. She didn't like not being able to see her face and look into her eyes, but she didn't want to spook Nan by asking her to take the sunglasses off just yet.

"How about this," Camille tried, "why don't you tell me what's on your mind right now? Right this instant."

Nan chewed on her lower lip. "You can't repeat what I say here, can you? It's all private?"

"That's right, I will not repeat what you tell me here," Camille explained. "However, if you reveal that you are going to commit a crime or are going to continue to commit a crime involving, say, a child or an elderly person, I'm required to alert authorities. But if you tell me about a past crime, I'm bound by secrecy."

Nan shifted uneasily in her seat. "I feel like I'm doing something wrong, that I'm being disloyal."

"You feel like by coming here, you are breaking someone's trust?" Camille asked. Nan nodded reluctantly. Camille leaned forward and lowered her elbows to her knees. "Many of my clients feel that way when they first come to see me, but come to realize that talking things through doesn't mean they are being disloyal, but are simply trying to make sense of what they are feeling."

Camille knew she needed to tread carefully. If she pushed Nan too hard, she would bolt. She was already looking toward the door. "You are feeling conflicted," Camille said. "Maybe if you told me a bit more about who you are worried about disappointing, I can better help you."

"It's my boss," Nan said, her voice thick with tears. "I can't eat, I can't sleep, but if I complain…"

"You are afraid you'll lose your job?" Camille asked when Nan didn't finish her thought.

"That and so much more," she said, rubbing a tattoo of a dragonfly on the inside of her wrist.

Camille wanted to ask Nan what she did for a living but didn't sense that this was the right time. Instead, she leaned back in her chair and crossed her legs and waited.

"I work so hard, but nothing is ever enough. I don't think I can take it any longer."

"You've tried talking to your employer?" Camille asked, wanting to know more.

Nan gave an angry laugh. "That would be impossible. She doesn't listen. She doesn't care."

"What about quitting?" Camille asked. "Is that an option?"

Nan considered this, again spinning the ring on her finger. "I don't know," she finally said. "I've thought about it, but I can't. Not yet. In this twisted way she needs me. I just wish there was a way I could make her see how important I am, the value I bring."

"What would be enough?" Camille asked. "Would make things right?"

Nan sniffed, sliding her fingers beneath the frames of the black lenses of her glasses and rubbing her eyes. "I don't know. It doesn't seem right that she gets to walk through life like I'm a no one. There should be consequences."

"Consequences?" Camille echoed. "What do you mean?"

Nan stood up abruptly and moved to the window that looked out at a stunning view of the bay. She was quiet for a long time. Camille let the silence hang. When Nan turned back to Camille, her lips were curled in anger. "I don't know—public humiliation, financial ruin sound reasonable to me."

"You're angry," Camille observed.

"Damn right I am," Nan shot back. "The way she treats me, others. How can I just sit back and take it? It's not right."

When Camille didn't fill the silence, Nan returned to her seat and sat down with a heavy sigh. "Have you ever read *The Count of Monte Cristo*?" she asked. "Or *Hamlet*?"

"It's been a while," Camille admitted. "But yes, I've read them. Both are about revenge," she added, carefully watching Nan's reaction.

"Yes, but it took Dantès and Hamlet years to dole out their revenge," Nan said, shaking her head. "I don't think it should take that long."

"You're thinking about revenge?" Nan asked, alarm bells beginning to ring in her head.

"No, of course not," Nan said in a rush. "Not really. Though I'd be lying if I said I don't fantasize about throwing my laptop against the wall and walking out."

"How about we brainstorm some other options?" Camille asked.

For the next thirty minutes, Camille tried to get Nan to reveal more about her work situation, but Nan was vague, elusive, not willing to offer concrete examples of what she was experiencing. Finally, the timer on Camille's watch beeped. Their time was up.

"I think I can help you, Nan, with what you are feeling," Camille said. "I can help you process your feelings about your employer and decide what, if anything, you can and should do. Do you think this is something you'd like to pursue?" she asked, picking up a box of tissues from a nearby side table and holding it out to her.

Nan plucked a tissue from the box. "I think so," she said, dabbing at her nose. "I think I would like that very much."

"Good," Camille said, bringing up her calendar on her phone. "Now, next week at this time is booked, but if it fits with your schedule, I'd be willing to see you after hours, say six o'clock?"

"That works," Nan said with obvious relief, standing up. "And—" she hesitated "—I prefer not to go through my insurance for my sessions. Cash is okay?"

"That will be just fine," Camille assured her. Nan handed her a slim envelope and Camille led her from the office, past Geraldine's desk, and out the front exit.

"Thank you so much, Dr. Tamerlane. This has been weighing on me," Nan said, reaching out to shake Camille's hand. Her fingers were cold and damp.

"It's my pleasure. See you next week." Camille watched as Nan walked away down the quiet street.

Once back inside, Camille set the cash atop Geraldine's desk. "You know what to do with this."

Geraldine looked up from her computer and nodded. "Will she be needing another appointment?" she asked.

"Yes," Camille said, not meeting her eye. "But off the books. I have a feeling I'll have several more sessions with her. That is one angry woman, but I think I can help her."

"Speaking of angry," Geraldine said. "I shooed Doug Weatherly away. Told him I was going to call the police if he didn't stop loitering outside the office. He was not happy."

"Well, there's a lot of that going around lately," Camille said, noticing with irritation the fresh bouquet of red salvia sitting atop Geraldine's desk. "No signature?" she asked, knowing they were from Travis Wingo.

"No signature," Geraldine confirmed, handing Camille the small card that accompanied the bouquet.

Camille retreated back to her office and closed the door to think. She looked down at the card and the two words written there. *Forever Mine.* She needed to do something about Wingo. Things were getting out of hand.

SIXTEEN

THE CONFIDANTE

Camille took in the sight in front of them thinking she might be in a fever dream. It appeared as if Armageddon had come to Napa and someone had built some sort of twisted playground atop a razed field.

A slight breeze was blowing, stirring up small dervishes of dusty clouds. Camille was so tired from the night before and the caffeine jolt from her latte hadn't kicked in yet. After losing the race through the hedge maze, she lurched back to her room, stumbled to bed, and fell into the deepest sleep she'd ever encountered. If it hadn't been for the Iowa mom's penlight or whatever she was holding, she would still be lost in the maze.

"It's an obstacle course," Samuel said. "I've done these before—it's like a Tough Mudder. They're brutal."

The tract of land was a sea of black dirt the size of two football fields. Above them, drones swept across the sky. Atop the field was a wall that rose three stories high, a mud pit, dozens of rubber tires, long steel beams, and, in the distance, what looked like bull's-eye targets. Samuel was right, they were going to be running an obstacle course. Camille also spotted what looked like a guard lookout. The towering cylindrical column had the all-too-familiar *One Lucky Winner* logo painted across it and sat off to the side of the course. An ideal vantage point for aerial camera shots.

Camille's eyes returned to the climbing wall and her stomach dropped. She was in excellent shape but might not be able to keep up with Samuel in the physical challenges. She had thought that after the hedge maze there were going to be puzzles and other competitions that didn't include being able to outrun her opponents.

At least she had stumbled across one of the Game Changers at breakfast. Camille had been the first one to the great hall. Sitting amid the bagels, pastries, and fruit, tucked beneath the top linen napkin, was an envelope. Camille looked around to see if anyone was watching her, and seeing no one, she slipped the envelope into her pocket. Moving to a quiet corner of the room, Camille opened the envelope.

Congratulations! You've discovered a crucial Game Changer. Memorize the four sentences below and in the presence of the cameras, work each statement into conversation with your fellow competitors.

Her stomach dropped in disappointment. She had been expecting some kind of earth-shattering advantage for the next challenge, but none of the statements made sense. Or rather, they didn't seem to mean anything. They were just simple, ordinary, everyday sentences.

"Good morning, Luckies," Fern called out, pulling Camille away from her thoughts. "Please join me."

In a single-file line, with the senator in the lead, the group followed the cobblestone path and came to a stop at the bottom of the dais. Atop the raised platform flanked by columns, Fern stood, wearing a beautiful white dress adorned with decorative crystal panels, a low-cut neckline, and a voluminous bubble skirt that fell just below her knees. Camille was impressed— the young woman had style and an impressive wardrobe budget. Her eyes fell to Fern's shoes. Pristine white tennis shoes.

That was certainly a bold choice, Camille thought, but something itched at the back of her brain. She kept feeling like she'd met Fern somewhere before, somewhere outside of the game.

Fern clasped her hands in front of her and smiled down on them. "Welcome to day two of your quest to become our one lucky winner. I trust you had a good night's sleep."

Everyone nodded, including Camille, though she felt like she hadn't rested at all.

Camille looked around, spotting Alfonso sitting in a director's chair off to the side of the course, legs crossed. For a director, he was certainly hands-off. Camille supposed that was the nature of reality TV—roll the cameras and see what unfolded.

"You won the Super Clue last night, Maire," Fern said. "Tell us—how important was it that you won that first challenge?"

"It was extremely important. I was lucky," Maire said. "I happened to get to the clue first, but I know I'm going to have to give it my all to win the other challenges. I know I can do it."

Before she could stop it, a bubble of laughter rose from Camille's chest. Maire sounded so innocent, but the way she made it through the maze last night made it clear that Maire was no Girl Scout.

"And, Camille." Fern turned her attention to Camille and the laugh died on her lips. "What is your strategy going into today's competition?"

"You know, Fern," Camille began. "Ten million dollars is on the line so there is only one strategy. To win every single challenge moving forward, and that's what I intend to do." Camille was relieved to hear the confidence in her voice. She almost believed herself. "And I'm going to make sure I find the next Game Changer before anyone else."

Fern nodded as if satisfied by the response. "Ah, yes, the elusive Game Changers. Would anyone like to share what they've found?"

Camille cut a glance to Ned. Everyone knew he had found

one the night before. Uncharacteristically, Ned decided to stay quiet on the subject, simply giving them a closed-lip smile. Camille studied the others. Had someone else found one? Camille looked around and noticed Maire's uncomfortable body language, how she stared resolutely at the ground. Camille would have to keep an eye on her.

"Well, then," Fern said. "I'm sure those Game Changers will be revealed soon enough. Let's get down to the business at hand. As you can see, today's challenge is an obstacle course. But this is no ordinary course. There are little surprises scattered throughout."

"What? Like Tasers? Maybe shotguns this time?" Samuel whispered. Camille chuckled, but was wondering the same thing. She liked Samuel. He was a competitor but less guarded than Maire, less obnoxious than Ned, and less, well, senator-like than the senator.

"First, you will run through the tires, making sure that your feet touch each one. From there, you will cross a balance beam without falling. If you do, you must go back and try again. Then you will army-crawl through a pit of wet ash and mud. Stay low, because there will be razor wire above you, so watch your heads. Once through the pit, you will come to a sandbox. In the sandbox, you will dig until you find a canvas bag that is the same color you are wearing right now."

Camille looked down at her yellow T-shirt.

Fern continued with the directions and Camille struggled to stay focused. This was only the second challenge. How was she going to make it through thirteen more days? "Once you get your bag," Fern explained, "you will open it and begin assembling the puzzle pieces you find inside. Once you assemble your puzzle, memorize it, because it's a clue. It will definitely come in handy for you later. After the puzzle, you will climb the forty-foot rock wall."

Camille eyed the wall; it didn't look like there were any

tethers or harnesses nearby. Did that mean they were going to have to climb with no protection? One misstep and someone could fall.

"Once atop the wall, you'll use a rope to climb down. Finally, you will run to the station we have set up as a shooting range. The first contestant who hits the target wins the Super Clue."

Chances were, Camille thought, she wouldn't be the first one through the obstacle course. She might not win the Super Clue but if she could get to the sandbox and find the puzzle pieces, she could solve it. And she'd search for as many Game Changers as she could find, in hopes that the others would be focused on hitting the bull's-eye first.

"Are you ready to face what could be the most grueling and dangerous hour of your life?" Fern asked.

"Well, it's not like any of us have an eight-year-old son," Camille said, deciding that this was the time to utter one of the sentences on the piece of parchment paper in her pocket.

Camille watched the others as they took in her seemingly random statement. Ned raised his eyebrows, Samuel gave her a sideways glance, and a muscle in the senator's jaw twitched, but that was all. Maire met Camille's gaze and stared back with resolute determination, maybe thinking of her own young child, but she had daughters, right? She tried to remember.

"Luckies, are you ready?" Fern asked from her perch. "On your marks." Everyone hurried to a spot behind the white chalk line. "Get set."

Camille inched her toe as close to the line without crossing it. Fern raised the starter's pistol, pulled the trigger, and Camille lunged forward.

She nearly stumbled right out of the gate. The crumbly soil beneath her feet was slippery and she couldn't gain traction. Somehow, she righted herself, but next to her, Ned wasn't so lucky. He fell to his knees, causing a mushroom cloud of dust to rise up around them. Camille was the first to make it to the tires, but Samuel, Maire, and even the senator were close behind her. Thighs burning, she carefully stepped through the eighteen tires. Camille wished she had spent a few minutes stretching that morning.

Once through the tires, Camille set her sights on the next obstacle: a steel beam, about forty feet long, four inches wide, and set about three feet above the ground. She hoisted herself up and threw a leg over either side of the beam, the tender flesh of her inner thigh slamming against the metal.

There she paused, looking down at the long strip of steel, trying to decide the best way to get across without falling. She maneuvered into a crawling position and considered trying to get across this way, but the beam was so narrow that she'd likely tip right off the side. No, she'd have to stand up. On wobbly ankles, she held her hands out to the side and stood. On the beam next to her, Samuel had pulled ahead, but she didn't dare turn her head to see where the others were.

One foot in front of the other, Camille told herself. She just needed to get to the puzzle. She would figure out how to get another Game Changer. She eased forward, trying to get the feel of the beam beneath her shoes. Maire moved past her, then Ned.

She was halfway across her beam when she heard the senator's heavy breathing on the beam next to her and then a cry, and a dull thud. The senator had fallen. Camille forced her eyes down and in front of her, stepping carefully until she was just a few feet from the end. From there, she crouched and leaped to the ground, the impact sending a shock of pain through her legs and a puff of powdery earth around her.

She paused in front of the next obstacle: the mud pit covered in razor wire. Ahead, she could see Ned, Samuel, and Maire struggling. On their bellies, they were already covered in the thick mud, barely inching forward. It was the warm-up suits,

Camille decided, that were holding them back. The minute they crawled into the pit, the fabric became slogged down with mud, making it nearly impossible for them to move forward.

Thinking fast, Camille unzipped her jacket, pulled off her T-shirt, and stepped out of her warm-up pants. She considered tossing aside her shoes, but the soles of her feet were torn up and sore from the hedge maze, so she kept them on.

Once again, she was down to a tank top and shorts. Who knew if it would make a difference, but she'd have to try. She was the smallest of the group, but she was strong. She could do this. Camille threw herself to the ground and began to army-crawl, trying to stay clear of the razor wire that hung ominously above her head. The thick, wet mud immediately enveloped her. It filled her ears, clung to her hair and eyelashes, and her limbs felt like cement, but she continued to inch forward. Somehow, she was gaining on the others.

Camille snaked past one mud-caked competitor and then another. It was impossible to tell who was who. Black dirt clogged her nose and worked its way into her mouth, the gritty muck thick on her tongue. She was neck and neck with her final rival, who was so covered in the ooze that Camille had no idea who it was. She could win this.

With a surge of adrenaline, she dug in her feet and pulled herself forward, the mud squelching noisily around her. She was now in the lead, so close to the exit. She might just pull this off and be the first one out of the pit. That's when she felt it, a viselike grip around her ankle.

The son of a bitch behind her was trying to stop her. Camille tried to wriggle free but the hand held tight, pulling her back.

"Hell no," Camille muttered. With a mule kick of her free foot, she struck out and was greeted with the satisfactory crunch of bone. Barely noticing the bite of razor wire against her scalp, Camille pulled herself through the final few feet of mud and, with a victorious smile, climbed out of the sludge.

She heard the impact first, a stomach-churning smack, before she felt it. Pain exploded through her ribs, a stabbing pain so sharp that Camille's breath lodged in her throat, and she fell to her knees. Gasping for breath, she looked down. Intermingled with the black mud smeared across her tank top was something else. She pressed her hand to her rib cage, vaguely cognizant of the sound of footfalls behind her, and groaned at the pain. Camille pulled her fingers from her side and stared down at her trembling hands, now covered in a sticky red substance. Blood. The realization clicked into place. Her hands were covered in blood. She had been shot.

SEVENTEEN

THE CONFIDANTE

Then

One week later, Dr. Tamerlane's doorbell rang. Though it was six o'clock and Geraldine was long gone, Camille was in her office preparing for the next installment of *Your Best Life*. She opened the door to find Nan wearing the same oversize sunglasses and a baggy sweatshirt. Instead of the slouchy hat, she wore a trucker's cap with *John Deere* embroidered across the front, the brim pulled low.

"Hello," Camille said, inviting her in. "How have you been since we last met?" she asked, after Nan had taken a seat.

"Okay. Fine," Nan responded. Again, Nan was perched on the edge of the seat cushion, her fingers gripping the chair's arms, the toes of her Converse shoes pressed into the carpet, her muscles rigid, as if ready to bolt.

"You seem quite tense," Camille began.

"There's a man outside," Nan said, chewing on a fingernail. "Just standing there, staring at the building. He was there last time too. Do you know who he is?"

Camille knew exactly who it was. Doug Weatherly trying to intimidate his wife, intimidate her. But Chelsea didn't have an appointment today and Camille was now meeting with her at a different location. He wasn't giving up. "No one you need to worry about," Camille soothed. "Tell me about your week."

"Awful, terrible, the same as always," Nan said. "I work twelve-hour days and my boss constantly tells me how much of screwup I am. She's ruthless and if you cross her, she'll bury you."

"Ah," Camille said, glad for the opening. "Sounds intense. What is your line of work? I don't think you mentioned it."

Nan twisted the silver ring on her index finger. "Do I have to say?" she asked.

"No, you don't," Camille answered. "But any information you can share will help me understand your anxiety, what you are going through."

Nan nodded but didn't answer Camille's question. "Half the time I feel like someone is sitting on top of me." Nan pressed a hand to her chest. "I can't breathe. I literally feel like I'm going to die."

"That sounds like it could be a panic attack," Camille observed. "Does something specific happen that precedes that feeling? Something that you can point to?"

"It's because of her," Nan said. "It starts just before I leave for work. I've been late twice in the last week alone."

"You don't feel like you can confide in your employer? Tell her what's going on?" Camille asked.

Nan gave a harsh laugh. "That's a no," she said. "My boss has no patience for ineptitude. She'll see a panic attack as a sign of weakness. I can't talk to her about this."

Camille wondered if Nan's boss, and Nan by default, had a high-profile position and this was why she insisted on wearing the sunglasses, the hats, the clothes that ate her up. Camille leaned forward in her chair. "I want you to know that having anxiety attacks has nothing to do with being strong. They are your body's way of telling you that something in your life needs to be attended to."

"And you think you can help me with that?" Nan asked skeptically.

"I do," Camille said. "But if I'm going to help, I will need to know more about your situation. I'm going to have to ask questions. Possibly ones that will make you feel uncomfortable. You are going to need to trust me, Nan. What do you think? Are you willing to give me that chance?"

Nan nodded, took a deep breath, and grasped Camille's hand. Her grip was much stronger, more assured this time. Camille once again caught sight of a dragonfly tattoo on the inside of Nan's wrist and wondered about its significance.

"I think I can do that," Fern said, her voice breaking.

"Very good," Camille said. "I know you are hesitant to talk about the work you do, but maybe you can tell me more about your fears. Are you worried if you quit you won't get another job?"

"We're in the middle of a big project and she'd kill me if I quit," Nan said. "I've worked for her for years and if I can't use her as a reference my résumé would be one big black hole." She rubbed her arms as if she was cold. "Besides, I don't know if I actually want to quit. I owe my boss a lot. She was there for me during a very difficult time. I don't think I could do that to her right now."

Camille longed to pull the sunglasses from Nan's face. It was so hard to get a handle on her patients without looking into their eyes.

"Your boss sounds like someone who is very important to you," Camille said. "So what I hear you saying is that you'd like some tools to handle your situation until you are ready to make a decision as to whether or not to stay in your current position. At least at this point."

Nan nodded.

"Why don't you tell me a little bit more about your boss…?" Camille held up a hand when Nan began to protest. "No specifics. I don't need to know who, when, or where. Just the basics—just the what."

Nan took a deep breath and began talking in her low, husky voice shaky with emotion.

Nan was right. Her boss was a piece of work. Verbally, sometimes physically, abusive.

Camille studied Nan's face. Though she couldn't see Nan's eyes, she was obviously tortured. Catching Camille looking at her, Nan self-consciously got to her feet and walked over to the Henni Alftan oil painting on the wall. A few years ago, on a trip to France, Camille discovered the artist's work and fell in love with the painting, which depicted an empty fig-colored chair sitting in the middle of a shadowed room. Though it was well beyond her budget, Camille had to have it.

"Okay. I know sharing that with me must have been difficult," Camille said soothingly. "So let's focus on your panic attacks. There are many strategies you can use to help ease your anxiety: exercise, a good sleep schedule, meditation. I can even write you a prescription for medication…"

"No, no," Nan said, in a rush. "I don't want medication. Not yet. I just want to know what to do."

Camille's watch beeped, signifying the end of the session.

"Next week we'll talk more about what you do have control over," Camille said, walking Nan to the door. "Determine what is healthiest for you. But I have to say, Nan, I do think we have to discuss whether this job is the best environment for you."

Nan smiled wearily. "Thank you, Dr. Tamerlane," she said. "I do feel better. I have no one else I can tell and it's such a relief to talk about it. But sometimes I think the only option I have is to deal with it on my own."

"But that's why I'm here. So you don't have to puzzle through this alone," Camille said.

Suddenly there was a loud crash and the sound of breaking glass. Nan screamed and covered her head with her hands while

Camille shielded her face. Then there was only silence. Camille lowered her hands to see a large, jagged hole in the window and a brick on the floor surrounded by shards of broken glass just a few feet away from where Nan was sitting.

"Are you okay?" Camille asked, leaping to her feet. "Were you hit?"

"No, no. I'm fine," Nan said, though she was trembling. "Who would do that? Was it the man standing outside?"

Camille didn't know what to say. Was it Doug Weatherly? It was out of character for him. Doug was more about intimidation through more subtle means: following his wife, and standing quietly by, glowering. He was also a man of considerable means, who appreciated the finer things in life and wouldn't deign to dirty his suit with a filthy old brick.

"I'm not sure," Camille admitted, "but I promise it won't happen again. Come on, I'll make sure you get outside safely. Would you like me to call you an Uber?"

"No, that's okay. I'm fine, really," Nan said. "I'm parked down the street."

Camille walked Nan to the exit, opened the door, and scanned the street for any sign of Doug. There was no one. It had started to rain and the drops hit the hot pavement in steamy splotches.

"It's getting dark," Camille said. "I can't let you walk to your car by yourself. Let me go with you."

"No," Nan said sharply, then added more softly, "I said I'm fine." She stepped outside, then turned. "Oh, I almost forgot," Nan said, reaching into her pocket. She pressed an envelope into Camille's hands. "Thanks again."

Camille stood in the doorway and watched as Nan moved down the street and out of sight. Camille peered into the envelope. Inside were seven crisp one-hundred-dollar bills. It would be a miracle if Nan decided to come back. "Dammit," Camille muttered. She needed her clients to feel safe or her practice would be ruined. She moved to go back inside, nearly tripping on something on the top step. A bouquet of flowers. Her stomach dropped. Travis Wingo. Camille bent over and picked up the bundle of delicate white petals surrounding a black center eye. She pulled out the small card tucked within the fern-like foliage. On it was written one word. *Forsaken*.

EIGHTEEN

THE BEST FRIEND

On the obstacle course, Maire had fallen into fourth place. How had that happened? She had let the earlier conversation with Samuel distract her and she needed to put him out of her mind and act like they were nothing but competitors.

She felt like she had swallowed more mud than she was wearing. As she crawled through the pit, she thought of Dani, the difficulty she often had with breathing. It humbled her, made her angry. No child should have to suffer in that way. It made her move faster.

She wanted another clue. The family tree she won the day before made no sense, no matter how long she studied the parchment. And she wanted another Game Changer. The more she could find and the more challenges she could win early on, the more power she had. She would have currency to barter. Right now, all she had was a tattered family tree with pieces missing and a sketchy pill. She thought of Camille's odd statement about how none of them had an eight-year-old son. What was that all about?

She was falling farther behind Camille and Samuel. *Think of the kids*, she told herself. They needed to keep their home, to stay together. Ten million dollars was an obscene amount of money. Maire would keep working. Or maybe she wouldn't. Managing Dani's health care was a full-time job. She wouldn't use the money for lavish vacations or fancy cars. She would only use what she needed to buy their house outright, to pay Dani's medical bills, to pay for the kids' education. She didn't care about the rest.

The image of her children's hopeful faces pushed Maire forward.

Maire reached the end of the mud pit just as the competitor in front of her staggered to his feet. It was Ned Bennett, recognizable by his orange warm-up outfit that peeked through the black dirt. He pinched the bridge of his nose with his thumb and forefinger and tilted his head back. His face was covered in blood mixed with slimy mud.

"She kicked me in the face," Ned gasped, spitting a wad of blood to the ground.

She had to be the psychiatrist, Camille. Maire didn't stop to see if he needed help. She could catch Camille and she could definitely beat her in the target shooting competition. She had grown up on a farm after all. But just ahead of her was Camille, on her knees. Her body was shaking so hard, it was vibrating.

"I think I've been shot," Camille cried, as Maire ran past.

It took a second for Camille's words to register with Maire, but when they did, she stopped short and turned. Maire didn't see any blood, but Camille was covered from head to toe with mud, so it was hard to tell. Should she stop and help her or was it just a trick? Behind Camille, Ned was closing in on them and the senator wasn't far behind.

It had to be a trick. Camille was just trying to slow her down. But still, Maire hesitated. Was she really the kind of person who would leave someone with grave injuries behind? No, the real question was—was she *still* that kind of person?

It didn't matter. This was just a game. No one was getting shot. Maire shook her head, disgusted with herself, and was just about to turn and run toward the next obstacle when a loud bang filled the air and the senator dropped. Maire screamed. Someone *was* shooting at them. She threw herself to the ground and covered her head with her arms but quickly realized her mistake. She was completely exposed and needed to run for cover.

Maire staggered to her feet and dared a glance up at the guard tower. There he was—a man holding a shotgun aimed directly at her. There was nowhere for her to go, nowhere to hide. Maire was frozen in place, her legs refusing to move. The ground erupted in front of her and thick, red blood splatted against her legs.

Had she been shot? She felt no pain, was still on her feet. Maire bent down and tentatively touched her shin. The liquid was too thick to be blood. She brought her fingers to her nose. Paint. They were being shot with paint balls meant to scare and slow them down. Relief and irritation flooded through her as Camille dashed past. She had figured it out too.

Maire turned and ran toward the next obstacle, still expecting to be pelted in the back with a paint bullet. In front of her was a huge sandbox the size of a tennis court. She needed to find the pink bag filled with puzzle pieces. The key was to dig up your own bag without revealing the locations of the other bags. Camille didn't seem concerned about that though. She was digging wildly, throwing sand over her shoulder in search of her yellow bag. Samuel was on his knees, looking around the sandbox and trying to decide where to dig next, his chest heaving heavily.

Maire chose the opposite side of the box to begin her hunt. She bent over, sank her hands into the soft sand, and then plowed forward as if pushing a wheelbarrow, trying to cover as much ground as possible in the shortest amount of time. Almost immediately, her fingers struck something. She dropped to her knees and yanked. Out came a kelly green backpack. Samuel's.

She covered the bag with sand the best she could but didn't want to waste time. She continued searching for the pink bag.

Across the sandbox came a sharp cry. Maire told herself not to look. She was moving more quickly now and didn't want to stop. There was another shriek and then a sob. *Keep going*, Maire told herself. *Don't look.* The heavy mud that encased her body was now being sloughed away by the sand. Again, her hands landed on something. Another bag. Maire shoved her fingers down deeper into the sand and caught a glimpse of bright pink. Her bag. She just needed to pull if free.

A figure dashed by Maire, kicking sand into her mouth, her nose, her eyes. Camille had found her bag and was moving on to the next obstacle. Ignoring the gritty bite of sand in her eyes, Maire kept digging, pulling. Her bag was slowly loosening.

There was another cry and a shout of, "What the fuck?" It was Samuel.

What was happening? Maire hadn't heard any more gunshots. She almost had her bag free, that was all that mattered. Suddenly, a flash of hot white pain struck her hand, so intense that for a moment Maire couldn't breathe. When she snatched her hand back, she expected to see blood but instead the pad of her ring finger was red and beginning to swell. The burning pain was excruciating. What was it? A spider bite? A beesting?

It didn't matter. With one final heave, she pulled her pink bag from the sand at the same time that another sharp stabbing pain hit her ankle. Then another at her calf. With a cry, Maire scrambled backward, still clutching the backpack. Emerging from the sand were a legion of crab-like creatures with a multitude of legs and snapping pincers, all coming toward her. It wasn't their clicking claws that terrified Maire, it was their curved tails with the needle-sharp barb. Scorpions.

She felt the skitter of something climbing her leg and frantically tried slapping it away. Another sting pierced her wrist.

The pain was disorientating. *Get up*, a voice said in her ear. *They won't follow you. Get up and run.*

Samuel was standing above her. He had his green backpack looped around his shoulders and held out his hand. Maire wasn't going to accept help from anyone, especially not him. She was going to win the money, scorpions be damned. She gritted her teeth and stood up, rushing to the edge of the sandbox and stepping over its wooden frame. The pain had ingrained itself deep in her skin. All her nerve endings were screaming but there was nothing she could do. From what she could tell, she'd been stung three times. Finger, wrist, ankle. She shook the heavy pink backpack, examining it for any remaining scorpions before sliding it onto her shoulders. She had to keep going.

Maire resolutely ignored Samuel, who had fallen into step beside her, and she set her sights on the pink flag next to a table, twenty yards away, where she would assemble her puzzle. She limped to her spot, removed the backpack from her shoulders, and unzipped the pocket, expecting more scorpions to come crawling out. The pain in her hand and ankle weren't fading. If anything, it was burrowing in, getting hotter. Scorpions were poisonous. Deadly, even. Maire gritted her teeth. She wasn't dead yet.

Ned, Samuel, and Camille were already at their tables assembling their puzzles. She dumped the puzzle pieces onto her table and began to flip them over to reveal the scattered image. The twenty-five puzzle pieces were thick, made of wood, and cut into irregular shapes. There were no corners, making Maire think that her puzzle was circular. She was decent at puzzle solving. She and the kids always had one on the game table in the basement and would periodically work on it, but there was never this pressure, these high stakes.

Unfortunately, Maire's puzzle was nearly monochromatic, chestnut brown with slashes of black, a little white and red thrown in. In its jumbled state, she had no inkling of what the final image could be. Next to her, the others were sliding their pieces around on their tables, deep in concentration. The senator finally appeared, breathing heavily, his red bag dangling from his fingers.

Maire focused on the round edges and an image began to emerge. Two ears, a scraggly chin. It was an illustration of an animal. The pieces with white quickly became a snarling mouth with sharp fangs. An uneasy familiarity fell over Maire as she pressed two red pieces into the puzzle that formed a heart-shaped tongue. She knew what this picture was. She just didn't know why. With shaky fingers, she continued to work until most of the pieces were in place. A bear. But not any bear. It was the mascot of her former college.

The Tanglefoot Bear—a ferocious, gaping-mouthed beast with red eyes. Why was Gil the Bear one of the clues in this game? She hadn't been to Tanglefoot in twenty years. She hadn't even graduated. Two weeks after that fateful night, she quit school, went home to Calico, and threw away all her college paraphernalia. She would have burned them if a bonfire in the yard wouldn't have raised eyebrows.

She stole a glance at the others. Camille had already moved on and her completed puzzle appeared to be an illustration of a purple chair sitting in an empty room. Strange.

Samuel plugged in his last puzzle piece and then immediately looked around, his eyes stopping on Maire. He looked as frightened as she felt. What was happening? He hesitated briefly and then took off toward the wall.

Maire knew she needed to head that way too, but she wanted to try to catch a glimpse of the other puzzles before she continued. Any clue was knowledge and would help her in the game.

She paused at the senator's puzzle, which was still incomplete, but it looked to be a photo of a woman in an orange jumpsuit of some sort—a mug shot? But it was Samuel's puzzle that made her breath catch in her throat.

An aerial image of a lake. But not just any lake. It was Tanglefoot Lake. What happened at Tanglefoot had been big news at the time, but all she wanted to do was forget every single minute of that terrible night.

Go, go, go, Maire told herself, not sure if she was ordering herself to run from this place, this strange, dangerous game, or to finish the challenge. She turned and dashed toward the rock wall. Camille was already at the top, hoisting herself over the other side with Samuel close behind. Maire could still win this. She placed her toes on the first foothold and reached above her for a handhold. She tried not to think about the puzzles, the scorpions, the throbbing pain in her hand and ankle, or the growing distance to the ground beneath her.

Soon she found a rhythm. Reach, step, reach, step. If she didn't look down, she would be okay. Her muscles groaned with the exertion and sweat burned her eyes, sending rivulets of blackened perspiration down her cheeks. She was almost there.

Behind her, Maire heard the puff and groans of someone gaining on her. She chanced a glance over her shoulder to find Ned Bennett and a wave of vertigo swept over her. One hand, slick with sweat, slipped from a groove in the wall and one foot followed. Half her body swung outward, the scorched earth thirty feet below.

Fear pounded in her chest like a drum. If she fell, she would break into a million pieces. Her children would be motherless. She swung back toward the wall and frantically reached for the nearest divot. *Don't think,* Maire told herself. Her breath came in ragged gasps and she waited until the world righted itself before she stepped up to the next foothold.

Just a few more yards to go. She and Ned Bennett made it to the top at the same time and she cried out as she pulled herself onto the sturdy platform. Below them, Camille was nearly at the bottom and Samuel was already running toward the shooting range.

Her limbs tingled with exhaustion, but she couldn't pause to catch her breath. The next step was to use the thick rope to scale down the other side of the wall. The ground below loomed, hard and unrelenting. Ned grabbed his rope first and began lowering himself.

Maire tried to ignore him and reached for her rope, pausing to thread it around her left leg, across her chest, and over her shoulder, securing herself in place. It took more time this way, but at least she would be safe.

Down she went, careful to keep some slack in the rope. Just below her, Ned was struggling as his sweaty, slick hands kept slipping down the rope. He dropped a few yards and then scrambled for a foothold. After one precarious drop, he pressed his body close to the rock face, his toes resting on a gap in the stone.

If Maire could get to the guns, she was confident she could hit the target. She grew up shooting at old beer cans and going pheasant hunting with her dad and brothers. Ned seemed like the kind of guy who would keep a gun in his glove box but had no idea how to use it. She couldn't see Samuel or Camille being gun owners, but who knew. The senator, a military man, surely had plenty of experience with firearms, but he hadn't even reached the top of the climbing wall.

She steadily lowered herself, the hemp scraping the inside of her thigh. Her fingers gripped the rope so tightly that they went numb. She passed Ned and then lowered herself a few more feet. She was halfway down, just twenty feet from the ground. The sound of a gunshot exploded from behind her. At first, she thought it was the sniper but then realized that Samuel and Camille were shooting at the bull's-eye. The challenge could be over at any second.

Maire continued to let out the slack and used her feet to bounce down the wall. Fifteen feet to go. Above her, Ned was once again gaining on her. The toe of his tennis shoe scraped the top of her head, prodding her to move faster.

The impact was unexpected and her head exploded in pain. At first, Maire thought Ned had slipped, accidentally striking her in the head with his shoe, but she quickly realized that wasn't the case.

"Sorry," he called out. Maire looked up and caught his expression. Cold. Calculated. Ned knew exactly what he was doing. Again, he crashed into Maire, sending her slamming into the wall.

Knocked off-balance, she began to swing in dizzying circles, the rope coiling tightly around her leg and chest. Maire gasped, trying to keep her hold on the rope. Once she stopped spinning, she looked up and she saw Ned gripping his rope with one hand and reaching into his pocket with the other. Out came a slim black object and then suddenly out popped a blade. Ned had a knife, sharp and curved. For one ludicrous moment, she thought he was coming after her. She thought he might stab her.

"What the hell?" Maire cried as she watched Ned begin to saw through her rope. "Hey! What are you doing?" She was stranded, hopelessly tangled so it was impossible to quickly scale the last stretch before Ned sliced through her rope. She squeezed her eyes shut and waited for the free fall. When it didn't come, she opened her eyes and looked up. Her rope was still intact, though barely. Ned hadn't completely sawed through the jute, but one wrong move and it would snap. Ned bounced past her, the knife still clutched in one hand. Where did the knife come from? And then it hit her. The knife must be a Game Changer. In the distance, there were more gunshots and then a whoop of celebration. Someone hit the target.

Maire had lost. There would be no Super Clue. The earlier adrenaline she felt leached from her body and the pain returned. Her hand and ankle pulsed hotly, and her muscles were cramping.

Should she wait for help? *No*, Maire told herself, *I'm going to finish this*. Maire slowly spun herself in the opposite direction, unwinding the rope, realizing that with each movement the rope was fraying more and more. She was almost free. Suddenly, the rope went slack in her hands, and she was falling, the earth coming at her with alarming speed. When she hit the ground, her shoulder detonated with white-hot pain and the air left her lungs like a popped balloon.

When Maire was able to open her eyes again, Samuel was standing above her.

"I think you might have dislocated it," he said sympathetically.

"What, so you're a doctor now too?" Maire snapped.

"Not a doctor, just a guy who has dislocated his shoulder once or twice," Samuel said, rotating his own shoulder. "Want me to try to pop it back into place?"

Tears were streaming down her face and Maire wiped them away with her good hand. She looked at him dubiously. "You know how?"

"Yeah." Samuel nodded.

She wanted to trust him. She couldn't ask Fern for medical help, or she'd be sent home. And if she didn't get her shoulder back into place there was no way she could compete in the next challenge.

"Lie down," Samuel said, and Maire eyed him suspiciously. "No really," he urged. "Lie on your back."

Gingerly, Maire lowered herself back to the ground. "Now relax," Samuel said and she glared up at him. She let out a shaky breath as Samuel carefully guided her injured arm away from her body and shifted so one foot was pressed against her ribs.

"Don't worry," he said, "I just need a little leverage. You are going to feel so much better in a few seconds." He grabbed her hand and wrist and gave a quick pull. There was a loud pop. Maire cried out in pain and then felt instant relief.

"How's that?" Samuel asked, kneeling down next to her.

"Better," Maire breathed. "Thank you."

"Did you see my puzzle?" Samuel asked quietly, kneeling next to her. "It was the lake."

"Hang on," Maire said, removing her microphone from her shirt and tossing it as far as she could with her good arm. Samuel did the same. "Yeah, I saw it."

"And I saw yours," Samuel said. "They know. Somehow, they know," he said. "Your puzzle was the mascot from college. The bear. And mine was a lake."

"Shh," Maire hissed, looking around to see if anyone was paying attention to them. "No. No one knows. It's just a coincidence."

"Tanglefoot Lake and our college mascot? Just a coincidence?" Samuel asked, holding out a hand to help her up. "I don't think so."

"They can't know it all," she insisted. "Not the whole story." Maire ignored Samuel's hand and got to her feet on her own.

"What are we going to do?" Samuel asked, his eyes filled with worry. They looked over to see Fern, Alfonso, the senator, and Camille in a small cluster, waiting for them.

Maire shook her head. "Nothing. It means nothing. Anyone could have found out where we went to school and the school was near a lake. Big deal. Just keep playing, that's all we can do," she finally said. "We just have to keep playing the game."

Samuel didn't look convinced.

Fern beckoned them forward. "Are you coming?" she called.

Maire lifted a hand to let Fern know they heard her. "Someone is getting voted out tomorrow. And it can't be me." She looked at Samuel. "It's just a game. You're reading too much into it. I'm sorry, but I have to focus on winning."

Maire strode toward the others, her fury toward Ned Bennett building. "You asshole," she cried. "You could have killed me!"

"I found a Game Changer so I tried to change the game," Ned said. "You would have done the same."

"Are you going to be okay?" Fern asked, her face a mask of concern.

"What the hell?" Maire turned her anger on Fern. "A knife? Really? What if I broke my neck? What if I had a bad reaction to the scorpion stings? I could have died. Any one of us could have died!" Tears of pain and anger filled her eyes. What good would ten million dollars do if she was dead? What good would she be to her children then?

"But do you need medical attention?" Fern asked with what seemed like genuine worry, but Maire wasn't sure. She couldn't be sure of anything anymore. Fern was the one who kept placing them directly in the way of danger. Fern didn't care about their safety. She cared about the number of people watching the show, and the more blood, the more drama, the more viewers.

Maire looked to Alfonso, the so-called director. Why wasn't he saying or doing anything? "You're okay with this? This can't be right."

"You signed the waiver," Alfonso said simply, though he kept sending furtive glances toward Fern. "We can call the medical team in, but if they determine that you need more expert care, you will have to exit the game. Is that what you really want?"

Did she? Maire wondered. She scanned herself for a serious injury. Every inch of her body hurt, especially her shoulder, but if she went to the hospital, Maire knew she would be out of the game, disqualified.

"No, I'm okay," Maire finally said. "But this is…" She paused trying to come up with the right word. "Wrong."

She wasn't ready to quit. Not yet, even though her shoulder was throbbing. Maire thought of the bear and the lake puzzles. Two items she had a very personal connection to. There was something more going on here and Maire needed to talk to Samuel again.

Maire thought of the pill hidden in her pillowcase. Her Game Changer. The first chance she had, she was going to use it. He was done. Finished. If Maire signed a waiver saying it was okay for someone to shoot paint bullets at her, to use a knife to send her falling fifteen feet to the ground, then one little pill dropped into a glass of wine wouldn't matter.

She was going to win this game and didn't care whom she had to take down to do it.

NINETEEN

DaniKryngle12 sat all by herself in the computer room. Lots of times, when her cough was acting up, she'd come here instead of going outside for recess. Dani wasn't supposed to be in here alone, but she never caused any problems. She usually just played a math game and the teacher would poke their head in every few minutes to see how she was doing.

No less than seven people, just that morning, had told her that they saw her mom online. They went on about some reality show called *One Lucky Winner* and how her mom had won the first challenge. Dani hadn't believed them. Her mom was away on a business trip. Something having to do with her jewelry. But when Mr. Hale, her music teacher, even mentioned it, Dani began to wonder.

So instead of playing Math Blasters like usual, Dani typed *One Lucky Winner* into the search bar. Up popped several videos and, to her shock, the thumbnail on one of them showed a picture of her mother holding something like a gun and aiming it at a man. Dani was just about to click on the link when a notification on the site announced that a live event was just about to begin.

Up popped a video and for the next twenty-five minutes, Dani sat in rapt attention, watching as her mother, along with four others, crossed a balance beam, crawled through a mud pit, got shot at with a paint gun, and climbed a wall. She held her breath when the man who was apparently called the Executive used a knife to slice through her mom's rope, and her hands flew to her mouth when her mother crashed to the ground. Thankfully, she seemed okay, but she was pissed and saying words that Dani would get in trouble for saying. Dani didn't know the last time her mother had been so angry. Except maybe when her dad left, and even then, she was more sad than mad.

Dani watched as the pretty lady called the Confidante pulled a piece of paper out of the blue pot she won. It didn't look like much of a prize. The lady didn't think so either because when she opened the paper she made a funny face and said, "Well, this makes no sense, it's a death certificate." That made Dani shiver. She didn't like to think about dying.

Her eyes widened when she saw the number of people who were watching the video. Over two million and counting. This couldn't be real. Her mother had lied to them. Why?

Her attention fell to the comments.

Pillowtalk_Morgan—I can't believe the Confidante won! I didn't think she was going to get up after she was shot.

EnchantingWeb—I can't believe the Executive tried to kill the Best Friend.

Summerrip5—He didn't try to kill her. He was just playing the game. I would have done the same thing.

Perfect_Prose—I love the Best Friend. I hope she wins the ten million.

Pillowtalk_Morgan—I wonder why the Confidante won a death certificate. Who do you think it's for?

GoKings2024—In any other situation, he'd be arrested for assault. This game is all kinds of wrong. The Executive is a fucking narcissistic asshole.

Dani looked around the lab furtively. She didn't know what *narcissistic* meant but she definitely knew the *F* word. If a teacher saw what she was doing, Dani would get in big trouble.

Strangely, her mother was called the Best Friend, which didn't make a whole lot of sense to Dani, but from what she could tell, a lot of people were rooting for her. And ten million dollars! That was a lot of money.

Summerrip5—She kind of deserved to get cut down. She did tase the Boyfriend and she cheated using the key chain flashlight.

Dani felt sick. This person was saying her mom deserved to get hurt? That wasn't right. And the accusation that her mom tased someone and cheated? No. Her mom was always telling Dani to be kind.

"Hey, Dani," came a voice from the doorway. It was Mrs. Waller, the computer lab teacher. "It's after noon, sweetie. You're late for class. You better scoot along."

Dani quickly exited out of the website and hurried from the room and down the hallway to her own classroom. Dani knew why her mother was doing this, why she was doing such dangerous things. It was for the money. They needed the money because her dad had run off and he had run away because Dani was sick and being sick was expensive. If only she would just get better, then her dad would come home, and her mom wouldn't have to worry anymore. She slipped into her chair and stared down at the top of the desk willing the tears not to fall.

TWENTY

THE EXECUTIVE

The Vault

"I do feel bad about cutting Maire's rope. That's why I stopped before I sliced all the way through. This game really messes with your head and I'm happy she wasn't seriously hurt.

"This is a tough game though, right? Look at my nose. Camille kicked me right in the face. It's going to take weeks for the bruising to go away. And don't forget I was tased too. Everyone will use whatever tools are available to win.

"Anyway, the game's really just getting started and I'm confident that I won't be the first one to be voted out. It will either be the senator or Samuel. It's a toss-up, really.

"Moving forward, I think my biggest rival is, and I say this grudgingly, Maire. She's the small-town mom with a sick kid— that's hard to resist. To win, I'm going to have to finish at the top of each challenge, but I'm smart and I'm driven.

"My passion project, *Cold, Hard Truth*, was the number one show for ten years and is in syndication throughout the world. I'm thrilled to announce that we're coming back.

"Next year, the premiere of the reboot of the show is coming your way. It will be bigger, bolder, and bloodier. The crimes will be more brutal, the investigations more in depth, justice will come down on the perpetrator like a hammer. And *Cold, Hard Truth* will be there for every heart-pounding moment.

"But, with all great ideas, there comes a cost. And to bring *Cold, Hard Truth* to life in the way it deserves, we need backing. The ten million dollar prize, once I win, will go directly toward creating our teams of investigators and private detectives, as well as resources to operate a twenty-four-hour tip line and a reward fund.

"People always wonder why I'm so passionate about finding justice for families. Most don't know that when I was five years old, my father was murdered. I spent most my childhood without a father. If it weren't for pictures, I wouldn't remember what he looked like. No one was ever arrested, and I think about that all the time. I may not be able to find justice for my family, but I can help families like mine."

TrueCrimePancake23—Wow! I never knew that about his dad.

DarwinSpaceDragon922—Have to play hard to win. He wants it more than anyone else.

ClassicBooksandCoffee—I worked for that jerk years ago and there wasn't an a$$ or a pu$$y he didn't grab.

Lordfuxalot84—Proof? You sound like a disgruntled employee. Maybe he didn't grab your ass and you're feeling left out. SMH—some people just can't appreciate hardworking men who get things done.

Ava_Rain—says the guy who gives himself a fake royal title and has to announce the frequency (you wish) of his sexuality activity.

TWENTY-ONE

THE BEST FRIEND

Then

Samuel raised an eyebrow. "What kind of fun do you have in mind?"

Maire slapped him lightly on the arm with her mittened hand. "I didn't mean that kind of fun," she laughed, but her stomach did a flip-flop. Why was she thinking about Samuel in this way? He was Lina's boyfriend. She needed to find her own guy. But still, why would he have come after her to see if she was okay if he wasn't a little bit interested?

"Uh-huh," Samuel said slyly, and she felt her face go hot in spite of the cold air.

"Come on," Maire said, stepping out into the icy road.

"Careful," Samuel said, snagging her elbow.

Maire moved to the center where the yellow dotted line split the road in half.

"What are you doing?" Samuel asked. "You could get hit."

"Showing you how we had fun in Calico," Maire said, lowering herself to the pavement, the cold seeping through her jeans. "Besides, it's dead out here. Like you said, we're in the middle of nowhere."

"Calico?" Samuel asked, standing over her and looking anxiously from left to right.

"Where I grew up," Maire said, pulling on his pant leg. "Now lay down or get out of the way, I want to look at the stars."

"This is stupid," Samuel said, but still he stretched out on the ground so that they were ear to ear but facing in the opposite direction. "When does it start getting fun?"

"Look at the sky," Maire said dreamily. "It goes on forever."

"Yeah, but we can see the sky from over there." Samuel waved his hand toward the side of the road. "And it's safer."

"But that's half the fun," Maire insisted. "We'd lay on our backs in the middle of country roads and wait until we saw headlights. Then we'd hop up and run to the side of the road and into the ditch and watch the driver of the car freak out."

"That's hilarious," Samuel deadpanned. "How many little old ladies did you give heart attacks?"

"Ha, I don't know, but we were chased by a few farmers through a cornfield a time or two," Maire laughed.

"That I would have liked to have seen," Samuel said. "But really, when does it get fun?"

Just then two headlights winked in the distance. "Right about now," Maire said.

Samuel twisted his neck to see the headlights in the distance.

"Yeah, hang on," Maire said. "Wait until they see us."

"No way," Samuel protested, scrambling to his knees.

"They're still far enough away. Don't panic," Maire said, laughing and grabbing his wrist to hold him in place.

"Don't be stupid," Samuel said, but he was laughing too.

Maire had forgotten the euphoria that two tons of metal careening toward her in the dark could bring. It was wrong, not normal, but it felt so good.

"Now?" Samuel asked.

"Not yet," Maire said. The car was not slowing down. The driver hadn't seen them yet. "A few more seconds."

Samuel scrambled to his feet. "Let's go, Maire," he urged, pulling her up by the arm.

She planted her feet. The headlights were mesmerizing, two yellow eyes bearing down on them. She could hear the car's engine now, which was her cue that it was just about time. She couldn't believe the driver hadn't seen them yet. They must be distracted, on a cell phone, or singing along with the radio.

Maire waited until she could see the silhouette of the driver through the windshield.

"Now!" Maire cried, clutching Samuel's hand as they dashed to the side of the road, the breeze from the passing car lifting her hair from her neck.

"That was crazy," Samuel said, bent over, hands on his knees and out of breath.

"It was amazing!" Maire exclaimed in delight. "See, I told you. Fun."

Suddenly, the sound of screeching brakes and the smell of burnt rubber filled the air. The car fishtailed wildly from one side of the road to the other before careening over a snowdrift and smashing into the trunk of a sugar maple. The sound of grinding metal and breaking glass rang in Maire's ears. Then the air went deathly silent.

The car's red taillights glowed accusingly as the engine continued to rumble and smoke from the exhaust pipe curled lazily into the air.

"Oh, my God," Maire said, covering her face with her hands. "Oh, my God." She began to move toward the wreckage but felt a tug on her sleeve.

"Shh, just wait," Samuel said, pulling Maire farther into the shadows. "Maybe he's okay."

The car door opened, the interior light illuminating the driver's face.

Maire breathed a sigh of relief. The driver was okay. Her gratitude was quickly replaced with a different kind of fear. They were going to be caught.

A man dressed in a khaki Carhartt coat and work boots stepped from the vehicle. "Hey," he shouted into the darkness.

Lurching around to the front of his car where a headlight cast a long river of light across the pavement, he bellowed, "You think this is funny?"

Samuel pulled Maire close to him and she buried her face in his chest, trying to muffle the sound of her panicked breathing.

"You think this is funny?" the man shouted again. His voice was slurred. Had he been drinking? The man's top half disappeared into his car and when he emerged, he was holding a long cylinder that glinted in the glare of the headlights.

"Oh, Jesus," Samuel murmured. "He's got a pipe. Hold still, and when I say run, go."

The man stumbled in their direction, pipe in hand. "Step out from behind the goddamn tree and we'll see if you're still laughing."

TWENTY-TWO

THE ASSISTANT

Fern stood beneath a vaulted ceiling crisscrossed with wooden beams painted white. In fact, the entire room was white—the woodwork, the furniture, the marble floor, the chandelier dripping with white lights. All pristine, Fern thought, but somehow soulless. Her least favorite room in the villa.

The contestants, now showered and cleaned up after the muddy challenge, sat solemnly on an overstuffed white sofa that curved into a half-moon shape. Their brightly colored *One Lucky Winner* gear looked garish against the white backdrop. Fern remained standing. A coffee table, a square slab of white marble rising out of the floor, formed a barrier between the host and the challengers. She half expected at least one of them to come lunging at her from across the table.

Fern waited for the signal from Alfonso and then spoke directly into the camera. "Welcome to the first elimination episode of *One Lucky Winner*. Sadly, we have to say goodbye to one of you tonight."

The obstacle course had been more grueling than Fern expected, even though she had known about most of the unexpected twists. She'd known about the snipers, the razor wire, and the scorpions. What she *hadn't* been aware of was Ned's Game Changer. Cat had neglected to inform her that deadly weapons would be in play. Cat had been insistent on handling this aspect of the game, and the idea that Ned Bennett was walking around the villa with a knife sent shivers down her spine.

At least now Ned sported two black eyes, courtesy of a kick to the nose from Camille. But all the competitors had bumps and bruises. Maire cradled her arm close to her body and the senator winced with the slightest movements.

"Each of you have competed like warriors," Fern said. "But only four can move on." She turned. "Maire, you used your wits to be the first one through the hedge maze and Camille, you made it through a brutal obstacle course before anyone else. You are therefore safe from elimination." Fern watched as both women's shoulders sagged with relief. "You both won a crucial Super Clue. Any ideas as to where your clue might be leading you?" Fern asked, with an arched eyebrow.

"At this point, I have no idea," Maire said. Fern noticed that Maire and Samuel sat as far away from each other on the sofa as possible, avoiding eye contact. She thought the two might have bonded after Samuel popped Maire's dislocated shoulder into place.

"And you?" Fern set her gaze on Camille.

"I have a few thoughts," Camille said coolly.

"Care to share them?" Fern pressed.

"I think I'll wait."

"Fair enough. Now," Fern said, "the time has come to say goodbye." She pressed her lips into a thin line. "Samuel, Ned, and Senator Crowley, one of you will be leaving us tonight."

A muscle twitched in Samuel's jaw and the senator shifted nervously in his seat.

"Over one million viewers tuned in live, and we are now up to three million views and growing. More than one and a half million watchers voted," Fern said, looking at the camera, "and one of our contestants received over one-third of the total votes."

After Ned sliced through Maire's rope, Fern was convinced that the viewers would not vote to save him. She certainly hoped that would be the case. She needed Ned to be gone.

Fern unrolled the scroll. "Tonight's one unlucky winner of a one-way ticket home is…" Fern paused, unable to speak. *No,* she thought. *There must be a mistake.*

Fern felt the heat of eyes upon her. The contestants, Alfonso, the crew. Everyone was watching, waiting to see what would happen next.

"The Senator," Fern finally said.

Samuel bent over, hands on his knees, letting out a rush of breath. Ned punched a celebratory fist into the air.

"Thank you, Senator Crowley. You competed valiantly," Fern said, trying to keep it together. She had to spend at least another night in the villa with Ned. She felt sick, angry at how bloodthirsty the American public was to save someone like Ned. "Do you have any parting words before you pack your things and exit the villa?"

The senator looked dazed as Ned slapped him heartily on the back. Camille leaned in with a side hug, but he gave her a little shove, creating distance between them.

"Senator?" Fern asked tentatively, a note of concern in her voice.

Senator Crowley slowly stood up and extended his hand to Fern. She took it and her fingers completely disappeared within his grip. He squeezed so tightly that her fingers were turning white. Fern tried to pull away, but the senator held tight and then drew her close to him, covering her lapel mic with one hand.

"I know what you're up to, and you won't get away with it," he whispered into her ear.

A flash of panic coursed through Fern. The senator knew.

He knew that she had locked Cat in the wine cellar. But that was impossible. He couldn't have known. After a brief pause, she turned and spoke directly into the camera. "Thank you, everyone, for joining us tonight. Please, tell your friends. If you can't join us live, you can watch every single thrilling moment on demand. Stay tuned because you never know what's going to happen next on *One Lucky Winner.*"

Fern rubbed her sore fingers as the senator strode from the room. What did the senator mean by *"you won't get away with this"*? It was understandable that he would be disappointed he was voted off the show, but Fern had nothing to do with that. She was the proverbial messenger.

"Go, go," Alfonso ordered, and the camera operators scurried after the senator. To Fern he said, "I really need to talk to Cat. I'm getting a little concerned about liability here. I mean, where did that knife come from? That wasn't in my copy of the script. And why isn't Cat answering her texts? I thought she was supposed to be on-site during production."

Fern hadn't thought things through clearly when she locked Cat in the wine cellar. Of course the director of the show would expect to be in contact with the executive producer. The longer Cat was radio silent, the more questions there would be. "You know Cat," she said lightly. "She's probably analyzing all the data, corralling more sponsors. As soon as we touch base, I'll let her know you want to talk."

Alfonso nodded his head in resignation and Fern relaxed. "Okay, after we get the final shots of the senator leaving, we'll pack up for the night," he said. "But tell Cat it's important."

Fern watched Alfonso exit and took a moment to catch her breath before heading to the great hall to see the senator on his way. She was shocked that Ned Bennett hadn't been the one eliminated. In fact, he had received most of the votes to stay, even beating out Samuel. Clearly the audience was bloodthirsty and wanted to see backstabbing, sabotage, and broken bones.

When Fern entered the great hall, the senator was already standing at the top of the steps, glowering down at her. He was an older man, but he was large and imposing. She tried not to shrink beneath his angry stare. "Senator," she said, keeping her voice strong. "Are you ready to go? Your car is waiting out front."

He gave a rueful shake of his head but said nothing, only began moving down the stairs, his suitcase thumping heavily behind him on the marble steps.

"May I help you with your bag?" Fern asked graciously when he reached the bottom, but the senator stared straight ahead, chin raised, the cameras pinned on his every move.

Fern led the senator through the great hall to the main entrance. The senator seemed ripe with anger. Surely, he couldn't be upset with Fern. If it were up to Fern, she would send Ned Bennett packing and keep Senator Crowley. The rules were the rules. The senator hadn't won any of the challenges—hadn't even come close—and he had been voted off by the viewers.

Fern picked up her pace. "Your driver will take you directly to the airport. We thank you for joining us and wish that your stay with us could have been a longer one."

"I think," he said in his gravelly baritone as he grabbed Fern's arm, forcing her to stop walking. "I think this is not over."

The disgust and hate in the senator's eyes were unmistakable. Fern shrank beneath his stare. It wouldn't be good for the show if the very first contestant voted off assaulted the host. It would only prove to Cat that she couldn't handle the job. No. Senator Crowley was a practical man. She would reason with him.

"I can see you're upset, sir," Fern said contritely. "But I think it's to your benefit if you leave the game with dignity."

The senator gave a harsh bark of laughter. "Dignity? A game? Is that all this is to you?" He squeezed her arm more tightly. "You have no idea who you are dealing with."

"Fern," a voice called out, and they both turned to see Maire striding toward them. "I was wondering if I could have a word."

She slipped from the senator's grip and forced a smile to her lips. "Absolutely," she said. "Let me get Senator Crowley on his way and I'm all yours." Fern pushed through the courtyard doors and was relieved to see that the SUV that would take the senator away was idling in the drive.

The senator, not waiting for Fern, began his descent down the stone steps. Shoulders hunched, he looked like a much older man than when he first arrived. Fern wanted to let him go without another word but knew that she needed to remain composed. She followed him down the steps, wishing that the cameras would follow them. Instead, they stayed behind getting a long shot of the senator's departure.

At the bottom, Fern held out her hand. "Again, thank you. Best of luck to you."

The senator's lip curled with disdain. He let her hand hang. "You don't understand that you most likely have ruined my life?" he asked, his face twisted in disbelief. "The picture of the woman in my puzzle was no accident. And what the doctor said just before the challenge, that was no accident either."

Why wouldn't he just leave? Fern steeled her spine. "Again, thank you for being here. Safe travels."

"This is not over," the senator said as the driver stepped from the car, took his bag, and stowed it in the rear of the SUV while the senator climbed into the back seat. Fern held her breath until the vehicle pulled away and its brake lights were swallowed up by the fog.

Aware that Maire had come down the steps behind her, Fern tried not to let her relief for the senator's departure show on her face.

"So, what can I help you with, Maire?" she asked, trying to push aside the panic she felt. Nothing was going right. Cat was locked in the wine cellar, the senator looked like he wanted to kill her, and there was another long night in front of her.

"Are you okay?" Maire asked. "I saw the way Crowley grabbed you."

Fern felt a lump form in her throat but swallowed it back. "I'm fine. He was disappointed. Understandably so. It's a lot of money and he's a man used to getting what he wants, I'm sure."

"I feel like that has to do with more than money," she said, noticing the bruises blooming on Fern's arm. "Be careful. People are dangerous when they are backed into a corner."

Fern looked up from her phone and studied Maire's face. It appeared to hold real concern and maybe a hint of a warning. If Maire only knew what Fern was capable of doing, how dangerous she could be, Maire might not be so calm.

Maire's face was exceptionally pale against the auburn of her hair. She cradled her right arm protectively against her body. "The real question is, are you okay?" Fern asked. She was genuinely concerned. Maire looked like she was in pain and Fern didn't know what it would mean for the show if a contestant would have to exit early due to injury. There would be only three players remaining.

"I'm fine," Maire said. "My shoulder is fine. But I have to talk to my daughters. I have to find out if Dani is okay."

"I'm sorry," Fern said, "I understand. I really do. But it clearly states in the show's rules that no outside communication is allowed."

"I don't give a fuck about the rules," Maire snapped. "This is about my daughter and her health. I don't think you understand how serious a lung infection can be for her. I want my phone. Now."

Things were spiraling and Fern needed to get the game and the contestants under control. "Maire, I sympathize with you," she said. "But if you insist on using your phone, you also forfeit the game. You will lose your chance at ten million dollars. Is that really what you want?"

Fern saw the bluster seep from Maire. "No. I don't want to leave, but I have to know that Dani is okay. Please, Fern," she begged, "help me."

Fern could see how anguished Maire was. Maybe breaking one little rule wouldn't be a big deal. Unless the other contestants found out. That would be chaos. Someone would call foul, say that Fern had given Maire an unfair advantage. She sighed and was just about to tell Maire she could use her phone, when she remembered something. She forgot to send out the press release about the elimination. Cat had been very clear. The email was to be sent out to all media outlets immediately after the vote was announced. "Dammit," she whispered. "I'm sorry, Maire," she said shortly, "I have to deal with something."

Maire shook her head in disappointment but didn't argue any further. She turned and went back inside.

Fern watched the doors close behind her and then headed to the hedge maze. She crossed the manicured lawn, past the marble nymphs, and entered the maze. She didn't worry about getting lost—she was familiar with every twist and turn. She sat down on a stone bench, the coolness penetrating her dress. Cat's dress. Everything was catching up to her. She had thought she was so smart, so prepared. But she wasn't. The fresh air felt good against her skin and Fern was glad to escape the villa for just a few minutes.

She pulled out Cat's phone until she found the draft of the email that Cat had written in the event that the senator was voted off the show. The subject line read: One Lucky Winner says goodbye to Senator Richard Crowley.

The recipients included a wide array of media outlets: *The New York Times*, *The Washington Post*, *People Magazine*, *US Weekly*, *Deadline Hollywood*, *Vulture*, and dozens of others.

For immediate release:
The *One Lucky Winner* family would like to extend its warmest
thank-you and gratitude to Senator Crowley for taking part in our
groundbreaking new show. We wish him the best of luck in all his
future endeavors.

Fern hit Send, hoping it wasn't too late to make the evening news cycle.

Then there was a second email that Cat wanted her to send
from an encrypted email address. The recipients were the same
as the first email and the message was brief. Just one line.

Please feel free to utilize the attached documents as you deem
appropriate.

Once again Fern hit Send, biting her lip as she tried to think
of how to respond to Alfonso's twenty unanswered texts to Cat.

Alfonso—enough already! Everything is FINE! Let me handle any
liability issues. Everyone signed waivers. Just worry about doing
your job and let me do mine. Or do I need to find someone else
to do it for you?

There. That should keep Alfonso quiet for the time being.

Fern needed to turn her attention to the next day's competition, the most challenging to date, but first she wanted to
check on Cat. She opened the security video app and clicked
on the feed that would take her to the wine cellar.

It was going on Cat's second day of captivity and she sat on
the large wooden box, knees pulled up to her chin, wrapped
in a thermal pallet cover used to protect wine bottles from ex-
treme temperatures during deliveries. On the floor were discarded water bottles and a nearly empty jar of snack mix. This
had gotten completely out of hand.

The bigger problem though, Fern thought, was what Cat would do when Fern finally opened the cellar door to let her out. It was too late to claim locking her in was all a big misunderstanding. It was all such a blur now. Why had she been so impulsive? That was so unlike Fern.

Would Cat call the police? If she was lucky, no. Cat wouldn't want the bad publicity. It would absolutely kill her if people found out that a lowly assistant managed to shove her in the wine cellar to hijack her show.

Fern guessed she probably wouldn't go to jail, but she would definitely be fired. Year after year of grueling hours, crappy pay, grunt work, verbal lashings, all for nothing. But was being fired really a bad thing? She'd be out from beneath Cat's thumb. She could make her own way in the world. Finally. Besides, Fern was now the face of *One Lucky Winner*. Cat couldn't take that away from her. And who had made the show into an overnight success? Not Cat. The more Fern thought about it, the more she believed that Cat had to be the one who brought Ned Bennett to the villa. For what—ratings? No matter the reason, it was twisted. Maybe a little more time in the wine cellar would do Cat some good. It would teach her that she can't play with people's lives for her own advancement or entertainment.

But wasn't that what Fern was doing right now? Playing with people's lives? She didn't like the thought and quickly pushed it aside.

Just one more night, Fern decided. Tomorrow evening after the next challenge, she would release Cat, greeting her with a warm robe, a steaming cup of coffee, and her favorite meal from La Toque, the Dungeness Crab Puffed Rice Bowl and two Meyer Lemon Squares. She'd pretend that nothing happened, that it was all an unfortunate misunderstanding.

Fern threw her head back and let out a long breath. What had she gotten herself into? Her phone buzzed, alerting Fern to a new text. It was probably Alfonso wanting to complain about Cat.

Fern frowned at the screen. The text wasn't from Alfonso. It was from the driver that was taking the senator to the airport.

FYI—the senator bailed before we got to the airport. Jumped out just outside the estate. I've been driving around looking for him. Downed a bunch of whiskey. Was going on about The Daily Beast or something or other. What do you want me to do?

"Oh, shit," Fern breathed, jumping to her feet. A new shot of adrenaline bulleted through her. Just what she needed. An angry, drunk politician roaming the countryside.

She quickly typed two words and hit Send. FIND HIM. She scurried out of the maze and across the lawn, her eyes darting from shadow to shadow. Above her, the gargoyles stared down from their perches. What could they see that she couldn't? Was the senator out there on the grounds, lying in wait? Would he try to finish what he threatened?

Fern dashed up the stone steps, glancing over her shoulder, half expecting the senator to come lurching out of the mist. Once at the top, she stopped to catch her breath. She needed to stay focused and remain in control. *What would Cat do?* she asked herself. Cat wouldn't have let this happen in the first place. She pushed through the front doors and into the courtyard, immediately feeling better sheltered inside the villa. The anxiety began to seep from her body, her muscles loosening, her breath steadying. She would shower, check in with the driver to make sure the senator was accounted for, and then get some much-needed sleep.

She walked beneath the bell tower, taking a moment to appreciate the earthy smell of rosemary and the piercing lemon scent of witch hazel in the herb garden from just outside the open-air windows. *Tomorrow will be better,* she thought. The shadows in front of her shifted and she caught the whiff of something different. Fern's pace slowed until she came to a stop. Someone was there in the dark blocking her entrance into the villa. The sweet, unmistakable smell of bourbon curled around her head, and she knew. After ditching the driver, he must have backtracked to the villa and lay in wait while Fern was down at the hedge maze. Fern inched her way backward, dared a look over her shoulder. If she turned and ran, she might be able to get away.

"I told you this wasn't over yet," the senator slurred. And Fern knew it was too late.

TWENTY-THREE

In Washington, D.C., ShanaLiveLaughLove was at her kitchen table reviewing her online appointment calendar while Caleb was doing his math homework. She had a meeting with a client tonight, the sitter would be there soon, and she needed to get changed.

Her phone pinged with an alert. Shana ignored it and returned to her calendar. If she left by seven, she could make it to the restaurant by eight. Then her phone pinged again and again and again until the alerts were coming in like machine-gun fire. Caleb looked up from his worksheet. "Jeez, Mom," he said.

"Sorry, honey," Shana said, ruffling his hair and lowering the volume. "It's probably just Aunt Stephanie. She must have some big drama going on."

Shana navigated to her messages and had to read the most recent message from Gabriella, a woman she worked with, three times before it registered. You've gone viral! And not in a good way!

She scrolled through the messages, all from different senders. Girls she worked with, her best friend, her sister, her mother. Another text appeared from Gabriella. It was a link to an Instagram video from JoJo Holt, an influencer who got second place in *The Queen of Cakes* baking competition series a few years back. Now, she recapped reality TV episodes on social media, all while offering baking tutorials. Shana clicked the link and JoJo's face appeared on her screen, nearly shimmering with excitement.

"Good evening, Luckies," JoJo said into the camera. "I'll get right to the point. You probably already know that former Senator Richard Crowley was voted off the show this evening."

Shana froze. Richard was on a reality show? She hadn't talked to him in over a week or seen in him in over a month. Since he retired from the Senate, he didn't get to D.C. as much. She glanced over at Caleb, who was once again immersed in his homework.

A flurry of comments filled the feed.

Travesty. I'm from Texas and Crowley was a godsend. Always put Texans first and foremost.

Shana heartily agreed. Amen, she typed.

Well, I'm from Texas too and Crowley always put himself first.

Shana watched as JoJo began measuring out cups of flour. "This latest news is bananas. But first, lemon squares. Since *One Lucky Winner* takes place in an Italian-inspired villa, I'm going to share my variation of the classic Italian lemon square with you. It's the perfect combination of sweet and sassy—just like me." JoJo gave a self-deprecating laugh. "For the crust, we add three and a half cups of all-purpose flour, a half cup of powdered sugar, and half a teaspoon of coarse salt.

"So, Luckies," JoJo said as she dumped all the dry ingredients in a large bowl. "I know that the senator was a controversial figure but wait until you hear this."

More heart emojis floated across the screen. Shana added her own heart.

"In case you haven't heard, Senator Crowley had an illicit affair, cheating on his wife of fifty years," JoJo said. Shana froze.

An image appeared above JoJo's head of a glamorous woman with shoulder-length blond hair and pumped-up red lips. She was wearing an expensive but tasteful black cocktail dress. Shana couldn't believe what she was seeing. It was a picture of herself.

"Caleb, sweetie," Shana said, her voice unnaturally high. "Can you please go clean your room up before Katie gets here?"

Caleb didn't need to be told twice. He leaped from his chair and rushed from the kitchen.

"But there's more," JoJo whispered conspiratorially. "So much more."

Shana felt light-headed. Sick.

"Apparently, the good senator's—" JoJo crooked her fingers as she said the word *good* "—mistress was a high-end escort from Washington, D.C."

"Please no," Shana whispered as her phone vibrated with more alerts. Another image of Shana appeared on the screen. In this one, a false eyelash hung precariously from her right eye, her lipstick was smeared, and she was wearing a deer-in-the-headlights expression. It was obviously a mug shot. "Luckies, meet Shana Stonehaven."

Shana prayed that would be it. That there would be no more. She could handle this. She could keep the photos from Caleb, could explain them away.

"Now combine the dry ingredients with one pound of chilled unsalted butter," JoJo went on. "That's right, four sticks of the good stuff. Press into a baking pan and parbake for about thirty minutes at three hundred and fifty degrees.

"But there is more, Luckies," JoJo said with delight. "So much more. Now for the filling. Four cups sugar, two-thirds of a cup of flour for thickening, a half a teaspoon of salt, the zest of one large lemon, and then whisk these ingredients together. This wasn't just a 'slam, bam, thank you, ma'am' sort of arrangement with the escort who has been identified as one Shana Stonehaven, but a full-fledged affair," JoJo said as she whisked. "A long-term relationship with jewelry, and vacations, and an expensive apartment in D.C."

Shana wanted to throw up. Her world was tilting on its axis.

JoJo held up an egg. "Okay, this recipe calls for eight large eggs. Thankfully, all I need to do is go right outside to my chicken coop and the ladies there have all the eggs I need. Mix the eggs with one and a half cups of fresh lemon juice. Fresh is key." JoJo began cracking the eggs against the side of the bowl and tossing the shells aside. "But sadly, there is more when it comes to the senator. Do you want me to tell you, Luckies?"

The comments came fast and furious.

Yes! 👏

How can there be more? 😮

Fake news! Where's the proof? It's incredibly irresponsible to repeat these baseless rumors 😤

"No, please, no," Shana begged out loud.

"Alright, I'll tell you," JoJo said, as if she weren't nearly bursting with glee.

"He paid for his side chick with campaign funds," JoJo said, widening her eyes and pressing her lips into a disappointed pout.

Oh, shit, Shana thought.

"Now a little tip. It's really important that you don't add the eggs to the sugar and flour too soon. If you do, you can get what we call sugar burn. Sounds dirty, doesn't it?" JoJo asked with a sly grin.

Shana wanted to smash JoJo's smug face.

"As for Senator Sugar Daddy, it looks like the feds have entered the building," JoJo said. "And there's going to be a thorough investigation of the senator and his...extracurricular activities."

Throw his ass in prison!

Lies!

Typical politician

"Now, as far as I can tell," JoJo said, "there has been no comment from the senator's camp. But his poor wife and kids, right?"

There was a knock on the door. The sitter was here.

"Oh, and one last thing," JoJo added as she poured the lemony mixture atop the cooled crust. "There's a kid. An eight-year-old that is the spitting image of the good senator."

Shana lowered her face into her hands.

TWENTY-FOUR

THE CONFIDANTE

Once again, Camille found herself lying in her bed, staring up at the ceiling. This time though she was sure the cherubs on the fresco above were staring down at her in judgment. It was after midnight and day three of the competition was looming.

The unfamiliar scents of strangers lingered in the air, and she could hear the night sounds of the other contestants. Rhythmic breathing, the rustle of bed linens, the soft murmurs of sleep. Camille couldn't sleep. She was too keyed up to rest.

She couldn't stop thinking about how the puzzle she put together in the challenge was a replica of the Alftan painting she had bought in France. Why? It made no sense. And then the senator had lashed out and given her a shove during the elimination. Yes, she had won the last challenge, but Maire had won the hedge maze and the senator hadn't turned on her. Was it what Camille had said just before the race began? *It's not like any of us have an eight-year-old boy.* But none of them had an eight-year-old boy, so what could that mean? It didn't make any sense. Nor did any of the other statements she was supposed to say in the presence of the rest of the contestants. All of them seemed ridiculously benign.

She waited until she was certain that the others had fallen asleep before rising from her bed. Every muscle in her body screamed in protest. The obstacle course had pushed her beyond her limits, but somehow she had solved her puzzle and won the Super Clue, which meant nothing to her.

Painfully, she lowered herself to her knees and her hand disappeared into the black abyss beneath the bed. Camille tried to quiet the thoughts of rodents and gnawing insects. Despite the lavishness of the estate, it was old and most likely attracted creatures that felt most at home in dark crevasses. Her fingers snagged on her suitcase and she pulled it out, quietly trying to unzip the front pocket. She reached inside for the folded sheets of paper. She pushed the bag back beneath the bed and moved to the door, wincing when it opened with a rusty creak. She slipped quickly from the room and came face-to-face with the long, dark corridor. Goose bumps erupted on her skin.

The obstacle course had been brutal. The razor wire, the sniper, the *scorpions*. Her ribs still throbbed from being struck by the paint ball and her calf ached from the scorpion.

Everything about the game seemed to be engineered to keep them off-kilter, unbalanced. Granted, this made sense. The prize was ten million dollars after all, and the creators couldn't make it easy. Still, there seemed to be something twisted, malevolent even, about the entire game, and it wasn't exactly bringing out the best in them.

Case in point: Ned Bennett. Ned had no qualms about slicing through their rope on a climbing wall. It was a miracle that Maire hadn't broken her arm, or worse. Though, Maire was giving as good as she got—she hadn't hesitated to tase Samuel. Even the seemingly mild-mannered senator looked positively venomous when he learned he was the first to go.

She thought of the two pieces of paper she had hidden in her pocket. The Game Changer and a Super Clue. She wanted to pull them out and examine them again, but it was too dark in the corridor to see.

The Super Clue was a death certificate with all the important parts blackened out. There was no name, no state, no cause of death listed. The only information that she could glean from the document was that the decedent was male and thirty-two years old. It could be anyone from anywhere, at any time in history.

Camille had known a man who had died when he was thirty-two. Or was he thirty-three? She should have remembered this detail, but had destroyed every last bit of the paper trail connecting her to Travis Wingo.

Last December 18 was their final unofficial session, the one where Wingo told her he had run out of money and Camille had told him she couldn't meet with him any longer. Wingo hadn't taken it well. The following evening, he was back. Then again and again. Night after night after night until he died.

No one knew about her private therapy sessions with Wingo, nor did anyone know how he had gladly paid cash. No one knew why Wingo was really at her office the day after Christmas. Camille made sure of that. No, this wasn't Wingo's death certificate, it couldn't be, but it made her think of him.

Camille followed the sinuous corridor past shut doors and shuttered windows trying to push thoughts of Wingo aside. She made turn after turn until she was hopelessly lost. The estate was even larger than she thought. *What kind of person lived here?* she wondered. There were no personal photos or children's artwork, no indication that a family lived here. So, who did?

The corridor curved once more, and she was back at the grand staircase. She must have walked in a complete circle. Camille put one hand on the iron railing and felt it rock slightly beneath her fingers. *Dangerous*, she thought.

A crash came from below, followed by a shout. Camille froze, waiting for more, but she was met with silence. Her heart skittered. Was it a cry of pain or surprise? She wasn't sure.

From the direction of the bedroom, Camille heard tentative footsteps. "What's going on?" Maire whispered.

"I don't know," Camille said, trying to peer into the shadows below. "I thought I heard someone yell."

Maire leaned over the railing to get a better look, the wrought iron tilting with the movement, and Camille pulled her back. "Careful there, the railing's loose."

"Thanks," Maire said. "I heard yelling too. Do you think we should go down there?"

"Shh," Camille ordered. "Listen."

Another far-off cry drifted up to them, again followed by a crash.

With a start, Maire grabbed Camille's arm. Her eyes were wide, frightened. Camille chewed her lip as if deciding what to do. "Ned? Samuel?" Camille asked.

Maire shook her head. "I think they're still in the bedroom. What should we do?"

The quiet was what spurred Camille down the steps. She nearly lost her footing on the slick marble but grabbed the iron railing before she fell. Behind her, Camille heard the clatter of footsteps. Maire was coming too. Whatever she was walking in on, she wouldn't be alone.

Once at the bottom, Camille spun around, trying to decide which direction to go.

"That way," Maire said, pointing toward the courtyard. They rushed forward and Camille pushed through the front door.

The fog had lifted, and the white glow of the moon spilled onto the courtyard floor where the marble statue of Aphrodite had been knocked from its pillar. Its disembodied head came to a slow stop at Camille's feet.

The senator had Fern pinned against the stone wall, his hands around her throat. Her eyes bulged as she searched wildly around the space, landing on Camille. Her fingers clawed desperately to loosen his grip, but he held fast.

Camille couldn't move. It was as if her feet were lodged in cement. She must have emitted a sound because the senator looked over his shoulder, his eyes feverish, his face a mask of rage.

Fern's face was turning blue, her arms dropping uselessly to her side as she began to lose consciousness.

"What are you doing? Stop!" Maire yelled as the two women spurred into action.

This time, the senator didn't even glance their way. If anything, his knuckles whitened as he pressed his fingers against Fern's throat.

"Let go," Camille cried, pulling at the senator's arm. He reeled back, striking Camille in the face, and she stumbled backward.

Fern went limp and slid to the floor; the desperate gurgling sounds she had been making moments before stopped. Momentarily shocked by the senator's backhand, Camille watched as Maire shoved him to the ground and then grabbed one of Fern's arms and began dragging her to safety.

"What the hell?" came a man's bewildered voice. Camille glanced up. Samuel. But the senator wasn't done yet. He was back on his feet and his eyes, glittering with rage, were still fixed on Fern.

"Stop him," Fern begged through clenched teeth.

"Hey, man," Samuel said, stepping between the senator and the women. "Take it easy."

"Take it easy?" the senator laughed. "Take it easy? She ruined my life," he said, pointing a shaky finger at Fern, who was gasping for breath. "Fucking bitch," he muttered and once again lunged toward Fern.

"Whoa," Samuel cried, snagging the senator around the waist and, in one swift motion, bringing the older man down to the ground, one arm wrenched behind his back. Maire left Camille with Fern and added the full force of her weight against the senator's legs until he stopped struggling. The only sound was their collective heavy breathing. The rancid odor of sweat and liquor rolled off the senator.

Camille, her cheek red from where the senator struck her, stood over them, a sharp shard of broken marble in her hand, ready to pounce if Crowley escaped.

"Why?" Fern rasped, massaging her fingers against her neck, already beginning to wreath with bruises. She crawled away from Maire and staggered unsteadily to her feet, trying to smooth the wrinkles from her white dress and leaving red smears of blood behind. "I don't understand."

"We need to call the police," Camille said, taking in Fern's bruises, her ripped dress. She sensed a new presence at her side and looked over to find that at some point Ned had joined them.

"No," Fern said, shaking her head from side to side. "Don't do that," she said softly, leaning heavily against the stone wall, the moon glistening off a wound at her temple.

"But that doesn't make sense," Camille said in confusion. "He tried to kill you."

"No," Fern said, swallowing painfully. "The show. If the police come, it will be over."

"I will *ruin* you," the senator slurred.

"Fern," Camille said, going to the younger woman's side. "He's unhinged. Look at yourself."

Fern looked down at her fingers, nails ragged and bloodied from fighting the senator. She had lost one shoe in the struggle. "No," Fern said, clearing her throat. "I'll get the driver to come back. Please, just get him out of here."

The senator lifted his chin from the floor and set his drunken gaze on Camille. "You're part of this too. How did you find out? Who put you up to this?"

"I don't know what you're talking about," Camille protested. "I'm just playing the game."

"This is no game," the senator snarled. "It's all over the news.

I'm ruined. My family is ruined. And did you even stop to think about what you've done to that poor little boy?"

"I don't know what he's saying," Camille insisted, looking to the others for support. "He's drunk."

"I'm saying—" the senator strained against the tight grips "—you told the world that I have an eight-year-old son. A son that my wife doesn't know about, that my boys don't know about."

"Who was in the picture?" Maire asked suddenly. "I mean in the puzzle you put together. The woman in the mug shot. Who is she?"

The senator didn't answer, just turned his head away from them and laid his cheek against the floor. That's when things clicked for Camille.

"That's the mother, isn't it?" she asked. "You have a son, that woman is the mother, and your wife has no idea either one of them exists."

The senator lifted his head again, tears running down his cheek. "We aren't playing this game, you know," he said. "The game is playing us. One of you will be next."

Fern stepped forward. "He's not making sense. Let's get him up and out of here. Now."

Camille looked to the others. "This is wrong, right? We need to call the police."

But if Camille thought she was going to get help from Maire and Ned, she was wrong. They all looked away, refusing to make eye contact. Then she got it. They wanted the game to go on. They wanted the ten million dollars. Only Samuel looked as reticent as she felt.

"Unbelievable," she said, throwing up her hands in defeat. But if she was being honest with herself, Camille wanted the ten million dollars too.

Fern bent down and picked up her cell phone that she must have dropped during the skirmish. Then, to Camille's surprise,

Fern picked up another phone just a few feet away. *Who needs two cell phones?* Camille wondered as Fern punched a few buttons and pressed one of the phones to her ear, wincing at the contact.

"Just wait," the senator said, bloody spittle dribbling from the corner of his mouth. "She'll get you next," he called over his shoulder as Samuel and Ned lifted the senator to his feet and began dragging him out of the courtyard.

A plastic rectangular card lay on the ground and Camille bent down to pick it up. It was a key card. It had a picture of Fern and her full name. Fernanda Espa.

"Come get him, now," Fern said coldly into the phone. "And make sure he doesn't come back."

She knew she had heard that voice before. It was all coming together. The Converse tennis shoes, sunglasses, the hat, the context, all explained why she hadn't made the connection before. She thought of her former client Fern. Fernanda. Nan.

Fern was Nan, the woman who came into her office months ago. The woman who confided to Camille about a ruthless boss who would bury anyone who crossed her. The woman who then disappeared without a trace. "Nan?" Camille whispered.

Fern covered the mouthpiece of her phone and narrowed her eyes at Camille. "What did you say?"

"Never mind," Camille said, stepping away from Fern, her heart slamming against her chest.

She wanted to shake Nan or Fern or whatever her name was and demand to know what the hell she was up to. What kind of dangerous game was she playing and why had she dragged Camille into the middle of it all?

TWENTY-FIVE

THE BEST FRIEND

Maire sat on the floor of the bedroom, the early evening light streaming through the window warming her face. She was trying to process all that happened over the last few days. The night before, the senator had tried to kill Fern. He had his hands wrapped around her neck and it took the four of them to pull him away. What could Fern have possibly done to summon such wrath?

Sleep hadn't come easily for any of them and no one spoke of the senator's exclamation that Fern was coming after them next. But was it drunken paranoia or the truth? Then there was Camille. How *had* she known about the senator's secret eight-year-old-son? Was she working behind the scenes, wreaking havoc and uncertainty among the contestants?

The day dragged on endlessly. There were no new challenges announced and the others had left the room hours ago, but Maire was content to stay inside the bedroom, to sleep, to think things through. Now it was nearing five o'clock and she would have to head downstairs soon.

She thought of the dangerous challenges and the strangely familiar clues, seemingly veiled threats. And it was no accident that both she and Samuel were chosen for the same reality show. But what could she do about it? Suddenly, Maire thought of the family tree. The Super Clue she had won after making it through the maze first.

She rose from her spot on the floor, reaching for her pillow. Inside the pillowcase was the family tree and the envelope holding the Game Changer—that small white pill. Maire unfolded the family tree and scanned the branches. At first glance, there seemed to be no connection to the senator. No surnames were listed and many of the first names were redacted. Maire turned her focus to the dates.

One blacked-out entry listed a birth date that could very well have belonged to the senator. She ran her finger down the page. Branching out from that entry showed four male children, all born over thirty years ago, matching what Maire knew about the senator and his wife. Jutting out to the right was another branch connecting the unknown patriarch to another woman and, from there, another single offspring. A boy named Caleb, born eight years ago.

So it was true. The senator had a secret son.

She felt the heat of eyes upon her and looked up to find Camille standing in the doorway. She was dressed in her yellow *One Lucky Winner* gear, and staring at Maire. "What?" Maire asked, unsettled. Everything about Camille was intimidating. Her intelligence, her beauty, her penetrating gaze, the way she dominated the obstacle course. "What?" she asked again, her voice tinged with impatience.

"Nothing." Camille shook her head. "Just freaked out about last night. I keep thinking about what would have happened if we didn't hear the senator attacking Fern. We could have woken up to a dead body."

"Yeah, it was scary," Maire agreed. She didn't trust this woman. Camille had somehow known about the senator's secret. Or had she? Maire had the same information and didn't realize what it meant until now.

"Do you know Fern?" Camille asked quietly. "I mean outside of the show? Have you ever met her?"

"Me? No," Maire said, surprised at the pivot their conversation had taken. "What makes you think that?"

Camille bit her lip. "You saw how upset the senator was. It seemed, I don't know, personal. Like maybe she had a past relationship or encounter with him."

"Losing ten million dollars was probably enough for the senator to turn on her." Maire shrugged, trying to cover her own suspicions about Fern, about the show. She needed more time to think things through. "He must have been desperate for the money. Do *you* know Fern?" she shot back.

Maire thought she saw something cross Camille's face. Guilt, fear maybe, but then it was gone. "No, I don't know her either," Camille said, getting to her feet. "Well, we better get downstairs. Ned and Samuel are already down there. The next challenge starts soon. And one of the crew members said we're supposed to wear our bathing suits today."

Once Camille left the room, Maire found a bathing suit buried beneath a clean *One Lucky Winner* pink warm-up suit. If today's challenge was like the others, anything could happen. Maire would just have to do her best and hope that would be enough. Before shutting the bedroom door behind her, Maire hesitated. The Game Changer, the pill, was still hidden in her pillowcase. Could she really drop an unidentified pill with unknown effects into a glass and watch one of her competitors drink it?

She could. She'd do just about anything for the ten million dollars and maybe even more to keep her own secret. Maire went back into the room, pulling out the envelope with the pill and sliding it into her pocket.

As she walked down the long corridor and toward the grand

staircase, a thought came to her. Maybe there was a way to get the money even if she didn't win. At least part of it. Five million dollars was just as good as ten million. If she could partner up with one of the other contestants, conspire to work together and against the others, maybe, just maybe...

But that would mean she would have to put her trust in someone else.

At the bottom of the stairs, Maire found the others standing around a buffet table filled with an array of food.

"Glad you could join us," Ned said, taking a drink from a soda can. The skin around his eyes was the color of eggplant and his nose was red and swollen from where Camille had kicked him during the obstacle course.

"Sorry," Maire murmured.

"No problem," Ned said mildly but his eyes flashed with irritation. "There's only a multimillion-dollar production waiting on you, but hey, don't mind us."

Maire was about to respond when Camille jumped in. "That's just lovely, Ned. I bet the people in your life just love your sense of humor."

"What?" Ned asked, innocently. "Everyone loves me."

"Oh, yeah, I'm sure," Camille said, selecting a bottle of water from the table. "It's not like you corner women in your office and shove your hand up their skirts."

Everyone in the room froze. Even the lingering crew members stopped their chatter to look.

"What did you just say?" Ned asked, his voice hard.

A flush crept up Camille's face, but she kept her eyes on Ned. "Nothing," she said, unscrewing the top of her bottle. "I didn't say anything."

"The hell you didn't," Ned said. "You need to watch your mouth."

"What?" Camille blinked her eyes innocently. "You must have misheard me."

But Maire had heard her. Everyone had. What was Camille up to? First, she had made the statement about the senator's eight-year-old son, and now this. Would this comment turn out to be true too?

After what Ned had done to Maire on the climbing wall, he was the one that she wanted to see go next. She slid her hand into the pocket of her jacket, feeling for the pill. Should she use it? Was this the time?

"How about we talk about what happened last night?" Samuel asked, wiping his lips with a napkin and setting aside his plate.

"Shh," Maire hissed, looking around. The camera operators were chatting and several crew members were rushing around the space, not focusing on them any longer, but Maire knew that there were hidden cameras everywhere. "There's nothing to talk about," Maire said as the group drew into a tight knot. "The senator was voted off and freaked out. We need to just forget it and move on."

"There is something seriously fucked-up about this game," Samuel said. Maire glared at him. She needed him to be quiet, to just keep on going like nothing happened. If he made a fuss, the game could be shut down.

"Shut up, man," Ned whispered, setting his soda can down. "Let's just play the damn game."

Maire shot Samuel a look, silently begging for him to stop. There was no way he was going to mess this up for her. Samuel shook his head in disbelief but closed his mouth.

Maire eyed Ned's drink sitting on the table. Had she lost the chance to put the pill in the can? If she dropped it in now, and he didn't take another sip, she will have wasted the opportunity. Maire palmed the pill and nonchalantly stepped in front of Ned at the buffet table, pretending to examine the spread of sandwiches, salads, and desserts. She reached for a turkey wrap with one hand while slyly slipping the pill into Ned's soda can with the other.

Maire stepped away from the table. It was done. Whatever came next was out of her control.

Alfonso's intern walked their way. "Good evening, everyone," she said, brightly. "I hope you were able to get some well-deserved rest today. It's time to head over to the next challenge."

Maire wondered if anyone filled Alfonso in on what had happened the night before. Somehow, she doubted it. Did the director of the show even know the contents of the Super Clues and the Game Changers, or was he just as much in the dark as they were?

Out of the corner of her eye, Maire saw Ned reach for the can and raise it to his lips. She held her breath as he took a sip, then another.

"We're heading outside again today," the intern said. "And I can guarantee this challenge will have viewers talking for years. Shall we go?"

Ned tipped his head back, drained the rest of his drink, and set it aside. "I'm ready, but the question is, is Maire ready?"

Maire bit back a response. She needed to keep Ned Bennett out of her head.

The intern led them through the grand hallway and through the same doors that they had exited the night of the first competition. They stepped out beneath an early evening tangerine-colored sky. Maire kept a close eye on Ned, looking for any signs that the pill was working. He appeared to be just fine and was walking with his usual swagger.

In the near distance, what looked like hundreds of black crosses filled an empty field. *A graveyard*, Maire thought. Seeing the disconcertion on her face, Camille leaned in and whispered, "They're grape trellises. They're supposed to support the vines."

Maire nodded but the image was so disquieting, she couldn't

pull her eyes away. With a growing sense of unease, Maire followed the intern along a cobblestone path.

Soon, the walkway opened up and Maire blinked several times, trying to understand what she was seeing. Ice. Part of the lake was covered in ice. Impossible. Fear coiled itself around Maire's heart.

"Are you okay?" Camille asked, putting a steadying hand on her arm.

Maire couldn't answer. She was transported back to Tanglefoot, could almost feel the wind biting at her cheeks, the sting of cold water against her skin. She forced herself not to look at Samuel. If she did, she would fall apart. She now realized that this whole thing was no coincidence. Maire wanted to run, but where could she go? The cameras were running, the world was watching. She was trapped.

Maire squinted to get a better look. Of course the lake wasn't covered in ice. It was a large white floating pond cover, about the size of a football field. She had seen the high-density covers many times, but never one as large as this. Maybe she had overreacted. Maybe this had nothing to do with Tanglefoot and was just another challenge. She had the nagging feeling that she had every reason to be scared.

Fern was waiting for them at the edge of the lake, dressed in a red, one-shouldered, high-collared gown that covered the bruises around her neck. She held up one hand. "Good evening, Luckies. I trust you had a good day. Let's go ahead and get started. As you can see, the sun is beginning to set and it's important we finish this challenge before nightfall."

Maire noticed that Fern had expertly camouflaged the bruises that her dress didn't cover. Despite her thick makeup, dark circles lined Fern's eyes and no amount of bronzer could conceal her exhaustion.

"The four of you have survived the first elimination," Fern said. "Welcome to your most intense challenge to date. As you can see, a portion of the lake behind us is covered except for a three-foot-by-three-foot hole."

Maire felt sick. Twenty years later and she could still feel the icy claws of the lake trying to drag her in.

"We'll walk out to the opening in the lake, but don't worry, it's sturdy," Fern said, and she moved on to the pond cover. Maire took an experimental step, then another. The hard plastic didn't even wobble beneath her.

In a single-file line, the group walked about fifty yards out onto the lake. Fern led them toward a large white marble gazebo with a domed roof and columns made from sculptures of Roman goddesses. It was an incredible sight. The amount of work and money to create the set had to be staggering. One camera operator was waiting in the gazebo and behind him was Alfonso, studying his clipboard.

Fern stepped up into the gazebo and faced the group. "Welcome to day three of *One Lucky Winner*! We're calling this challenge The Polar Plunge. Right behind you is a large hole. This will be your portal in and out of the lake. You'll also see that a few feet beyond the hole are four flags, each corresponding to the color of your *One Lucky Winner* gear. Pink, green, yellow, and orange. Your task is to dive into the hole and swim until you find a pouch." Fern held up a black cloth bag about the size of a fist.

"How are we supposed to see those?" Ned asked, incredulously. "It's going to be pitch-black down there."

Maire's head snapped to Ned. Had she heard a slur in his voice? Was the pill starting to work?

"Don't worry," Fern assured him. "You can't miss them. When you find a pouch, untie it from its mooring and swim back to the hole, climb out, drop the pouch at your designated spot, and then go back in. The person who collects the most pouches wins the challenge and will win a Super Clue."

"Got it," Ned said, and he swayed on his feet. The pill was

working. Then a new terror surged through her. What if Ned passed out in the water? What if he drowned? She would be a killer. Again.

Maire dreaded jumping into the lake, but she was more afraid of someone else getting the Super Clue. If the clue held incriminating information about her, she wanted to get to it first. Maire's shoulder ached, but she was a strong swimmer. She could do this.

"It sounds dangerous," Camille observed. "Is the water warm enough for swimming?"

"And there's only one way out," Samuel added, gravely. He caught Maire's eye. So many clues pointed to Tanglefoot and that cold night so long ago. They both knew it. Would Samuel quit? Maire couldn't, no matter what.

"You mean, like someone could drown?" Camille asked, her eyes narrowing. "Certainly that's not the case," she insisted.

"The choice of whether to participate or not is yours, Camille," Fern said. "As you know, with every challenge there is risk. Now, if you're all ready, we'll get started."

"What precautions are being taken?" Camille pressed. "Are there lifeguards nearby? EMTs? Who's going to sweep in and save us if something goes wrong?"

Maire wanted to clap a hand over Camille's mouth, even though she had the same fears.

"Jesus, Camille," Ned said. "Do you want to play or not?"

Fern gave Camille a sympathetic smile but there was a glint of irritation in her eyes. "You are welcome to sit this one out, Camille, but that puts you at risk for being voted off the show. Only you can decide if ten million dollars is worth the risk."

"Well, it's worth it to me," Ned said, unzipping his warm-up jacket and stepping out of his pants. "Let's do this."

"I don't like this," Camille whispered in Maire's ear. "Something is very wrong."

Camille was right. This entire competition was twisted and

masochistic, but Maire was in too deep. If there was even one sliver of a chance of winning the money, she had to take it.

"So quit," Maire said shortly, kicking off her shoes and peeling off her warm-up suit until she was down to her bathing suit. She walked gingerly to the edge of the lake, the rocky shoreline sharp against the bottoms of her feet, and joined Ned. She was followed by Samuel and Camille.

Off to the right was a black hole that stood out starkly against the white expanse. She tried to swallow back her terror. The entire setup was eerily similar to the way Tanglefoot Lake looked that night. Even Fern's crimson dress reminded Maire of the blood that had pooled at the edge of the broken ice.

She peered down into the hole. The water was murky and still. How were they going to see where they were going? The thought of being trapped beneath the lake with no light made her pulse quicken. She wouldn't be able to go in there. There was no way. Suddenly, something in the chasm blinked back at her. Maire pulled back in surprise, but just as quickly realized it was a light. She stepped closer to the hole, bending down to get a better look. Soft glints in the water bobbed lazily.

"There are fourteen pouches. Each is marked by a light and connected to a rope that is tethered to the surface," Fern explained, and Maire felt a wave of relief come over her. They wouldn't have to go into the water completely blind. "And make sure you always know where you are in relation to the hole. It can be disorienting down there and it's your only exit," Fern warned. "Any questions?"

"What's in the pouches?" Camille asked. "Clues?"

"Just bobbers, to keep them afloat," Fern said. "The Super Clue goes to the winner who collects the most pouches. Anything else?"

No one spoke. Fern handed them each a pair of goggles and Maire hurried to pull hers onto her face. "Alright, then," Fern said, lifting the starter's pistol.

This was really happening, Maire thought. A crack filled the air, followed by the squawk of some startled birds.

Samuel was the first one into the water, immediately disappearing beneath the surface. Maire lunged for the hole, but Ned was quicker. Now only Camille and Maire remained. Camille looked unsure, afraid.

"Come on," Maire said. "We can't let the guys win."

"Okay," Camille said, her voice shaky. She reached for Maire's hand. Together they leaped, feetfirst, into the hole. The shock of the cold water was like a million shards of glass piercing Maire's skin. She lost her grip on Camille's hand and immediately lost her equilibrium. For one awful moment, she had no idea which way was up or down. Then she saw it, the tiny spark of light. Then another and another. The pouches were visible, connected to varying lengths of buoyed rope.

Samuel and Ned already had a pouch and were swimming back toward the hole. That meant there were only twelve left. Camille swam past her with a thumbs-up. She had gotten a pouch as well. Now there were eleven. Something smooth and slippery brushed against her legs and bits of debris floated past. Maire shuddered, reassuring herself that there was nothing down here that could hurt her.

In that moment, Maire made a decision. It could backfire with catastrophic consequences, but right now, she was at her strongest. She swam past each of the remaining pouches one by one, counting them as she went. Fern never said that they had to come up for air between each pouch. Ten, eleven, twelve, thirteen. At the fourteenth pouch, Maire stopped and began untying it from the rope it was tethered to. Once free, she stuffed the bag into her bathing suit and swam up a few yards to the thirteenth pouch. Again, she worked the knot and it released easily. She shoved the pouch inside her bathing suit with the other one.

Maire knew she would have to gather eight pouches to ensure a win but figured if she could get at least five she would have a good chance. While the others battled against each other for the pouches closer to the surface, Maire would gather the ones farther down. She moved on to the next pouch. The pressure in her chest was growing, but she focused on untying the knot. Her fingers were numb now and she clumsily picked at the tangle of rope that held the pouch in place. After what seemed like an eternity, the knot slipped loose, and she moved on to the next bag. Above her, the water swirled and churned. The others were getting closer.

Her lungs were screaming now. How long had she been below the surface? One minute? More? She had no idea. She snagged the next pouch and now had four stowed inside her bathing suit. She tried to do the math. If she had four and Samuel, Camille, and Ned each had one, that would mean there were seven more bags left. If she could get two more, she figured she would be okay.

Her arms felt as if they were tied down by an anchor and the muscles in her calves clenched painfully. She could do this. She had to. She moved upward to the next light, but suddenly it disappeared. No, she thought. She was so close. The light reappeared and through the gloaming, she could see that someone else was closing in on the pouch too. It was all Maire could do to keep from gasping for air—air that she knew wouldn't be there.

With all the strength she could muster, she kicked her legs and surged toward the light. Her hand snagged on the pouch, but it was knocked away.

Ned.

Her throat was burning and every bit of oxygen she had left in her lungs was gone. Again, she reached for the bag and, again, Ned blocked her, this time knocking the goggles from her face.

She flailed, reaching out blindly, but miraculously she gained purchase on the bag and it slipped from its tether. She had it.

Maire began to swim toward the opening but was pulled back by a tug on her ankle. She jerked her leg, but Ned held tight. If she didn't get away from him, she'd drown. Despair overtook her, and Maire began to flail.

This was it. There was no way she was going to be able to outlast him. She had to get to the surface or she would die. Her children would be without a mother. They would only have Shar to take care of them, or worse, their father.

Ned dragged her down but an unseen force grabbed her hair and was pulling her upward. Pain seared through her scalp. It was Samuel. Samuel was trying to free her from Ned's grip. Ned's fingernails scraped against her skin as he lost hold and the pain in her scalp faded. She was free. Samuel swam downward past her, but all Maire could think about was getting to the surface. She kicked and tried to use her arms to thrust herself upward, but the water felt thick. Every kick and stroke was like moving through mud.

Above her, Maire could see the ghostly hole in the pond cover that meant she would be okay. Her lungs screamed for air. She was so close, but her arms wouldn't work anymore, her legs were useless, and she began sinking again, slowly this time. Gently. She thought drowning would be a cold, terrifying death, but once the panic passed, her limbs were pleasantly warm and as water filled her nose, her throat, and her ears, she was oddly at peace. There was nothing more she could do.

The hole disappeared. *How fitting*, Maire thought, *to die this way*. She deserved nothing less. She had tried to play God that night. She thought of her sweet daughters and her tears joined the lake water. *I'm sorry*, she thought over and over. *I tried to be better, tried every day to be a good person, a good mom*. Maire prayed her children would never learn about what she had done, how she was a murderer and a coward.

Suddenly, Maire felt hands grabbing and pulling at her and she was yanked from the lake and thrown onto a hard, unyielding surface. After the blackness of the water, the light hurt her eyes and she still couldn't breathe. Two faces, etched with worry, loomed above her. Camille and Fern. Fern appeared to be just as wet as Camille, her dark hair plastered against her head. Had they both jumped into the water to save her? *Strange*, she thought. Wasn't it Fern who was trying to undo her? Make her pay for her sins?

A surge of lake water erupted from her gullet, and Maire could breathe again. Her chest heaved with the effort of gathering as much air into her lungs as she could. Every nerve ending was on fire. Pain exploded throughout her body. Her lungs burned and her limbs were frigid. Someone wrapped her in a dry warm blanket and Maire moaned with relief.

"Are you okay?" Fern asked, her own teeth chattering and her beautiful gown clinging to her skin.

Maire nodded, still unable to speak. Camille, wrapped in her own blanket, placed an arm around Maire. "I didn't think you were coming up," Camille said. "We thought you were dead."

"Me too," Maire managed to eke out. She looked around. The colored flags hung limply. Beneath Samuel's green flag were five pouches, beneath Ned's and Camille's were two. "Samuel? Ned?" she asked.

Fern had migrated back to the opening in the water and was staring into its black depths.

Camille shook her head. "They haven't come back up yet. We have to do something."

Maire thought of Samuel, how for a few blissful moments all those years ago she thought she was falling in love with him. And she thought of the pill she dropped in Ned's drink. Without thinking, she scrambled over to the hole and jumped back in.

TWENTY-SIX

THE BEST FRIEND

Then

"Run," Samuel urged, but Maire was frozen, unable to move, her eyes pinned to the pipe the man held in his hand. As he came closer, Maire could see the man was swaying unsteadily on his feet.

"You little shits," the man slurred. "You think you're funny," he said, raising the pipe a little higher. Maire closed her eyes, bracing herself for the impact, but then felt a strong yank on her arm.

"Run!" Samuel cried, trying to pull her away. Maire opened her eyes. The man had stopped advancing, the pipe slipping through his fingers and falling to the ground.

A strange gurgling noise rose up from the man's chest and Maire watched in horror as the man fell to his knees, his eyes widening in fear just before a stream of vomit erupted from his throat. His head lolled and he fell onto his side, knees bent, one arm stuck awkwardly beneath his body.

With Samuel still holding her by the elbow, Maire took a step forward and stared down at the unmoving man. His eyes were open, his right pupil unnaturally large. "Is he dead?" Maire whispered.

"I don't know," Samuel answered, his voice cracking with emotion.

"We have to get help. The twins have a cell phone," Maire said, turning in the direction of the bluff. "One of us should go…"

Samuel bent over and gave the man a tentative shake. "Hey, man," he said. "Get up." There was no response.

"Is he breathing?" Maire asked.

"I don't know," Samuel snapped. "I can't tell."

Heart slamming into her chest, Maire pulled off her mittens and placed two fingers against the man's neck, nearly gagging at the stickiness of the vomit, at the rancid smell.

"I think he's dead," Maire whispered. "We killed him."

In the distance came the wink of approaching headlights. Someone was coming. "We should flag them down. Get help." But Samuel was already shaking his head.

"No," he said sharply. "We need to get out of here. People will ask questions. We can't let anyone know we did this."

"But it was an accident," Maire said. "We didn't mean for this to happen."

Samuel shook his head. "Maire, we're not kids. You're what—twenty? I'm twenty-two. I'm trying to get into law school. We screwed up, and if we get arrested…"

"Arrested?" Maire's chin shot up. "For what?"

"I don't know, Maire," Samuel said, his voice rising. "Criminal mischief, reckless endangerment, criminal injury, destruction of property, harassment. Do you want me to go on?"

She glanced down at the body at her feet. Samuel was right. They needed to go. Someone would see the wreckage, find the man. She looked back to Samuel, his dark eyes pleading with her. Maire nodded and he grabbed her hand. They started running. Soon, they were enveloped by rows and rows of slender river birch, each a ghostly white replica of the next.

They ran until Maire couldn't take another step. Gasping for air, she leaned against a tree.

"I don't understand," Maire said breathlessly. "How did he get hurt so badly?"

"I don't know," Samuel said, bending over, hands on his knees, his breath ragged. "Maybe he wasn't wearing a seat belt. He was going really fast. Hit his head on the windshield. Jesus, I have no idea where we are."

"I'm really sorry," Maire said, the reality of what they had done settling over her. "It was so stupid. I wasn't thinking."

"Yeah, well, it was stupid, but I did it too," Samuel said. He examined the ground. "I don't think we left much in the way of footprints. It's too cold, the snow too hardpacked. Which way do you want to go?"

"We can't go back that way." Maire waved a hand in the direction from which they came. "Let's find the lake. Maybe we'll be able to see the smoke from the bonfire there."

Samuel nodded. "Okay. It looks like the ground starts sloping down that way. It makes sense that the lake would be in that direction."

"I think it's getting darker," Maire said, looking to the sky. The stars had dimmed, barely illuminating the path ahead.

In silence they began walking, glancing furtively over their shoulders. The only sound was their feet moving along the icy ground and the uneven hitch of their breath as their heart rates slowly steadied.

The trees up ahead seemed to be thinning out, replaced with scrubby brush. Maire prayed it was the lake. It was getting colder by the minute, and she dug into her pockets for her mittens.

"What are we going to tell everyone?" Maire asked, slipping the mittens over her fingers, grateful for the warmth and even more grateful to cover up the blood that stained her skin.

"I know what we're not going to say," Samuel said, pushing

aside a prickly shrub and stepping aside so Maire could move past. "We're not going to tell them that we ran a guy off the road and he came after us with a metal pipe and died. Definitely not that. Let's just say we got turned around and forget this ever happened."

"You think Figgy will let it go at that?" Maire asked, wanting to think about anything but the dead man. "She hates that you're dating Lina, you know."

"Figgy?" Samuel asked, genuine surprise on his face. "Why should she care?"

"You two used to go out, right?" Maire asked.

"Oh, no," Samuel said, drawing out the words. "That girl is all drama, all the time. No, thank you. We hung out a few times, but that's it. Figgy may have wanted more but I was definitely not interested."

"But she said you two hooked up," Maire said. "Why would she lie?"

"Why would I?" Samuel said. "Never happened. Never will." He said this with such finality that Maire almost believed him. "Finally," Samuel said with relief.

Maire stepped out from behind Samuel. Stiff winds had swept away any lingering snow and Tanglefoot Lake lay in front of them like a polished silver platter. Instead of feeling relief, Maire was again reminded of how very alone they were.

"Do you see the bonfire?" Maire asked, scanning the horizon for smoke.

"There," Samuel said, pointing off to the west. White tendrils of smoke rose above the trees. "I think if we just follow the shoreline, we can get back to them. It's not far." He began moving down the rocky incline and then turned back, offering his hand to Maire. She took it and, together, they picked their way down a staircase of slippery rocks until they reached the lip of the lake.

"You think it will hold us?" Maire asked. The lake looked

frozen, but just the day before the temperature had been well above thirty-two degrees. She didn't relish the thought of her foot breaking through thin ice and into the frigid water.

"It's like zero degrees out. I'm sure we're fine," Samuel assured her, and they began walking.

It was a slow journey. Chest-high frozen bulrushes and canary grass snapped as they trudged along the frozen shoreline. Maire stuck close to Samuel, and though she knew no one was coming after them, every rustle and swish made her heart jump.

Samuel, sensing her trepidation, reached for her mittened hand. "It's okay," he whispered. "We're close."

Maire smiled up at him gratefully. Was it wrong to be holding Samuel's hand? They were just trying to steady one another, keep each other from stumbling. But what would Lina say if she found out? Maire pushed away the image of Lina's hurt expression, pushed away Figgy's self-satisfied smirk. She liked the feel of Samuel's hand in hers, wishing the woolen fabric of her glove wasn't a barrier to the warmth of his skin.

Something had passed between the two of them. A connection. But maybe that was because of the dangerous prank of chicken they had played. Their senses were heightened but maybe Samuel and Lina's relationship had run its course. Maybe Maire had a chance. She stopped walking.

"What's the matter?" Samuel asked, stopping along with her.

Maire pulled off her mittens, shoved them in her pockets, and then reached for Samuel's hand. His skin was cold but still a current of electricity passed between the two of them.

"Maire," Samuel said gently. "What are you doing?"

She knew this wasn't the time. It was morbid, wrong. But she didn't want to talk, didn't want to think about the dead man, about Lina or Figgy or Damon and the twins. She reached up and touched his face, traced his lips with her finger, then leaned in. Their lips touched and Samuel's hand slid beneath her coat, searching for skin.

That's when she saw him. The silhouette of a man crouched among the reeds. Maire froze as the man slowly rose unsteadily from his hiding spot.

"You think you're going to get away with this?" His voice was low and dangerous. He was ageless in the murky light from the stars; she couldn't see his face. He was only shadows and words.

It was impossible. He was dead. Maire was sure of it.

"We're sorry," Samuel said, raising his hands, palms out.

From behind the reeds, the man's breath came out in white swirls and was tinged with the stinging scent of whiskey. Maire eased backward, her hand still clutching Samuel's.

Suddenly she was being pulled from the reeds and out onto the lake. "Run," Samuel said through clenched teeth. She let him pull her along until they were running, struggling to stay upright on the ice, not daring to look over their shoulders, certain that the man with the pipe was not far behind.

TWENTY-SEVEN

THE ASSISTANT

Fern watched as Maire and then Camille jumped back into the lake before sliding in after them. The water wasn't quite as piercing cold as the first time she went in to rescue Maire, but it still sent a jolt of adrenaline through her. How long could someone stay beneath the surface before losing consciousness? Ned and Samuel had been down there for quite a while. Three minutes, maybe more.

She felt something brush against her arm. Camille. She was pointing through the murky water and that's when Fern saw the large shadow moving toward them like a great school of fish. Three figures. Two kicking their legs furiously, one being pulled limply through the water. Samuel, Ned, and Maire. Ned appeared to be unconscious.

Camille patted her chest, as if indicating she was out of air, and pointed upward, then disappeared, churning up the water as she moved to the surface. The others' progress was slowing and Fern swam toward them, knowing that all of them could end up dead at the bottom of the lake if they didn't get out of there now. Fern reached for something to snag onto, an arm, a leg, anything that would help her pull one of them to safety.

Her fingers found the hard muscle of Samuel's bicep. She waved Samuel and Maire off and they released Ned into her arms, swimming upward to take a breath.

Fern reached her arms around Ned's chest and began swimming toward the hole, using the rope that tethered the bags as a towline. Upward they went, the surface shimmering above her. Suddenly hands were on them, grabbing fabric, skin, anything possible to pull the two of them to safety. Ned was yanked first from the water, followed by Fern. She crawled from the hole, trying to gulp in air. Fern saw Camille on her knees and watched as she pinched Ned's nose shut, covering his mouth with her own, and breathed. She started chest compressions and Fern found that she was counting out loud right along with her. "Twenty-eight, twenty-nine, thirty."

After what felt like an eternity, Ned coughed, turned his head and vomited lake water. He was going to be alright.

Why hadn't she just let him drown? After what he had done to Fern all those years ago, he deserved nothing less. Someone wrapped a blanket around her shoulders and Fern glanced up to find Samuel looking down at her, disconcerted. Had he caught the look of disappointment on her face when Ned finally took a breath? Fern nodded to thank him.

"Those lifeguards would have come in handy right about now, right?" Samuel said darkly.

Fern ignored him as the medical team that was on standby moved in. She watched as they tended to Ned, who, like a roach, couldn't be drowned. He was quick to refuse a recommended trip to the hospital to get a more thorough examination. He wanted that money. Maire, Camille, and Samuel were wrapped in blankets, shivering from the cold. Maire was nearly inconsolable. Even after it was clear that Ned was going to be alright, she buried her face in her hands and sobbed.

One of them could have died in the lake. Ned Bennett nearly died. Not that she would have mourned his loss—the world would be a better place without him—but the optics would be terrible. God, that sounded awful. She hated Ned Bennett and rightly so, but she didn't wish anyone dead, did she?

Fern could hear Cat's voice in her head. *"I knew you would fuck this up, Fern. Jesus, you took a brilliant concept and ran it into the ground. Worthless."*

The thing was, Cat would be right. Fern *had* fucked everything up. She had this unbelievable, golden opportunity that landed right in her lap and she destroyed it. In the short span of three days, Fern had locked her boss in the wine cellar, had hijacked a reality show, had nearly been killed by a former U.S. senator, and had watched four near drownings. She wanted to walk back to the lake, slip into its welcoming arms, and disappear. Now, *that* would be must-see TV. The ratings would go through the roof.

She wasn't sure how she had gotten here. Ambition? Greed? Probably both. But there was something more. There had to be. Fern hadn't been the one to plan the dangerous challenges, hadn't curated the strange clues, hadn't been the one to invite Ned Bennett. But it didn't matter. In the end, Fern would be the one holding the bag. Her name would be the one people remembered, the one that would be the butt of a thousand jokes. She could already see the memes.

It was time, Fern thought. It was time to quit, to make a new plan. Time to tell the contestants to go home, to free Cat from the cellar, to face the consequences. She would go home, maybe go back to school. Better yet, go to a far-off country and disappear into anonymity. First, she would go pack a few things, grab her passport, maybe help herself to a little of Cat's cash. It wouldn't be stealing—it's not like Fern hadn't earned it. Consider it payment for services rendered.

She would leave a note for the contestants, along with their cell phones, letting them know the game was over. But how to get Cat out of the wine cellar without being caught? That was a little trickier. She was tempted to leave her there, but that would be murder. Fern was many things, but she wasn't a murderer.

She could let Cat out and then leave the villa. Cat might even be too weak and tired to make much of a fuss. But knowing her boss, the moment she was free, she would raise holy hell and call the police, the FBI, and a SWAT team to come after Fern. Fern would have to get a message to someone to let Cat out after she had made her getaway.

"Fern," came a voice. Fern was pulled from her thoughts to find Samuel standing next to her. "This is unacceptable," he said, his face furrowed with frustration. "This is pure negligence."

"It's for ten million dollars," she said mechanically. "You knew the competition was going to be challenging. You signed a waiver."

"Nothing is worth this," Samuel said, throwing up his hands. "I quit."

"But you won," Fern said. "You won the challenge. You get the Super Clue." She lifted a blue urn from its spot on the gazebo. "Here."

Samuel shook his head, refusing to take the urn.

"You won. You came in first place, Ned in last. Take the urn."

Samuel reached inside the urn. "A letter opener?" Samuel asked in disbelief. "What the hell am I supposed to do with this?" He walked away shaking his head.

Still dripping wet, Fern led the way across the lake toward the shore. The sun was long gone. The navy sky was pricked with a million stars, the camera operators' drones buzzing above, taking in every single second of this shit show.

They trudged forward. The walking wounded. Fern would get them to their room to take steaming showers and put on dry clothes. She would ensure that they got dinner and hot coffee. This game was seriously twisted, and she wanted no part of it

any longer. She would get them to settle into their beds for the
night and when they woke up in the morning, Fern would be
gone, and they would be free to go.

Once at their bedroom door, Fern paused. "We were sched-
uled for one more challenge tonight, but in light of this evening's…" She struggled to find the right words. *Disaster?
Near-death experiences? Clusterfuck?* "Events," she finally settled
on, "I think we will postpone until tomorrow."

"Hell no," came a soft voice. It was Maire. Her pale skin
was now nearly translucent. "We've come this far, and I want
to play."

"I don't know," Camille said doubtfully. "I think maybe
we all need to get a good night's sleep. Talk about this in the
morning."

"I agree with Camille," Samuel said, his eyes heavy with
weariness.

"Then you forfeit," Maire said, her voice rising. "You quit.
I want this on camera. I want people to know that I want to
keep going. That I'm not giving up."

"Hold on now," Samuel said, raising his hands. "No one's
quitting. We are just coming to a mutual agreement to pause
things for the night. To regroup."

"I agree," Camille said. "Ned? How about you?"

"I nearly fucking drowned tonight," Ned said. "So a break
would be welcome."

"Then you quit," Maire said, triumphantly, setting her gaze
on Fern. "What does your trusty rule book say about not taking part in challenges?" she asked.

Fern pressed her lips together. If a contestant refused to take
part in one of the challenges, they essentially bowed out of
the game. "Technically, she's right. We have to stay on schedule," Fern conceded. In reality, it didn't matter. She was leaving. Let them think the game was going to go on forever for
all she cared.

"So what's it going to be?" Maire asked. "Are you in or out?"

There was silence. Everyone cast looks at one another, trying to gauge each other's thoughts. "I guess I'm in, then," Ned said. "But Jesus this game's going to kill me one way or another."

Samuel nodded grimly.

"This is a big mistake," Camille said ruefully.

"Fine, then," Fern said. "We play." She checked her watch, now frozen on 6:31 p.m. It had stopped when she was in the water. She glanced up at a clock on the corridor wall. It was nearing eight o'clock. "We'll meet on the veranda at nine. The good thing, I guess, is that this challenge isn't as physical as the other ones. But just so you know, there will be a vote to send someone home tonight too. And, Maire, the intern is waiting for you in The Vault. Head on down and she'll get you set up."

Fern left the contestants staring after her. The first thing she needed to do was get herself warm. Well aware of the cameras watching—always watching—she kept her back straight and her chin up as she tried to move casually through the hallway to her quarters. Once safely inside her room, Fern stripped off Cat's red dress, now ruined, and tossed it to the floor. She ignored both cell phones, lighting up with alerts, and stepped into the shower, letting the hot water roll over her skin. As Fern washed the lake water from her hair, she realized that her life as she knew it was over.

Skin red and pleasantly aching from the hot water, Fern reluctantly turned off the spray. She needed to keep moving. She wrapped her hair in a towel, riffled through her suitcase, and threw on a pair of wide-legged black jeans, a gray turtleneck, and her favorite Converse shoes.

She sat on the edge of her bed and scrolled to the security camera app on her phone. Cat was lying facedown on the stone floor, covered in the insulated blanket. A fist of panic struck Fern in the chest. Why wasn't she moving?

Fern poked at the intercom button on her phone. "Cat," she

called out. "Cat, wake up. Are you okay?" She was crying now. Hot tears of regret. How had things gotten so completely out of hand? "Please, wake up," she pleaded. "I'm so sorry."

Fern was crying so hard she almost missed the twitch of Cat's fingers. "Oh, thank God," Fern breathed. "Don't worry, Cat," she said. "I'll get you out of there. There's something wrong with the lock," she lied. "I'm working on it."

Cat lifted her head from the stone floor and looked up. She struggled to a sitting position and Fern could feel her desperation through the camera. Cat cleared her throat and a sound like fingernails against sandpaper emerged. "Why are you doing this?" she rasped. "After everything I've done for you."

"I'm so sorry," Fern said, wiping the moisture from her face.

"You're sorry?" Cat repeated, getting to her feet and coming closer to the camera, her eyes blazing with anger. "If you're so sorry then get me the fuck out of here!"

"Okay," Fern cried, unable to stop the tears. "I'll be right there. I promise."

Fern turned off the camera. She had betrayed the one person who had come to her defense. Cat could have left Fern to contend with Ned Bennett in that executive office ten years ago, but she didn't. Cat had understood that Fern was in danger, in need of help, and she had stepped in with no regard for herself. Cat had walked away from a great job and took Fern with her.

Fern had been blinded by her own ambition. But no more—she would put an end to all of this. She would let Cat out of the cellar and take care of her like she had taken care of Fern. The game could wait one more night. Once Cat got something to eat, had showered and slept in her own bed, Fern would hand back the reins of *One Lucky Winner* to the rightful person. Relief flooded through her. It was going to be okay. Cat would make things okay again.

Fern's phone vibrated again and she glanced at the screen, anxious to keep moving. It was Alfonso.

Have you seen the reach yet? he asked.

Reach? It took a moment for Fern to understand what Alfonso was talking about. Fern's stomach dropped.

Record-breaking! Alfonso texted. Sixteen million viewers and growing.

Fern froze. Sixteen million?

People are watching. Millions of people. It's all anyone is talking about. I've texted Cat but haven't heard from her at all. Where is she?

Fern paused. This changed everything. Sixteen million. And she had been the one to do it. Fern had brought the viewers. A few more hours in the cellar wouldn't hurt Cat, would it? She had to tread carefully here. She couldn't claim to know where Cat was at this moment in time and then feign ignorance about her whereabouts later. Fern needed a story and had to stick to it, no matter what Cat said when she came out of the cellar.

I just talked to her. She's locked away in her office working on the next press release.

If you see her, tell her congrats. This is HUGE! And congrats to you too, Fern. You're famous.

Fern felt her face grow warm. Famous. She had never dreamed that the show would be seen by so many people. Everyone was watching now. Everyone. Maybe there was a way out of this after all. Maybe she wouldn't have to leave the country. Thanks, she typed. We're going live with the next challenge at nine.

Sixteen million viewers. Fern had to find something to wear.

TWENTY-EIGHT

THE BEST FRIEND

The Vault

"Anyone would have jumped in the water to try to save someone, don't you think? Everyone but Ned, that is. He was the one trying to drown me.

"I don't think I did anything special. Was I scared? Yeah, I was scared—it was terrifying being underwater and not knowing if I was going to make it to the surface. All I could think about was my girls and how I need to get back to them. But I have a job to do here first.

"What do I think of my competitors? Well, you already know how I feel about Ned. But after Camille jumped into the water to save me, it really made me think differently of her. At first, I thought Camille came across as very arrogant, but I don't think that's it now. She's self-assured and seems to have a good moral compass. I'm not going to say I like her, but I respect her.

"On Samuel Rafferty, I have no comment.

"Listen, I don't need ten million dollars, but I need money. I'm not going to buy a big house, fancy cars, or go on exotic vacations. The only thing I need are my daughters, Keely and Dani. My youngest, Dani, has cystic fibrosis. She's ten. Some days, she is so sick that she can't get out of bed.

"I'm sorry. I don't mean to cry. I hate it when people cry on these things. But Dani should be going to school and playing outside with her friends. Instead, she spends weeks in the hospital, taking plates full of medication. And some days…some days she has to fight for every single breath she takes.

"No, I don't need ten million dollars. But I need to be able to pay for Dani's medications, the hospital stays, the nebulizers, the pancreatic enzyme replacement therapies, the blood tests, the bone density tests, the ultrasounds, the chest CTs, the X-rays, the lung biopsies. And eventually, most likely, a lung transplant. Keely needs her sister and I need my daughter. So please, I'm begging you, keep me here as long as possible. For my family, *One Lucky Winner* is life and death."

ChapterandVerse1990—I'm crying. Someone give her all the money!

This_Is_Not_A_Drill—She should set up a GoFundMe and be home with her kids. Why is she even here?

ChapterandVerse1990—I can think of ten million reasons.

Frankie_Gee—Color me skeptical… Forget the Best Friend, the Executive is the real deal.

ChapterandVerse1990—I'm skeptical of anyone who starts a sentence with color me…

CaitlynCBB—Did anyone else notice that the Executive looked a little off? He was weaving all over the place.

CisterPower—You can also make a donation to the Cystic Fibrosis Foundation at https://www.cff.org/—together we can find a cure!

IowaBornAndBread—I know the Best Friend and the Boyfriend.

I mean I know who they are but never met them. We went to the same college a loong time ago. LOL. If I remember correctly, something really bad happened on Tanglefoot Lake. Someone died or almost died—I'm not sure of the details. Eventually, the Best Friend and Boyfriend just kind of disappeared from campus. It was weird.

FiggyPudding13—Oh, I was there that night. I know what happened.

TWENTY-NINE

THE CONFIDANTE

Camille sat on her bed, hands wrapped around a steaming mug of coffee. Dressed head to toe in white *One Lucky Winner* gear, she was still shivering from the disaster in the lake. Also dressed in white, Ned, Samuel, and Maire sat with their cups of coffee, waiting for nine o'clock and the next challenge.

If only she could have convinced them to hold off until tomorrow for the next challenge, maybe she'd be able to puzzle through what was actually happening here. But there was no convincing Maire or Ned. Despite nearly being killed, they were intent on moving forward.

The more Camille thought about it, the more she was sure that the five of them were brought here for a reason beyond battling it out for ten million dollars. How could they not understand this?

Fern was the key. The senator had played the game, lost, left the estate, and came back prepared to kill her, claiming that Fern had leaked a very damning piece of information about him. Did that mean Fern had dirt on all of them?

Camille was pretty sure that all Fern could know about her was the debt that she'd accrued over the years. So what? Big deal. Lots of people maxed out their credit cards or mortgaged their homes to the hilt. Fern couldn't possibly know about the patients she saw off the books and didn't keep records on. And she definitely didn't know about Wingo.

Camille was certain that Fern was Nan, her former patient who said she worked with some truly awful people who needed to pay for what they had done. Were she and the other four contestants these awful people? It had to be the case. Fern, posing as Nan, would have seen the Alftan painting in her office. She felt light-headed at the thought of her misdeeds splashed all over the news.

"I wish you would rethink things," Camille said. "We need to talk things through, figure out what's really happening here."

"Drop it," Maire snapped. "We're playing."

"Maybe it's best we don't talk to each other," Ned said from his spot next to the window. "Just shut up and let's get through tonight."

"Easy to say for the guy who tried to kill me," Maire said, shooting Ned a dirty look.

"Who tried to kill who? I'm the guy who ended up needing CPR!" Ned snarled.

"You swallowed a little water," Maire sniped back. "You were going to be just fine no matter what."

"Stop," Samuel said, rising from the edge of his bed. "Just stop. It's our own fault we're in this situation. It's a brutal game—what did you expect for ten million dollars? Did you really think it would be a walk in the park? Let's just all agree it's not worth dying over, okay? Whoever wins needs to win fairly."

"I don't think anyone is going to win," Camille said softly.

"What was that?" Ned asked. Out of the four of them, he looked the most wrecked. Despite his awful behavior, Camille had to wince at the sight of his broken nose and bruised face.

"I said I don't think anyone is going to win," Camille repeated. "I think it's a setup. I think Fern brought us all here for a very specific reason."

"A setup?" Ned asked. "But why? Because the senator said so? Nah." Ned shook his head. "He was just looking for someone to blame for his own bad behavior. Why in the world would she want to set *me* up?"

Camille didn't know how much to reveal about her theory. Even to her own ears it sounded unhinged. "Never mind," she said. "I'm tired and cold. Just ignore me. I'm not making any sense."

"I think we can all agree on that," Ned said, standing up. "It's almost nine. I'm going downstairs."

Camille watched as he limped from the room.

"That man needs to go home. Tonight," Maire said, walking over to Camille. "Every single close call was his fault. Think about it. He plays dirty. He cut my rope and almost drowned all of us."

"The only way to make that happen is to make sure he doesn't win the next challenge," Samuel said, rubbing his eyes and heading toward the exit. "Fern said it wasn't a physical game, thank God."

"Yes, but simply beating him won't be enough," Maire insisted. "He has to be voted out. Ned is famous and popular. That's a hard combination to beat. The audience rules in this game."

"You don't think the audience sees Ned for what he is?" Camille asked. "You don't think they see how he plays dirty?"

"They either don't see it or don't care," Maire said, with a rueful little laugh. "I don't understand. But if I lose to that son of a bitch…" Maire got to her feet and slammed her coffee cup on a side table.

This was not going to end well. "Wait," Camille said, getting to her feet. "Let's just lay it all on the line. What did you do?"

Maire looked back at her blankly, but she thought she saw a spark of fear in Samuel's eyes.

"Listen, I know her. I know Fern and she's not who she says she is."

Maire crossed her arms over her chest. "What do you mean? You said earlier you didn't know who she was. You said you never met her."

Camille held up a hand. "I know, but I wasn't sure then. I am now. She was one of my patients."

"A patient?" Samuel stared at her in disbelief. "None of this is making sense."

"A woman came to my office wearing a baseball cap and big sunglasses. She said her name was Nan, but I think it was Fern. I saw Fern's ID. Her full name is Fernanda."

"You're saying she wore a disguise?" Maire gave a chuckle of disbelief. "Like in some stupid movie? Come on, Camille, I may not be a doctor, but I'm not an idiot." She turned to Samuel. "Do you see what she's doing? She's trying to fuck with us. She's screwing with our heads so she can win the money."

"I want to hear what she says," Samuel said.

Camille saw the hard look Maire gave him. A warning.

"I want to hear," he repeated more forcefully and sat back down.

"Fine," Maire finally said, throwing up her hands in defeat. "Tell us about *Nan*."

Camille knew this could be her last chance to make them see. Make them understand. "About nine months ago, out of the blue, a woman came to see me at my practice. She said her name was Nan and that she was struggling with her boss."

Maire rolled her eyes, but Camille kept going. "Think about it. Why haven't we met Fern's boss? Why don't we have any idea who the person behind the show is?"

"You're losing me," Samuel said.

"Nan… Fern said that her boss was ruthless, would do anything to get back at people who wronged her. Look at what happened to the senator."

"And you think she created this reality show to get back at us?" Samuel rubbed his forehead. "I'm sorry, that, that..." He shook his head.

"Makes no sense," Maire finished, but Camille could tell she had hit a nerve. "Who would want revenge against all of us?"

"I know," Camille said, hearing how ridiculous it sounded said out loud. "But I'm sure it's her. I think I recognize her tattoo." Camille pointed to the inside of her wrist. "A dragonfly."

"I didn't see a tattoo," Samuel said. "Camille, come on."

"She covers it up with makeup for the show, I think." Camille was losing them. "I know it's hard to believe. But think about it. Think about the puzzles. Did yours relate specifically to you? To a certain time or event in your life?"

Samuel's face turned stony, and Maire shook her head impatiently.

"My puzzle was of a painting in my office," Camille confessed. "How would anyone know that unless they've been there? Fern was there. I know it." When neither of them responded, Camille knew she had one more try. She thought of her Game Changer. She had two more statements to utter in front of the cameras and she was sure they related in some way to Maire and Samuel.

"Have you ever experienced the thrill of laying down in the middle of the road and waiting for a car to come speeding toward you?" Camille asked softly.

Samuel froze like an animal caught in the crosshairs of a rifle.

"What did you say?" Maire asked, her eyes narrowing.

Camille knew they had heard her loud and clear.

"But have you ever been kissed in the woods next to a frozen lake by a boy that didn't belong to you?" Camille said, keeping her eyes on Maire.

"This is bullshit," Maire said, shaking her head. "You're play-

ing head games. I'm going now. Ten million dollars is waiting." Maire stormed from the room, slamming the bedroom
door behind her.

"We better go," Samuel said, looking at the floor. "We're
late."

She had lost him for now. It was time to go. The next challenge was about to begin.

"Okay," Camille said. "Let's just agree to do whatever we
can to make sure that Ned Bennett goes home next. Then we
can regroup. Talk more and try to figure out exactly what's
happening. And, Samuel." She grabbed his hand. "I don't
really want to know what you did. I don't care. I just want to
get out of here in one piece."

He shook her off. "That's easy, then," Samuel said, his eyes
boring into hers, "because I didn't do anything."

Fear dragged a cold finger down her back and Camille nodded and let him pass by her. She lagged behind Samuel as they
moved down the stairs where an intern was waiting for them.
She led them through the atrium with its gurgling fountain.
The marble goddess smiled down benignly on her as dark water
poured out of the mouth of the mask she was holding.

"It's this way," the intern said, holding a wrought iron door
open for them. Camille stepped over the threshold and nearly
gasped at the beauty of the veranda. It was like transporting
into old-world Italy. It was a more intimate space, unlike the
other rooms in the villa. Smaller, warmer. Dozens of candles
of various heights sat on the sills of the open-air windows.

The walls were made of stone and Camille looked up to see
a pergola with massive wooden beams laced with grapevines.
The vines, interlaced with twinkling lights, and heavy with
black grapes, hung so low that Camille could reach up and grab
a handful. Alfonso stood in a corner of the room and gave Camille and Samuel a distracted nod as they passed. "Fern will
be here momentarily and then we'll get started."

"No cameras tonight?" Camille asked, noting that there were no camera operators in sight.

Alfonso gave her a knowing smile. "There are always cameras."

Camille searched for the telltale evidence of cameras but saw none. But she knew they were there, she just couldn't see them.

A harvest moon splashed through the leaves and puddled on the blue stone floor. A round table with five high-backed chairs sat in the center of the room. Atop the table, crystal wineglasses glittered in the candlelight. Rows and rows of wine and liquor bottles sat behind a bar cut from the same stone as the walls. Soft classical music played from a hidden speaker and the spicy scent of California fuchsia filled the night air. Ned paced across the blue stone and Maire sat on a cracked windowsill, looking out at the black lake.

Camille fought the urge to run. Despite the soothing music and the ambient lighting, tension crackled in the air. There was still time. She could forfeit and Fern would call a car for her, and she could be home in her own bed within a few hours. But Camille had to admit she was equal parts terrified and curious as to what the night would bring.

The only sound was the gentle lapping of the lake's water kissing the shoreline and Ned's footfalls on the stone. After a few minutes, Fern made her entrance dressed in a white silk jumpsuit with a cross-halter neckline that covered the bruises around her neck. "Camille, you sit right here, next to me," Fern said, pulling out a chair for her. A pit grew in her stomach. Fern was planning on putting on a show tonight.

Camille walked over and stood next to Fern. Fern's eyes shone brightly in the candlelight, giving off an almost feverish glint. It was as if the terrifying events at the lake never happened. She glanced at Fern's arm. Once again, the tattoo was gone.

"Samuel and Maire, sit there and there," Fern directed. "And,

Ned, you're over there." *She's taking back some of the control that she lost during the lake challenge,* Camille thought. Fern wanted everyone to know who was in charge, who was the master of the game. "And, Alfonso, I think we are all set now. You can go."

"He's leaving?" Samuel asked. "Why?"

"It's in the script," Fern said simply.

Camille watched, stomach twisting, as Alfonso and his intern went inside, leaving them all alone with Fern.

Fern took a seat and Camille settled into the remaining empty chair. "Our uniforms," Camille said. "We're all in white. Why?"

"Why not?" Fern countered. "Something different for a different kind of challenge."

"I was thinking maybe it had more significance," Camille said. "Everything on *One Lucky Winner* has been so methodically planned out. I thought it meant something more."

Fern tilted her head and a thoughtful furrow between her eyes appeared. "Such as?" she prodded.

"Such as...perhaps we're all wearing the same white uniform because we're meant to think that we're now on the same team."

She smiled. "Or, Doctor, a white jacket is just a white jacket." Camille nodded as if acquiescing the point and eased herself into her chair. "I took the liberty of pouring you each a glass of cabernet sauvignon. It's our best wine, and it only comes out for the most special of occasions." Fern picked up her glass and looked at them expectantly.

Maire followed suit and reached for her glass and took a sip of the deep red wine.

"Do you taste the vanilla?" Fern asked. "It comes from oak aging."

"I taste it," Ned agreed, taking another thoughtful sip. "And hints of black cherry and green pepper."

"Yes!" Fern cried in delight. "So fun to have another wine connoisseur in our company."

Camille and Samuel exchanged a look. How could Maire and Ned not feel the tension in the room? Or maybe they did and were just playing the game better than she and Samuel were.

"Shall we get started?" Fern asked. "Like I promised, this challenge does not have the physical element that the others had, but you will need to be mentally sharp and make split-second decisions. This is a game of wits."

Camille released an internal sigh of relief. Every single muscle in her body hurt from the last two challenges. There was no way she could run, swim, or climb anything.

"This game is called Spin, Speak, Shoot," Fern said, then paused.

"Shoot?" Samuel asked. "Shoot what?"

This was Camille's immediate question as well.

Fern gave an enigmatic smile and Camille was surer than ever that Fern was the woman who called herself Nan. The woman who said that her boss was obsessed with retribution. Camille watched as Fern reached beneath the table and pulled out an object and set it in the center of the table.

A gun. A long-barreled, sleek revolver.

This wasn't a Taser or even a shotgun used to strike a paper target like in the earlier challenges. This was a weapon that was meant to kill.

"Don't look so scared," Fern said, teasingly. "Obviously it's not loaded." To prove her point. Fern lifted the gun, barrel pointed straight up, and pulled the trigger. Camille flinched but the only sound was an anemic click, like a tongue clucking the roof of the mouth. "See," Fern said, setting the gun back down. "Empty."

"So, what's the game?" Ned asked.

"You've heard of spin the bottle, right?" Fern asked.

"I'm not kissing anyone," Maire said, flatly.

"I bet you would for ten million dollars," Ned said.

"You wish," Maire shot back.

"Not really," Ned said, offhandedly.

Camille wished they would just shut up.

"No kissing," Fern said. "But it's called Spin, Speak, Shoot for a reason. But instead of spinning a bottle, you spin the gun and wherever the barrel ends up pointing, that is who must answer a question." Fern once again reached below the table and pulled out four decks of cards. Each deck was a different color: pink, green, yellow, and orange. "If the barrel of the gun stops in front of you, I'll draw a card from your pile and then you will answer the question written on the back."

"Sounds easy enough," Samuel said. "What's the catch?"

"Excellent question," Fern said. "A question may pop up that you don't want to answer. That's perfectly acceptable, but if you choose not to respond, that's when you must pick up the gun and put it to your head and pull the trigger."

The room became thick with stunned silence.

"That's sick," Camille said, finally speaking.

Fern kept her face passive, businesslike. "Obviously, it's symbolic. But if you refuse to answer three questions, you lose. You are out of the competition and at risk for being voted off the show."

"What kind of questions?" Camille asked, noticing the way Maire kept looking across the table at Samuel.

"Well, why don't we find out?" Fern said, giving the revolver a spin. "Shall we begin?"

Camille watched as the gun whirled, a black-and-silver pinwheel. It spun past her again and again. She didn't want to be the first one to answer a question and willed it to pass her by. There was nowhere to go, nowhere to run. The gun flew past Ned, Fern, and Maire before beginning to slow. At first, she was sure it was going to stop in front of Samuel, but it crept past him and came to rest right in front of Maire, its barrel pointing directly at her.

"Maire," Fern said, with delight. "You are the lucky one. I'll draw a card from your deck, read it, and you'll decide whether or not you'd like to Speak or Shoot."

Camille watched as Maire nervously dug her fingers into her thighs, her face tight with anticipation. Fern pulled a card from the top of her deck and read it silently. Fern glanced from the card to Maire and back to the card, building the suspense. "So tell us, Maire, where did you go to college?"

Camille breathed a sigh of relief. She hoped all the questions would be this easy. There was really no reason that Maire shouldn't answer it, Camille thought, but if she didn't, she would have one strike against her.

Maire was hesitating for too long. "What will it be, Maire? Speak or Shoot?" Fern prodded.

"Speak," Maire said. "I went to Tanglefoot in Iowa. I was an art student there."

"See," Fern said, looking at each of them in turn. "Easy, right?" Maire released a breath. "Okay, Maire, your turn to give it a spin."

Using her thumb and index finger, Maire gave the gun a spin. It was an awkward attempt and the gun only rotated around the table twice before stopping in front of Ned. Camille felt some of the tension leach from her body.

"Ned," Fern said, pulling a card from the orange deck of cards. "Your question—have you ever committed a crime?" she asked tightly. "What will you do? Speak or Shoot?"

Camille noticed the way Fern seemed to stiffen in every interaction she had with Ned. Camille couldn't blame her; she had the same reaction. Ned was boorish and arrogant.

Ned chuckled. "A crime? I mean, I've gotten my fair share of parking tickets, but beyond that, no. I can honestly say I've never committed a crime."

Fern stared at Ned for a time, her head cocked to the side as if inviting him to say more.

"And that is my final answer, Fern," Ned said, deadpan.

"My turn to spin?" Without waiting for Fern's response, he twirled the gun with gusto. It seemed to take forever to slow and come to a stop and, when it did, it returned to its last resting spot in front of Ned. "Oh, hey," he said. "I get to spin again, right?" he asked.

"I'm afraid not," Fern said. "Wherever the barrel points, that's the person in the hot seat. You get another question."

"Okay," Ned said looking around with a nervous laugh. "Let me have it."

Camille eyed her deck of cards. What kinds of questions were in store for her? Questions about her past? Her debt? Her patients? Wingo? If Fern read a card asking about one of her patients, she would have to choose the Shoot option. Maybe, Camille thought, she should just bow out now. Purposely tank in hopes of being the next one voted off the show. Then, at least, she would be free of this strange, torturous game.

Camille noticed the slight tremble in Fern's fingers as she slid the top card from the orange deck. Why was she so nervous? Camille felt sick at the possibility of what might come next.

Fern paused before speaking, her dark eyes darting from Ned to the card and back again. "Have you ever had an employee sign an NDA before?" Fern asked.

Ned's eyes narrowed. "An NDA?" he repeated.

"Yes," Fern said with mock patience. "A nondisclosure agreement."

"I know what it is," Ned retorted lightly. "I'm just not sure why it's relevant."

"Is that a pass?" Fern asked with an arched eyebrow.

Ned stared long and hard at Fern, his eyes flashing with anger. Alarm bells began clanging in Camille's head. *We need to get out of here*, she wanted to scream. She wanted to sweep her arm across the table, knocking the candles, the wine, and the decks of cards to the floor. She looked at the twinkling lights above her and there it was—a small red light. The cameras. The damn cameras were everywhere.

Finally, Ned spoke. "Of course my employees signed NDAs. It's standard practice in the entertainment field. We couldn't have employees giving away crucial information about *Cold, Hard Truth* and its episodes before they aired." Ned shrugged. "I imagine my NDAs were very similar to the one all of us had to sign to be on *One Lucky Winner*."

"Fair enough," Fern said, breaking eye contact with Ned. He smirked and gave the gun a spin. Instead of watching the gun twirl, Camille observed the others. Samuel, Maire, and Fern were watching the gun rotate while Ned was studying Fern. Camille saw the moment his face transformed from irritation to sick realization. It was clear to Camille that Ned suddenly recognized Fern. Did he know her as Nan, like she did? Or as someone else?

Camille had a sinking feeling that she knew what Ned's crime was. *Degenerare.* Degenerate. Today, NDAs seemed to be synonymous with sexual misconduct in the workplace. Had Ned done something to Fern?

Suddenly, all eyes shifted toward Camille. She glanced down to find the gun pointing at her. Cold sweat gathered at her temples and her empty stomach roiled. Which of her secrets would be teased out by the cards? Because, for as much as Camille tried to believe that she was here as a spectator, a witness of some sort, she did have her share of secrets that she'd rather keep undiscovered.

Fern flipped a yellow card and looked up at Camille, a sly smile on her face. "So, Dr. Tamerlane, have you ever lost a patient?"

Camille's heart seized. Fern had done her homework, she had to give her that. No one knew about Wingo, or at least Camille thought no one knew. He wasn't really her patient. Not on paper anyway. How could she answer the question?

That was key. Play dumb? Pretend that Wingo never existed? Or was it better to answer in a vague, offhand way? *No. Don't acknowledge, don't evade. Just don't answer.*

"I'm afraid that confidentiality prevents me from answering any questions pertaining to the work I do," Camille said, feeling her lips tremble. Would Fern notice? Would the people who were watching notice?

"So you refuse to speak?" Fern asked.

"That's right," Camille said, pushing professional confidence into her voice. "I will not answer any questions regarding my practice."

"Then Shoot it is," Fern said, picking up the gun and offering it to Camille.

Camille stared down at the weapon and found that she couldn't lift her hands. How could something so relatively small look so ominous, so heavy. *There are no bullets*, she reminded herself. *The chamber is empty.*

"Take the gun, Camille," Fern urged softly.

Camille reached for the revolver. It was even heavier than she thought it would be. A cold, dull weight in her hands. She looked to Fern for help. What was she supposed to do next?

"Just put the barrel to your head and pull the trigger," Fern said. Despite the confident set of Fern's jaw, Camille could see in Fern's troubled eyes that this didn't set well with her either, but still she pressed. "Don't worry. It's not loaded. Remember, this is just a game."

"This is sick," Samuel said, pushing his chair away from the table. "You don't have to do this, Camille. We can all just refuse. What is she going to do then? Do we all lose?"

The truth was, Camille had lost patients. All doctors did. Just maybe not in the way she lost Travis Wingo. A bullet for a bullet.

"No," Camille said resolutely. "It's okay, I'll do it." Best to get it over with. She lifted the gun and found that she needed both hands to support its heft. With quaking hands, she guided the barrel to her temple, the steel burning cold against her skin.

"Jesus," she heard Maire breathe.

It's not loaded, Camille told herself. Her finger found the trigger. *It's not loaded.* Closing her eyes, Camille pulled the trigger.

THIRTY

THE CONFIDANTE

Then

Icy rain pecked at Dr. Tamerlane's bedroom window. She looked up from the patient file she was reading to glance outside. The night sky held the threat of snow, unusual but not unheard of in San Francisco. The faint scent of smoke tickled her nose. It was hard to believe that the wildfires could still be burning in this weather, but Camille knew the smell could travel for miles and miles.

She set the file on the pillow next to her, knowing that bringing work home, even if her office was just down the stairs, was a bad idea. Camille had promised herself that she would take a few days off, but the holidays were difficult for many, especially for some of her clients. So here she was, thinking about Chelsea Weatherly. She had finally decided to leave her husband and remarkably, Doug appeared to have accepted her decision and was leaving Chelsea alone. However, he was still showing up wherever Camille happened to be. Popping up outside her office and home, the grocery store, the gym. He never said a word, just made sure Camille saw him. Doug Weatherly was letting her know that he blamed Camille for the death of his marriage.

And since the night the rock went through her office window, there had been several more acts of vandalism and more bouquets of flowers. Camille knew the flowers were coming from Wingo, but the property destruction was another matter. It wasn't like Wingo to be destructive. That fit more with Doug's more mercurial personality. Camille didn't know.

Camille reached for the cup of tea on her bedside table. It had grown cold while she was reading. Reluctantly, she slipped from her warm bed and moved through the dark hallway, mug in hand, to the top of the steps that led downstairs to her kitchen. The smell of smoke was stronger out here. Had she inadvertently left a window open? Earlier in the day it had been warmer, mild even, until the rain and sleet muscled its way in.

Camille's three-level Marina District home was too big for one person and much more than she could realistically afford, but she loved every nook and cranny. And once she had seen the office with its private entrance, it had to be hers.

Gripping her mug in one hand and the banister in the other, she carefully made her way down the creaky hardwood steps that led to the pitch-black front living room. At the bottom, she shivered. The temperature was markedly lower down here, cementing the thought that she left a window open. Maybe two. She felt around for the lamp on the antique rosewood table where she set her mail each day and fumbled beneath the shade and finally found the switch. When she turned the small knob, no light appeared. She tried again. Still nothing.

Had the power gone out? No, she could still see the faint glow from her bedroom light on the upstairs landing. She set her mug down on the table and moved blindly through the room toward another lamp. Again, she floundered for the switch, and no light appeared. Weird. Camille felt around for the bulb, thinking a quick twist would tighten the connection and instead found an empty hole. The light bulb was gone.

Confusion gave way to fear, and Camille froze in place. She

hadn't been the one to remove the bulb, so then who did? She had used that lamp just the night before. Geraldine hadn't been in the office since just before Christmas, so it couldn't have been her. What if the person was still in the house?

Her phone. She needed her phone. It was upstairs, on her bedside table, charging.

She could run upstairs and grab it, call 911. Or there was her office phone. It was a landline. It was closer and she could call for help. Or should she just get out of the house? Camille was frozen with indecision.

Camille heard a soft click. Then another and another. She couldn't place the sound, not until a small yellow flame appeared in the dark and was then extinguished. It appeared once again, then disappeared. A lighter. Someone was sitting on her sofa, flicking a lighter.

"I know you don't allow smoking in your office," a voice came from out of the dark.

It was Wingo, the man who was her client but wasn't her client. One of the several who paid cash so as to leave no paper trail. Mutually beneficial, she had always told herself. Cash meant no paper trail, but it also meant she didn't have to claim the income and didn't pay taxes. It worked great until Camille understood that Wingo didn't want help. Never wanted help. He had become obsessed with her while listening to her show and now wanted only Camille.

"Wingo," Camille said, once she caught her breath. "We talked about this. I asked you not to come here anymore." He was a confused, lonely man who had come to rely too heavily on Camille. "I told you, you need to find another therapist. I gave you some names."

Wingo flicked the lighter again. This time the flame stayed, illuminating his broad, pale face. "I know," he said. "But I really think we were getting somewhere. I was feeling better. I know I shouldn't have come inside, but the window was open."

"No, Wingo," Camille said, her voice impatient. "You shouldn't have come in. That's against the law. You need to be invited in."

"I know, I know. I'm sorry," he said. The flame went out. "Are you going to call the police?" he asked miserably.

"No, I'm not," Camille said, taking a seat next to him on the sofa. "But this has got to stop. You need to go home."

"What if I promise to call first and make an appointment? Will you start seeing me again?"

"No, Wingo, I can't. We talked about this." She could almost feel the despair coming off him in the dark. "Are you thinking about hurting yourself, Wingo?"

"No," he said. "I just want to talk."

"Good, I'm glad to hear that. But there are better ways to ask for help. Go home. Call one of the other therapists. They'll be able to help you." Wingo didn't answer. "Why did you remove the light bulbs?" she asked.

She felt him shrug next to her. "I didn't want you looking at me. I knew you'd be mad."

She sighed. "I'm not mad, Wingo, just concerned. You're not my client. I thought I made that clear." In the distance, came the wail of a siren. "Needing help is nothing to be ashamed about," Camille told him for what must have been the hundredth time. "We all need to talk to someone at one time or another."

The sirens were growing closer. She could see the flash of red lights just outside her living room windows. Her neighbors must have seen Wingo crawling through the window and called the police. *Dammit*, she thought. This only complicated things.

"I don't want to talk to anyone else. Only you. But I can pay you. I promise I can get the money. My dad said he would give it to me," Wingo said, his voice taking on a note of hope.

Alarm bells sounded in her head. She heard the sound of a car door being slammed. "No, Wingo," she said tightly. "We talked about this, remember? You can't tell anyone about our arrangement. I was doing it to help you. I could get in trouble for seeing you after hours, for not keeping an official file on our visits. You wanted it that way, remember?"

"Yeah, but you said I shouldn't feel bad about asking for help," Wingo said, getting to his feet.

"You need to call one of the other therapists that I referred you to, Wingo," Camille said. "They will be able to help you and that's what we all want. For you to feel better."

"Is that the police?" Wingo asked. "Why did you call the police?"

"No, it wasn't me, probably a neighbor," Camille said, trying to think fast. How was she going to explain Wingo's presence in her home this late at night? Wingo's father was a local judge. If he found out that Camille was seeing his son off the books, he could ruin her. There would be an investigation, an audit of her practice. She could lose her license or worse. What had happened to her? Camille wondered. Somewhere along the way she had traded her professionalism for self-preservation.

"We'll just tell them you were confused," Camille said. "That you came in here by accident. You just have to remember we don't know each other."

There was a rap on the front door. "Police," came a deep voice. "Everything okay in there, Dr. Tamerlane?"

"But I wasn't confused," Wingo whispered. "You have to tell them you're my doctor. Otherwise, they'll arrest me."

"Just a moment," Camille called out. Her voice shook with fear, but it wasn't Wingo that she was afraid of. It was of the world finding out she was unethical, a thief.

"I can't do that, Wingo," Camille said. "Your dad is a judge. He'll help you. Just say you're sorry. That you came in the house by mistake. That we don't know each other. I promise I won't press charges."

There was more pounding on the door. "Dr. Tamerlane," the officer repeated. "Please open the door. We got a call that someone broke into your house. We need to know that you're safe. Are you safe?"

Wingo flicked on the lighter so she could see his face. "Tell them you're safe," he whispered, his eyes begging. "Tell them you know me."

She couldn't. She couldn't do it. This was her career. Her life.

Panic filled his face. He dropped the lighter and it clattered to the floor and the room went black. "I'm not safe," Camille called out shrilly. "Please help. He's somewhere in the house. And I think he has a gun."

THIRTY-ONE

THE BEST FRIEND

Maire flinched as Camille pulled the trigger, expecting to hear a loud bang, expecting to see an explosion of blood and brain matter. But there was nothing but a whispered click.

With shaking hands, Camille returned the gun to the center of the table. She looked so small, so defeated. This game was cruel, sadistic, and it was becoming clearer that perhaps there wasn't really ten million dollars at the end of this twisted rainbow. But...if there was one iota, one sliver of a chance that the money was real, Maire wanted to be the one to grab it.

"Okay, then," Fern said, her voice shaking. "We have one strike against Camille. And remember, three strikes and you're out. Go ahead and give it a spin, Camille."

Camille didn't move. Just sat there, face and shoulders slack.

"Camille?" Fern repeated, but still Camille didn't reach for the gun. Instead, she gave a slight shake of her head.

"No, I'm done. I'm not playing," Camille said, her eyes shining with tears. "This is psychological torture. And I want no part of it."

This development was good for Maire. It meant there was one less barrier to the money, but she thought of the way that

Camille came to her rescue at the lake and felt a twinge of guilt. No, it was Ned who was the one who was supposed to go home next.

"Spin the gun, Camille," Maire found herself saying. "They want us to panic, to break us down. It makes for better television. Don't quit."

"What the hell?" Ned scoffed. "Don't encourage her. If she wants to quit, let her quit."

"Shut up, Ned," Maire said, keeping her eyes on Camille. "It's okay," she said softly, wanting to reach across the table for Camille's hand. "Remember, it's just a game."

Camille held Maire's gaze. Tears brimmed in her eyes and Maire could see that Camille had secrets of her own. Secrets that she couldn't reveal. They had that in common at least.

Maire looked at Samuel. He had aged in the three days they had been at the villa. His eyes had taken on a haunted, hunted look and his skin was sallow and tight in the candlelight. After two decades of keeping their secret, if the right question was asked, he might be the one to break. She willed him to look at her, but he was transfixed on the gun.

Finally, Camille reached for the pistol and gave it a half-hearted spin. One rotation, two, three, and on the fourth, it came to a wobbly stop in front of Ned again.

"No fucking way," Ned said, in disbelief. "Is there a magnet under there?" He bent down to look beneath the table and when he popped back up, he rolled his eyes. *He still hasn't gotten it yet*, Maire thought. He still didn't realize that someone was coming for them. For him. "Hit me," Ned said, slapping the tabletop as if he were at a blackjack table in Vegas.

Fern reached for the top card on Ned's deck, but he reached out and laid his hand atop hers. A spasm of revulsion spread across Fern's face and Maire could feel the anger radiate off her as she jerked her hand away. Camille was right. This game was personal, at least to Fern. But not to Maire. She was positive that she had never met Fern before walking onto the estate the other day. Revenge by reality show? It was too ludicrous to believe.

"Can I pick from the deck?" Ned asked. "Just to mix things up?"

"Fine," Fern said, rigidly. "But no peeking."

Ned made a show of fanning the remaining cards in his deck across the table, then turning his head away, eyes closed, as he chose a card. He held it up in triumph and handed it to Fern with a flourish.

Fern took the card gingerly from Ned's hands. She wobbled in her seat and, for a moment, Maire thought she might slip from her chair. Using one hand, Fern steadied herself and began reading.

"Have you ever been…" Fern began. "Have you ever been…" she tried again but faltered.

"Spit it out," Ned said. In some twisted way, he was enjoying this. Ned was a powerful man who was probably used to not having to be accountable for the way he treated people. Hadn't he shown that over and over during the competition? He had no problem trying to knock Maire from the climbing wall, cutting her rope, or letting her drown in the lake.

"Have you ever been accused of sexual misconduct in the workplace?" Fern asked, her voice cracking.

"No," Ned said, staring back at Fern defiantly. "My spin." He moved to give the gun a turn, but this time Fern held her hand up to stop him.

"Wait. That was only part of the question. There's more to it," Fern said. She paused to take a sip of her wine. When she spoke again, her voice was stronger, steadier. "Have you ever held a subordinate against a wall…"

"No," Ned said.

"And have you ever taken a letter opener…"

Ned's eyes squinted in suspicion. "No. No I haven't." But

Maire could see that the words struck a chord with him. "This is getting ridiculous," he said, looking at the others for support.

No one met his gaze. Samuel rubbed his hand across his scalp. Camille couldn't take her eyes away from Fern's face. Maire watched, a shroud of dread settling over her.

Fern forged on as if in a trance. "And ran that letter opener along her thigh, drawing blood...and using that letter opener to cut a subordinate's underwear from her body..."

"No!" Ned shouted, his face reddening. "You better shut your mouth right now. This is defamation. I'll fucking sue you." He slammed his fist against the table, sending ripples through the wine in their glasses.

But Fern raised her voice to match Ned's. "And using that letter opener, cut the subordinate's underwear from her body, even though she was crying, begging you to stop?"

Maire wasn't sure she had heard Fern correctly. A letter opener? She felt sick.

"No, I did not," Ned said, folding his arms across his chest. "That never happened."

"This needs to stop," Maire heard Camille whisper.

Fern leaned forward in her seat, her eyes pinned to Ned. "Are you sure? Is that your final answer?"

The room went quiet. The only sound was the desperate quickening of breath.

"What are you doing?" Samuel asked, finally breaking the silence and getting to his feet. "This isn't funny."

Samuel was right. Camille was right. This had gone too far. "Fern, stop it, please," Maire begged.

Fern ignored them all. "Ned? Speak or Shoot? The choice is yours."

Ned lifted his chin, defiance flashing in his eyes, as he calmly reached for the revolver and pointed it at Fern. Everyone gasped.

"That's not funny," Maire said. "Put it down."

"Don't worry, it's not loaded, right, Fern?" Ned asked. "It's just a game."

Fern crossed her arms over her chest. "Speak or Shoot?" she asked again. A dare.

"I choose Shoot," Ned said, getting to his feet and pressing the barrel to his temple. "Maybe here," he said, with a twisted smile. "Or how about here?" He slid the gun down the side of his face and beneath his chin.

"Stop!" Maire cried. "Just stop!"

"But if I had my way," he said, pointing it once again toward Fern, "I'd choose here." He pulled the trigger and Maire expected the soft click of an empty chamber. Instead, the gun exploded, and a bullet ripped past her ear and a hailstorm of glass rained down. The gun cracked again and again. Eyes squeezed tightly shut, Maire dropped to the floor, arms covering her head, ears ringing. She felt the vibration of bodies landing next to her and warm liquid seeping into the fabric of her clothes.

Had she been shot? She couldn't tell. Every nerve ending was on fire and her heart was beating so hard it threatened to burst from her chest. Maire dared to open her eyes and found herself lying in a puddle of red. She felt the scream slide raggedly from her throat but couldn't hear it, couldn't hear anything over the ringing in her ears.

She turned her head to find Samuel lying next to her on the cold tile floor, his eyes closed, blood oozing from a gash at his temple. She reached out to touch his face. It was here. The day had come. They were finally going to pay for what they had done, just like she knew they would one day.

THIRTY-TWO

THE ASSISTANT

Fern cowered on the floor, barely registering the broken glass, the shattered wine bottles, the smell of gunpowder in the air. The gun was loaded. How was the gun loaded? She had checked it herself just before the competition began four days ago.

By the terror on Ned's face, he was just as shocked as she was. His mouth was moving frantically, but the gunshot blasts had left her ears ringing. She couldn't decipher what he was saying. Ned threw the revolver to the floor and fell to his knees.

Fern was vaguely aware of the others also dropping to the floor. Had they been shot? Why couldn't she move? Her limbs were numb, heavy. Had a bullet hit her spine? She rubbed her legs, willing the feeling to return in them. No bullet wounds.

Ned was still on his knees, his face contorted in anguish. Fern didn't care. She hated him, hated him for what he had done to her, hated the scars that he left behind.

She needed to see if a bullet had struck one of the others and call for an ambulance. But she couldn't seem to stand up and she was so cold, she couldn't stop shivering. She must be in shock.

Fern watched as Camille pushed herself up from the floor and crawled over to Maire and Samuel, helping them both sit up, her hands running over their bodies as she checked for bullet wounds. Camille pressed a white linen napkin to a cut at Samuel's temple. They were sitting in a puddle of red wine that at first glance Fern thought was blood. She should go get help, but she couldn't move.

Who loaded the gun? Cat? One of the dozens of crew members and contractors who had been in and out of the estate? But why? It made no sense.

"Fern," came a distorted voice. "Fern." Camille's face floated into her line of vision. "Are you okay? Are you hit?"

"I'm fine," Fern said, the tingling feeling leaching from her limbs. "Is Samuel okay?"

"No one was shot. But you're bleeding." Camille nodded toward Fern's arms. Fern looked down to find her arms covered in small cuts. The broken glass. She must have landed on it when she dived for cover. Small bits were embedded beneath her skin. She pulled a jagged fragment from her palm and tossed it aside. She would need tweezers to get the rest out.

"What the fuck was that?" Ned snarled. "Why the fuck would you give us a loaded gun?"

Fern jumped at the venom in his voice. "I didn't. I swear I didn't know," Fern said. "I don't know what's happening."

"Yeah, right," Ned said, getting to his feet and shoving a chair aside so that it clattered against a wall. Fern shifted, keeping the table between them. "I could have killed someone!"

"I'm not up to anything. I swear," Fern cried. "Why would I give you a loaded gun? You could have killed me. You almost killed *me*."

"We were supposed to point the gun at ourselves," Samuel said, accusingly. "It was a miracle that Ned didn't shoot himself. Why are you doing this? Why are we here?"

Oh, God. The cameras. This entire fiasco was being streamed live to millions of phones, TVs, tablets, and computers. The viewers must have seen the gun go off. She swiveled her head in search of the cameras. The one placed among the wine bottles was now somewhere among the shattered glass. The one above their heads was shot clean away. It looked as if half of the veranda was destroyed.

Fern felt her cell phone vibrating, an incessant buzz that itched against her hip. Cat. But no, Cat was still in the cellar. It was over now, her chance to show Cat that she could host, produce, manage a hit show. It wouldn't matter that millions of people watched, that advertisers were clamoring to place their products with *One Lucky Winner*. A shooting on set would be the death knell for the show. For Fern.

"This isn't a game," Ned said. "Not anymore. Nothing is worth this amount of money. Nothing. I'm done. I don't care, I'm finished." He turned and stormed back into the house.

Fern's phone continued to vibrate. In frustration, she pulled it from her pocket. A dozen missed calls and texts from Alfonso. Of course, he was too much of a coward to come out to the veranda himself to see what was happening. She had to think fast.

We're fine, she typed. Prop malfunction. Are the cameras still on?

Alfonso immediately responded, No, we shut them down. Social media is freaking out. You have to let them know. When do you want us to flip the cameras back on?

She couldn't concentrate, couldn't think. Camille, Maire, and Samuel were staring at her accusingly. Ned was nowhere to be found. Thank God everyone was okay, but everything Fern had worked for was destroyed. Ruined. She would never work again. She would be sued, arrested. She needed to get out of here, get in her car and drive. She had fucked everything up. The game was over, wasn't it?

Another text appeared. What do you want us to do? She looked at her watch. How long would it take for her to figure things out? One hour—that's all she needed.

Go live in 60 minutes, she texted and Alfonso sent a thumbs-up emoji.

"Are you going to tell us what's going on?" Camille asked, her face hot with anger.

"I honestly have no idea," Fern said, pressing the pads of her fingers to her eyelids.

"How did you not know the gun was loaded?" Maire asked, as she dabbed a napkin against Samuel's cut. "This game has been fucked-up since the start."

"I'm out," Samuel said, peeling the cloth away from his head. The gash was long but not deep and had finally stopped bleeding. "It's not worth getting killed. I quit." He stalked from the patio and into the house with Maire at his heels. At the last minute, Maire stopped and turned.

"Whatever you think you know, you're wrong. There's no proof. Nothing. We've led good lives. We're good people. At least Samuel and I are." Maire pointed a finger at Fern, tears streaming down her face. "And for what? Ratings? You're not doing this just to us, to me. You're doing this to my daughters."

Fern was covered with broken glass and wine, her head ached. She rubbed her forehead, wishing they would all just go away. She needed to think. But Maire and Camille just stood there, waiting for her to speak.

"Did you really think I wouldn't recognize you?" Camille asked. "That I wouldn't finally put two and two together? I don't care what these people have done. I want no part of your revenge plot."

"Revenge?" Fern repeated, getting unsteadily to her feet.

"You're just going to stand there and deny walking into my office nine months ago and giving me some bullshit story about your name being Nan?"

Fern held up her hands. "I have no idea what you are talking about," she said, trying to sidestep Camille and go back inside the house, but Camille blocked her path. Fern needed to get the hell out of here and to the airport.

"Come on, Fernanda. I know it was you behind the sunglasses," Camille said in exasperation. "Same hair, same voice, same mannerisms, same shoes." She looked down at Fern's white Converse. "You came into my office and rambled on and on about terrible people and how they needed to pay for their crimes. I know you're Nan."

"Stop it!" Fern cried. "I never, ever came to your office. I've never met any of you before." Fern faltered. She was lying—could they tell? She had met Ned before. But he hadn't even recognized her, had he? He had no idea who she was. Was she that insignificant, that forgettable?

Camille grabbed Fern's arm, flipping it over so that the inside of her wrist was exposed. Fern tried to pull away, but Camille held tight. "Where's it at? Where's your tattoo?" Camille rubbed roughly at Fern's skin, trying to wipe away the makeup that hid the ink.

"Let go," Fern said, pushing against Camille with her free hand. Camille dropped her arm but stood her ground. Fern needed to calm everyone down and somehow get through the next hour. "I have no idea what you are talking about. I haven't met any of you before the other day. I don't know why the gun was loaded." She bent down and retrieved the revolver from where Ned had dropped it. Fern remembered hearing three shots. Were there more bullets in the chamber?

Maire held out her hand. "Let me check," she said. Fern hesitated, not wanting to relinquish the gun to someone who was so angry. "Give me the gun, Fern," Maire said. "I'll make sure it's not loaded. We don't want it to go off again."

Fern allowed Maire to take the gun and watched as she opened the chamber, looked inside. "It's empty," Maire said, setting the revolver on the table.

"Good," Fern said. "Now, if you'll excuse me, I have to send out a press release letting everyone know that a prop malfunctioned, and that everyone is okay."

Maire and Camille exchanged looks. "Is there even ten million dollars?" Camille asked. "Is any of this real? And while you're at it, why don't you tell us who your boss is?"

Fern gave a sharp laugh. "Of course it is. Look around you. Look at this estate. Look at the obstacle course, the hedge maze. Does it look fake to you? It's real, every bit of it. Look! Look at what people are saying about the show." Fern began reading from her phone.

"This is the real deal, best show I've ever seen, I can't get enough. Amazing! Can't wait to see who wins." Fern looked up, trying to force an air of confidence into her voice. "We are up to more than twenty million viewers now and it's growing. It's up to you, but the last person standing wins the ten million dollars. We'll meet in the library in one hour. Stay, go, I don't care. The cameras go back on in one hour. With or without you." With that, Fern pushed past Camille and Maire and entered the house.

Heart pounding, she rushed past Ned, who was sitting on the floor in the corridor with his back against the wall and his face in his hands. She couldn't worry about him now. Let him wallow in the knowledge that he could have killed someone. Let him suffer. By the time they figured out she'd left, she'd be long gone.

THIRTY-THREE

THE CONFIDANTE

The Vault

"I don't even know what to say. The fact that I'm sitting in this room talking to millions of people after nearly being shot should say enough. Yes, everyone is okay. No one was seriously hurt, but having an unsecured, loaded weapon on the set should have never happened. Never. Was it an accident? I hope so. Nevertheless, this is a cruel game. It's twisted, and sick, and dangerous. I don't know if we'll ever find out who is really behind the show, but whoever it is, brava, you did it. You managed to bring your own Roman Colosseum to life and we're just your unwitting gladiators, turning on each other for personal private enjoyment.

"And everyone out there watching right now, those of you sitting at home reveling in every second of the drama unfolding in front of you, don't forget this is real. We are real people, and someone could have died tonight. Someone could still die.

"So, what happens next? I don't know and honestly, I don't really care. If I win the money, great. I'll use it to support mental health and wellness for the disadvantaged. If I don't win, fine. I just want it all to be over.

"That's it. I have nothing else to say. I'm done."

★ ★ ★

BlahBlahBlah1000—Wow, dramatic much?

BlackLicoriceBaby—Dramatic? She was nearly SHOT! I can't believe the show hasn't been shut down yet.

BourbonBaublesandBirthdayCake—I have no sympathy. They all signed up for this. It's ten million dollars! What did they expect? If she wants to go home, I say we send her ass home.

PickleBallQueen65—I love Dr. Camille. Her podcast is amazing. She's smart, funny, and she really cares about people. All you haters need to go listen to her show right now. You'll change your mind.

EasyBreezyLeezie—Anyone notice how all these people say "a portion" of the winnings will go to their cause? That could mean ten bucks for mental health and $9,999,990 for the doctor's pockets for all we know. The only person who really told us exactly what the money is going toward is the Best Friend—for her daughter's care. I hope she wins—she seems the most genuine, the most real out of all of them.

BlackLicoriceBaby—cynical much?

SanFranTreat—She's full of shit. I know who this lady is. She acts like she is this caring doctor, but there is much more to her. My friend was a patient of hers (though she'll deny it), and she told me there was a client who was shot by the police at her office. The Confidante accused him of having a gun on him. He did NOT have a weapon—it was a tiny little pocketknife, and it was in his pocket when he was shot. Not dangerous, he was harmless and wouldn't hurt a fly—he was bringing her flowers for fuck's sake.

DogMom4—I heard about that on the news a while back. I'm sorry, but I don't see her as the villain here. He broke into her house, he had a weapon. It was sad but the police were only protecting her.

SanFranTreat—There is much more to this story, but no one will listen. #justiceforwingo

THIRTY-FOUR

THE CONFIDANTE

"Do you believe me now?" Camille asked, coming into the bedroom after her time in The Vault. She had still been picking pieces of glass from her hair when some intern whisked her away to talk about her feelings.

"I don't want to believe it," Maire said softly from her spot by the window. "Why us? I've never met Fern before. I don't understand why she's doing this."

"Does it matter?" Samuel snapped, zipping up his carry-on bag. "I just want to get my phone and get out of here."

"You know it's not going to end when we leave the estate," Camille said, dropping the shards of glass into a waste basket. "Fern thinks she has dirt on us. She has to have files somewhere."

"But what about the money?" Maire asked, still looking out the window. Camille came to her side. Maybe Maire was ready to listen to her.

"I really needed that money," Maire said, and Camille could see the sadness in her eyes, the desperation.

"Jesus, Maire," Samuel said. "Can't you see this is bigger than ten million dollars? Fern is after us. At the very least, she wants us ruined. She's been trying to kill us or get us to kill each other since we got here. So no, Maire, I hate to tell you this, I don't think you're getting any money."

Maire rounded on Samuel. "You think I wanted to win for myself? My daughter is sick and if she doesn't get the best treatment, the best doctors, she could die." Maire was crying now, and Camille felt the burn of shame rising on her cheeks.

Camille had wanted the money for purely selfish reasons—to pay for cars, homes, and to cover her out-of-control spending, to help bury any hint of professional impropriety. But here was a woman who only wanted one thing—to save her daughter.

"There are resources for that," Camille said. "Organizations. I'll help you sort through it when we get out of here."

"Why would you do that?" Maire asked. "You think we're awful people. You said it yourself."

"We all have our secrets," Camille said. "We saw the clues." When Maire and Samuel didn't say anything, she threw her hands up in frustration. "How many times do I have to tell you I don't care what you did? It doesn't matter to me. Let's just lay it all on the line, go through all the clues. If it has something to do with you, don't say anything, I don't care. But if you found a clue that relates to me, I want to know." They wouldn't meet her gaze. Camille shook her head. "Fine, I'll go. The Super Clue I won after the obstacle course was a death certificate with the name and location crossed out." When Maire's head snapped up, Camille hesitated. How much should she share with these two, knowing they were being so closemouthed about their own clues?

"Did you get any other information from the certificate?" Samuel asked.

"Just that the deceased was male and thirty-two years old," Camille said.

Maire and Samuel exchanged a look. *Interesting*, Camille thought.

"Maire, during the shooting game, Fern asked you where you went to college. That had to mean something, am I right?" Camille looked for some sort of confirmation but got none.

"So, because of the questions Fern was asking Ned, he's a predator," Samuel said. It wasn't a question. They knew it was true. "When I won the lake challenge my Super Clue was a letter opener," he finally offered. "It made no sense until Fern asked Ned about it."

"Then there are the wine bottles with the odd labels," Camille said, lifting Ned's now-empty bottle from the trash can. "Ned's says *Degenerare*. When we first saw it, we all thought degenerate, right? That fits. Mine says *Sfasciafamiglie*," Camille said, shaking her head. "I don't know what that means."

Samuel walked over to the bureau next to the senator's vacated bed. "And the senator's says *Imbroglione*. He had an affair and a secret son. I don't know, maybe adulterer? Cheater?"

"That makes sense," Camille agreed. "And yours?"

"*Traditore,*" Samuel said, going to his suitcase and pulling out the bottle.

"It sounds like traitor to me," Camille said. "Does that make any sense to you?"

"It makes zero sense," Samuel said with finality. "How about you, Maire?"

Maire's forehead furrowed. "*Uccisore,*" she said impatiently. "But who cares? They're just wine bottles. It doesn't prove anything."

"Listen," Camille said. "I don't think people are all good or all bad. Whatever you've done, I don't want to know what it is, just like you don't want to know about me. It's better that way. What we need to do right now is figure out how to convince Fern not to take this any further."

"And how do you propose we do that?" Samuel asked, sitting at the edge of his bed. "She's in too deep. Think about it—everything she's put into this, all the money and resources. What's she going to tell all the viewers? Sorry?"

A terrible or maybe wonderful thought came to Camille. "What if there is no show?"

"What do you mean?" Maire asked, dropping on the bed next to Samuel.

"I mean what if there really is no show? What if it was just some weird piece of her revenge plan?"

Maire and Samuel sat in stunned silence.

"But the comments on the show," Maire said weakly. "Fern read some of them to us. She said it was a hit, that millions of people were watching."

Samuel rubbed his eyes and shook his head. "So all this time we've been playing for an audience of one?"

Camille shrugged. "Maybe. I don't know. Nothing about this makes any sense. But what I do know is if we want our personal business quiet, we need to get our hands on Fern's computer."

"Yeah, and how are we going to do that? Corner Fern and hold her captive until she hands it over?" Samuel asked. "I don't particularly want to add kidnapping to my list of chargeable crimes."

Camille caught the look Maire sent Samuel—soft, almost wistful. Yes, those two definitely had a history. "I don't think it will have to come to that," Camille said. "The cameras are down, right?"

"If they were actually recording, yes, they are," Samuel said. "Fern said for about an hour. We have about—" he checked his watch "—another thirty minutes."

Camille held up a thin, rectangular piece of plastic. It was Fern's key card with her photo and full name printed across it. Fernanda Espa. "I think this will take us to where we need to go," Camille said.

THIRTY-FIVE

THE ASSISTANT

Once in her bedroom, Fern locked the door behind her and looked around frantically, not sure what to do first. She needed to clean her cuts, change from her blood-splattered clothes, and send out that press release explaining that the show was continuing. That had to come first. She opened Cat's phone and typed a cursory update: An unfortunate mishap occurred on the set of *One Lucky Winner* this evening. Blanks from a prop gun went off, startling everyone and causing one of the contestants to accidentally bump into a display of Bella Luce wine, sending bottles crashing to the ground. We look forward to continuing the game. Live coverage will resume shortly.

Fern reread the message. It wasn't perfect but it would have to do. She hit Send.

As for Cat, once she was well away from the house, she would call someone to unlock the wine cellar. If Cat went to the police and she was detained, she would feign ignorance. She would claim she had no idea that Cat accidentally got stuck in the cellar, that she only noticed it once she was at the airport and checked all the security cameras from her phone. Cat was notorious for hiding away in her office for long hours and it was no secret that she wanted to stay behind the scenes during the production of *One Lucky Winner*, that she didn't want her involvement to be a distraction from the show.

Then Fern needed to leave, to disappear.

She would get in her car and head straight to the airport. Portugal sounded nice.

Fern washed bits of dried blood from her skin from where the shattered glass left tiny cuts. She changed and threw some clothes in her suitcase. It was time to go. She looked down at her bed where she had tossed Cat's phone.

Money. She needed money. She picked up the phone and toggled to Cat's bank app. How much to transfer? Too much and Cat would notice. Too little and she'd only get as far as Chicago. She typed in $12,000. It wasn't enough and was too much all at once. She couldn't do it. It was stealing and Fern may be a lot of things, but she wasn't a thief.

Then there was Cat's phone. She couldn't leave it in her room, and she couldn't take it with her. She'd have to drop it off somewhere it wouldn't be easily found. Beneath a sofa, behind a shelf, maybe.

She slowly opened her bedroom door and peeked up and down the corridor. It was empty. Pulling her suitcase behind her, Fern headed toward the back staircase, the scent of dead flowers in the air. In the hecticness of the game she had neglected to put fresh flowers in the vases. Both phones suddenly started vibrating. Probably Alfonso again.

Fern opened the narrow door that led to the back staircase. She flipped the light switch and paused atop the iron spiral staircase that would take her downward in a tight corkscrew. Here. This is where she would leave Cat's phone. It would take her forever to find it. Fern shut down the phone and used her shirt to wipe any prints, then set it on the top step.

Her head pounded. It was all so surreal. She carefully navigated the winding staircase, her feet echoing on the iron steps, certain that everyone in the house could hear. At the bottom, a door opened to the laundry room that was adjacent to the kitchen. She gathered a breath. *Think*, Fern told herself. Did she have everything she needed? She would never be coming back here again. Ever.

Her passport was back at her apartment. She would have to make a stop there and grab a few other items as well—the necklace that once belonged to her mother, a few photos. She didn't have much. Then she thought of Cat's laptop sitting on her desk in the office. That laptop held Cat's entire life. Her emails, her files, her secrets. And maybe it would hold the answers to *One Lucky Winner* and how it had gone entirely off the rails. Fern wanted that laptop.

Fern left her suitcase by the back door and quietly made her way through the kitchen to the corridor. She searched for any evidence that Alfonso had already turned the cameras back on but found none. The house was hushed and dark, the remaining crew gathered on the veranda, cleaning up the mess. She had just about twenty minutes until they were back online. All she needed to do was get to Cat's office, grab the laptop, get in her car, and then be on her way.

Where were the others? Back in their rooms? Lurking around a corner? Maybe they had left already, scaling the wall and flagging down rides. She couldn't blame them. Moonlight shone through the windows, casting distorted shadows across the floor as she crept slowly down the hallway. She could hear the drip, drip, drip of water coming from somewhere.

Just turn around, she told herself. *Go back to the kitchen, go out the back door, and don't look back.* But she wanted that laptop. If anything, it would be insurance. If Cat threatened to have her arrested, Fern could pull up a few documents, and reveal that she had found a few of Cat's own dirty little secrets that were worth staying buried.

Just a little farther to go. Up ahead was a corridor of closed doors, except for one. It was Cat's husband's old office. The door was ajar. Hadn't she locked it? She must have forgotten. Another task she had neglected. At least there was nothing of real value in there. She patted her pocket. She didn't have the old skeleton key with her. With a gentle push, she shut the heavy door.

Get it over with, Fern told herself. *You're just wasting precious seconds.* She forced herself to move down the hallway, ignoring the feeling that someone was in the shadows watching, waiting.

Holding her breath, she hurried around the final corner until she was standing in front of Cat's office door. She shoved her hand into her pocket, fumbling around for her key card. It wasn't there. Fern slid her bag from her shoulder and began digging through the contents. Her phone was still inside, her wallet that held some cash and some credit cards, ChapStick, some loose change, but no key card. Panic filled Fern's body. She must have dropped it. She needed that key. The laptop and its contents were her only leverage against Cat.

Fern stopped worrying about making noise and rushed down the corridor, her footsteps a desperate beat against the floor. She stopped short when she once again came to the old office. The door was open again. She had closed it. She was sure she had.

Her hand went to the knob to close the door, but she couldn't help peeking inside. The room was pitch-black. Unable to stand the dark any longer, Fern pulled out her phone and enabled the flashlight. She swept the light across the room. Everything looked the same as it did the last time she was in here—a mess of sawdust, old paint cans, and abandoned tools. Only one thing was out of place—a large black iron grate that covered a floor vent had been removed and was leaning against a wall.

Strange, Fern thought, wondering where the vent led to. Suddenly, the plastic sheeting that hung from the ceiling rustled and a figure stepped into view. Fear, thick and oily, slid through her. She turned to run but a hand closed around her wrist and pulled her more deeply into the room.

Her phone tumbled across the floor, landing face up and extinguishing the beam of light. Fern opened her mouth to scream, but a hand clapped across her lips, muffling the cry. She couldn't see who grabbed her but knew who it was. His smell, his touch would be ones she would never forget. Ned Bennett. He'd always wanted to get her alone. And this time, Cat was nowhere around to save her.

THIRTY-SIX

THE BEST FRIEND

"You stole Fern's ID?" Maire asked, eyeing the hard plastic card printed with Fern's full name and photo that Camille held tightly. Fernanda Espa. Camille was right about Fern's name. Could Fern really be this Nan she told them about?

"Which door does it open?" Maire asked, reaching for the card.

Camille pulled her hand away before Maire could grab the key. "I saw Fern going in and out of a few locked rooms. I figure one of them is her bedroom and the other might be an office. Her files or laptop have to be in one of them. If we get them, maybe we can reason with her."

Maire bit her lip, considering. It was risky, dangerous. What if they were caught? What if they were wrong and blew any chance at getting the money?

"No," Samuel said firmly. "No. I draw the line at breaking and entering. We can try talking to Fern or simply just leave, but I'm not breaking the law."

Camille laughed, but there was no humor in it. "Really, Samuel? After nearly getting your head shot off, you're worried about stealing a laptop?"

"It's not just that," Samuel said, his voice rough with emotion. "If I could go back and change things, I would. I would have never have... We would never have..."

"Samuel," Maire said sharply, and he stopped speaking. Camille was staring at them, her eyes hungry for more details.

A terrible thought came to her. Maybe Camille was in on it. Maybe this was all one big double cross. Camille always seemed to be two steps ahead of everyone else, and she was the one who kept planting the seeds of doubt in their minds. She needed to get Samuel alone and make sure he stuck to their story.

"Like I said," Camille said, holding up her hands. "I don't want to know any details. Let's just go look for the laptop and files and go from there. We have to hurry."

"Why don't you two go look for the laptop and I'll look for Fern," Samuel said. "Maybe I can talk some sense into her. She could go to prison for extortion."

"No, we all stay together," Maire interjected. She needed to keep Samuel close, if only to make sure he kept his mouth shut. They needed to be a united front. "And we should find Ned," Maire added. "God knows what he's up to."

"No," Camille said. "I say we forget about him. He's poison. You saw the questions Fern was asking him about sexual assault and NDAs. We already know he's dangerous. Let's focus on the laptop for now."

Maire had to admit that Camille was right. It was probably better to have Ned off on his own somewhere right now. He was too unpredictable, too volatile. She glanced at Samuel. He simply nodded and the three of them moved into the hallway. They all looked around in search of the red lights of the cameras. They weren't being filmed—for now.

Camille led the way down the dark corridor and stopped in front of a door with a key card entry. "I've seen Fern go in and out of here. I think it's her room," she whispered. She tapped the card against the entry panel but the indicator light glowed red. The key didn't work.

"Where now?" Maire asked, her heart thudding. She was only supposed to come here, play this stupid game, win as many challenges as she could, and go home with enough money to pay Dani's medical bills. Seeing Samuel... She hadn't expected that. Hadn't expected the stir of old emotions. He wasn't a bad man, just like she wasn't a bad woman. They had just made some really bad decisions that haunted them through the years. Old ghosts looking for retribution.

"Downstairs," Camille said softly. "There's another room I saw Fern going in and out of. Let's try that."

The group moved swiftly but quietly down the marble steps, pausing when they heard the murmur of voices. Maire was sure they would be caught. Then what? Would the whole world learn what she and Samuel had done? She thought of Keely and Dani. They would never look at her the same way again. So what if they lost the house? They could find somewhere else to live. Shar would gladly open her home to them. She should have stayed home and found another way to get the money.

Maire vowed to herself that if she got out of this mess, she would go back to Calico and find a different job, one with health benefits and a good retirement plan. She belonged home with her girls.

Camille slowed her steps. "It's that one," she said. "Keep an eye out for anyone coming and I'll go in and get the laptop."

Samuel rubbed a hand over his goatee and nodded. He had finally given up the pretense. He wanted that laptop as much as the rest of them. Camille waved the card in front of the entry panel and a green light popped on. "It worked," Camille said with relief. "If the laptop is in there, I'll grab it."

"Wait," Maire said, snagging Camille's sleeve. "Give me the card."

"Why?" Camille asked in confusion. "I'll be just a second."

"We don't know what you're going to do once you're in there. Give me the key," Maire said more firmly.

"Fine," Camille said, handing it over. "But I'll be right out." She opened the door and slipped inside the dark room.

"What do you think?" Samuel asked.

"What do I think?" Maire repeated angrily. "I think we've been screwed. But by who? There's no way Fern was behind all of this. Not by herself. She's barely holding it together as it is."

"Then who?" Samuel asked. "Why?"

Maire didn't know if she could trust Samuel, but what choice did she have? "It has to be someone the five of us all have in common. Someone who wants us to pay for what we've done."

"So someone who was at the lake that night," Samuel said. "But no one saw us. We were nowhere near there when he was found. We were so careful."

"No," Maire said. "We weren't. We weren't careful at all, and I think it might be too late. We're already dead."

"You think you know who it is," Samuel said. "Who?" he grabbed Maire roughly by the arm. "Come on, tell me."

"Think about it, Samuel. It can only be one person," Maire said sadly.

"No," Samuel said, shaking his head. "No way."

Maire opened her mouth to argue but a cry pierced the air.

"Fern," Maire said instead. "That has to be Fern."

THIRTY-SEVEN

THE BEST FRIEND

Then

Maire's feet slipped on the slick ice and she went down hard, ripping the knee of her jeans, but Samuel was right there and yanked her back to her feet. "Keep going," he huffed.

The man they had run off the road was coming after them. But how? He had died right in front of them, but somehow he had gotten to his feet and was coming after them with a pipe. She had been so stupid, so reckless dragging Samuel into the middle of the road and waiting for an unsuspecting car. She was trying to show off, trying to prove to Samuel that she knew how to have fun.

If they kept going, maybe they could outrun him and he'd give up. Maire clutched more tightly to Samuel's hand. She had lost her mittens along the way and the weight from Damon's flask was gone, but she didn't care. They needed to keep running. The stars above were quickly being overtaken by snow clouds, snuffing out the little light they had. She felt the ice below her feet creak and moan. Would it hold them? They were nearing the middle of the lake and the water beneath the ice had to be at least thirty feet deep and bitterly cold. They had to keep running and get to the other side and up to the bonfire where the others were. The cold air burned her lungs and her legs felt like concrete. Was the man still behind them?

"I can't," Maire gasped. "I can't." She slowed, half expecting the man to strike her in the back of the head with the pipe. She needed to try to reason with him, beg for forgiveness. "You go ahead," she told Samuel. "Keep going."

Samuel slowed right along with her. "I'm not leaving you," he said.

Maire dared a glance over her shoulder and nearly stumbled. The man was gaining on them. Samuel grasped her hand, urging her forward, but it was no use. He was going to catch them.

"I'm sorry," Maire said, coming to an abrupt stop and turning to face their pursuer. "We didn't mean it." Cold air whistled through Maire's chest as she bent forward, hands on her knees, trying to catch her breath, struggling to speak. "It was an accident."

In front of her the shadowy figure slowed to a jog and as he came closer Maire registered that something wasn't quite right. The man from the wrecked car was broad-chested. The one in front of her was taller, leaner, and wore a stocking cap.

It was Damon, breathing hard, eyes wide. "What the hell?" he gasped. Maire could smell the alcohol on his breath. "You thought no one would find out?"

"No," Samuel said, weakly. "It wasn't like that."

"I saw you," Damon said with disgust. His gaze flicked between Samuel and Maire. "You are so dead."

"It was an accident, Damon, we didn't mean for it to happen," Maire began. "We tried…"

"Accident?" Damon repeated in disbelief. "You call that an accident? Lina won't believe this. I'm going to tell."

Damon would go to the police; they would be arrested. Samuel would never get into law school; Maire would never get into art school. Their lives were ruined. But they had killed a man. They were going to get what they deserved.

"No, no, no," Samuel said in a rush, hands up in supplication. "Just wait. We can explain. We were just playing around. Things got out of hand and he crashed. We were going to get help, but it was too late. He was already dead."

Damon looked back and forth between Maire and Samuel, his forehead wrinkled in confusion. "Dead?" he repeated. "Who's dead?"

Maire's head was spinning. Damon hadn't seen the crash and what caused it? Hadn't seen the man stumble from the wreckage and collapse? Then what was he going on about and what had he seen?

"You're telling me there's a dead body back there?" Damon asked, turning to look back across the lake. "You fucking killed a man? I thought you were just screwing around on Lina."

But she could see the fear on Samuel's face, the realization that Damon hadn't seen anything and they had just told on themselves. They'd been caught.

"Shh," Samuel said, sharply. "Listen."

Maire cocked her ear, but all she could hear was the wind. A soft snow started to fall, drifting down in lazy circles.

Then Samuel's face shifted from fear to panic. "Hold still," Samuel said, grabbing her hand. "Don't move."

Damon was still prattling on. "How the mighty have fallen. Wait until everyone finds out you two killed a guy."

"Shut up," Maire cried and gave Damon a shove. He stumbled back a few steps, his arms windmilling. When he regained his balance, he still had that smug, hateful look on his face.

"Ouch, Maire," he said, rubbing his shoulder. "I think you can add assault to cheating and murder on your list of fuckups for tonight."

"Be quiet," Samuel ordered, his voice low, frightened. "Something is happening."

Then she heard it. A mournful moan beneath their feet. Spidery cracks shot out toward them and then Damon was gone, dropping into the lake with only the slightest of splashes. It was as if a trapdoor had opened. He just disappeared.

Maire looked down into the jagged black hole, hoping to see Damon's gloved hand reach up or the top of his burgundy Tanglefoot stocking cap, but there was nothing. He was just gone.

"Oh, my God," Maire whispered. "Do you see him? What do we do?"

"I don't know, I don't know," Samuel said, still clutching her hand.

A clawlike hand burst out of the water and clambered to grab on to the lip of the ice.

"Help me," Damon cried, his voice thick with cold as he went down again.

Maire looked at Samuel and her question hung heavily between them. No one would ever know about the crash or what they had done behind Lina's back. If Damon died, their secret would die with him.

Maire stared into the abyss until she couldn't stand it any longer. She couldn't do it. She plunged her arm into the black, watery hole, but Samuel pulled it back. She looked at him in surprise and disappointment. Samuel was willing to let another person die tonight. He wasn't the person she had hoped him to be.

"Wait," Samuel said, "he'll just pull you in. When I lie down, just grab my feet." When she opened her mouth to question him, Samuel stopped her.

"Just trust me, we need to distribute our weight," he said, lying on his stomach and grasping one of Damon's flailing arms. "I've got you," he told him. "Hold still. Maire, grab my feet, but if I go under, get to shore."

Maire moved behind Samuel, carefully lowering herself to the ice and wrapping her hands around his ankles, hooking her fingers into his bootlaces.

"Now pull!" he shouted. Maire yanked with all her might.

She had visions of Damon dragging them into the water, pulling them down to the rocky bottom. But to her surprise, the ice didn't break and Damon was somehow with them atop the ice, panting and shivering.

"We need to get to shore," Samuel said. Maire knew he was right. The lake could collapse beneath them at any second. "We need to crawl, spread out our body weight. He's going to need help."

They army-crawled slowly and methodically across the ice with Damon between the two of them, urging him forward. The snow began to fall harder, the wind growing in intensity. The cold penetrated Maire's jeans and her coat until her entire body was numb. They didn't speak. Each second felt like an eternity, but finally, they reached the bulrushes and collapsed.

"Thank you," Damon said, through chattering teeth. "You saved me. I could have died."

"Of course," Samuel said. "We would never have left you behind." Maire was too relieved, too cold to answer. Instead, she wrapped her arms around Damon's shoulders. They sat there for a moment, catching their breath.

"I won't tell," Damon said, through chattering teeth. "I won't say anything about what you did. I promise."

Maire and Samuel looked at one another. During the trek across the lake, Maire had resigned herself to the idea that she would lose everything. Her future was gone.

"About what?" Maire asked to be sure.

"About the man who died. That you're cheating on Lina," Damon said. His lips had taken on a bluish tinge. "That I saw you two together. I thought I was going to die. You could have let me die. I won't say anything about any of it. I promise."

"Thank you," Samuel said softly.

Maire couldn't find words big enough to tell Damon how grateful, how relieved she was.

"I can't feel my feet," Damon said tearfully.

In the distance, they heard voices. It was Figgy, Lina, and the twins running toward them. Maire struggled to her feet. "Hurry," she cried out. "He fell through the ice. We need to get him to the car and to the hospital."

Wes and Wade peeled off their coats and wrapped them around Damon's shoulders. With Figgy's help, they began carrying him toward the car.

"Are you okay?" Lina asked with concern. "What happened?"

"Damon fell through the ice but we're fine," Samuel assured her. Maire nodded in agreement but was unable to meet her eyes. "Go on ahead, help him. We're coming."

Lina bit her lip uncertainly. "You sure? You're not hurt?"

When Samuel and Maire both shook their heads, Lina gave them both a tight squeeze. "I don't know what I would have done if something happened to one of you." With that, Lina ran off toward the others.

"What do we do?" Maire asked when Lina was out of earshot, her teeth chattering.

"Nothing," Samuel said. "We never lay in the road, never saw the man crash into the tree."

"We never kissed," Maire added.

"Right," Samuel said after an excruciatingly long moment.

"Do you believe Damon? That he won't tell say anything?" Maire asked.

"I don't know," Samuel admitted. "But we saved his life, that's something."

"Yeah," Maire said. "That's something. But what if the police start asking questions? If they ask why we were gone so long, what will we say we were doing?"

"Walking. Talking. We got lost and we didn't see anything."

"We got lost," Maire agreed.

Samuel looked into her eyes, brushing the snowflakes from

her eyelashes. She slipped her hand into his for just one brief moment. They fit perfectly.

After this night, they would never speak, never see each other again. Maire would never feel his lips on her hers, never feel his skin against hers. She might never know what happened to Samuel, where he would go, what he'd become, and out of all the terrible, horrifying things that had happened tonight, that was the worst.

THIRTY-EIGHT

THE ASSISTANT

Fern tried to twist from Ned's grip and, with her free hand, felt around for something to use as a weapon. But she found nothing. It was too dark. She tried to scream but Ned clapped a hand over her mouth. "Shut up," he said through clenched teeth. "I'm not going to hurt you."

She didn't believe him. Why should she? Her abuser had her trapped in a dark room.

"I just want to talk to you away from the cameras," he said. "Don't scream and I'll let you go. Promise, okay?"

Fern wanted to scream, kick, and fight but what if no one heard her? Ned was an awful person, but she didn't think he would kill her, not with people around.

She nodded and Ned slid his hand from her mouth and down her chin, coming to a rest at the nape of her neck. Fern felt her stomach roil.

"I know you," Ned said, his breath hot against her ear. "You worked for me." It wasn't a question.

Fern nodded, still afraid to speak.

"I fired you. That's why you're doing this?"

Fern didn't respond. Anger bubbled in her chest. He didn't

remember who she was. To Ned Bennett, Fern was just one of many young women he assaulted.

"I think there may have been a misunderstanding between the two of us. In the past, I made some missteps—" he paused "—some mistakes. But I've changed. I swear I have. What do you want from me?" he asked, his voice begging, pleading. "What can I do to make it right?"

Fern nearly laughed. But she needed to focus on getting out of this room, getting away from Ned. Time was ticking away. The cameras were going to come on soon. She was running out of time.

"Say you're sorry," Fern finally said. She knew that it wouldn't be enough, would never be enough, but the more quickly she could get out of here, the better. "Apologize and leave. Then it will be over."

Ned let out a breath. "I'm sorry," he said. "I'm truly sorry. And I've really changed. I've gotten professional help. That's why I've been out of the limelight for so long. I've been working on getting better."

Fern wanted to call bullshit. He hadn't been working on himself, more likely he'd been dodging legal problems. She couldn't worry about that now. She just needed to get rid of him so she could leave.

"I'm sorry," he repeated, sounding more desperate than contrite.

"Okay," Fern said, though she wasn't moved by his emotion. "I'll get your phone and you can go."

"Thank you," Ned said with relief. "Thank you." Fern felt him step back and she took the opportunity to reach for the doorknob, open the door, and step out into the corridor. Now she could leave.

She still needed the key card to the office. That's where the phones and the laptop were. She looked toward the end of the hallway and saw Maire and Samuel standing in front of Cat's office. What were they doing? Then she saw it. Maire was holding the key card. Without waiting for Ned, Fern hurried down the corridor and reached to snatch the card from Maire's hand, but she pulled it away.

"We just want to get our phones and leave," Samuel said.

"You can't go in there," Fern said, vaguely aware that Ned was right behind her. "The locked rooms are off-limits." Maire and Samuel exchanged a look. "Where's Camille?" Fern asked, looking up and down the hallway. Then she realized Camille was already in Cat's office.

Fern wasn't worried about the laptop anymore, not for the moment anyway. It was the video monitors. What if Camille started pushing buttons and found a woman locked in the wine cellar? Cat would tell her that she was being held captive. Fern's life would be over.

Fern grabbed for the key again, this time wrenching it from Maire's hand. She waved the card over the sensor and pushed through the door. Her first sight was of Camille sitting in a chair across from Cat's marble desk. Fern's gaze shifted and that's when she saw her. Cat.

Cat was sitting behind her desk, her back straight and her hands steepled beneath her chin. She had never seen her boss in this office looking anything but perfect, but now she was downright disheveled, exhausted-looking, and angry.

She had escaped the wine cellar. Somehow Cat had gotten out.

Cat turned her sly smile on Fern. "Ah, Fern, there you are. I'm so glad you could join us."

THIRTY-NINE

THE CONFIDANTE

As shocked as Camille was at finding Cat James sitting behind the marble desk, it looked as if Fern was equally surprised.

"Cat," Fern began, "I'm so sorry. I didn't mean…" But Cat shut her up with a searing look.

"Don't speak," she snapped. "You didn't think I would figure out a way to get out of the cellar? Please," Cat sniffed. "You aren't smart enough to outwit me. You forgot about the ceiling vent. It took me a while to loosen the screws but once I did, I was able to climb out." Fern seemed to shrink beneath Cat's words and retreated to a corner of the room. Samuel, Maire, and Ned stood in the doorway, speechless.

Cat turned her attention back to Camille.

The last time Camille had seen Cat was when? Two years ago? They had been in Camille's office, sitting across from each other, much like this, but on that occasion, Cat's husband, Jack, was with them. And it was Camille who was in control, who had the power. She was their marriage counselor. Week after week, Camille had sat in sessions with Cat and watched the way she berated and humiliated the man. The way she took absolutely zero ownership in the state of her crumbling marriage.

Cat would go on tirade after tirade until Camille cut her off and turned her attention to Jack, Cat's husband. She told him to walk away, to get out. Camille told him that there was nothing healthy or redeemable about the relationship with his wife. *Run*, she told him. And Jack had. He had stood up from his chair and walked out of her office, away from Cat. Camille saw news of the divorce on X. *Good*, she thought. Cat James was toxic.

"*Sfasciafamiglie*," Cat said. "Home-wrecker."

The wine bottles. So that was what they were for. To label each contestant based on their crime.

"So, all this. The game, *One Lucky Winner*—" Camille nodded toward the bank of video screens on the wall "—was all some big charade to—what? Get back at me because you feel I betrayed you?"

"You destroyed my marriage. The minute that last session was over, Jack packed his bags and left. I never heard from him again, except through attorneys."

"Well, this is all well and good, Cat," Camille said, getting to her feet, "but I'm afraid I'm not your therapist any longer so I don't have to sit here and listen to this."

"Cat James?" Ned asked and Camille froze. Ned knew her too.

"Ned Bennett," Cat said smoothly. "*Degenerare*. Degenerate."

Ned looked at Cat in confusion. Then his eyes darted to Fern. "You two quit the same day. The two of you are in this together? You wanted to come for me after all these years?"

"*Please*," Cat said snidely. "There's no way Fern could have pulled this off. Until you showed up, she thought another contestant was going to compete. She had no idea what I was doing. You are a disgusting human being, Ned," Cat said. "You've been pulling this shit on women for years. You did it to me. And at the time, I thought there was nothing I could do about it, that I had no recourse. That sexual harassment and assault was just part of the job. But when I walked in on what you were doing to Fern…" Revulsion spread across Cat's face. "I'd had enough. I knew you weren't going to pay right then, but I thought someday someone would come forward. They never did, so I realized that it was me. I was the one who was supposed to come forward. And, Ned, today's that day."

"So you were behind Spin, Speak, Shoot. You loaded the gun?" Ned asked. "You had a bad day at work, what like ten years ago, and you set me up to shoot myself or someone else?" Ned shook his head. "Sounds reasonable," he said sarcastically.

Cat laughed. "Men always think they can do whatever they want and there are no consequences. The senator is a perfect example."

"What did he ever do to you?" Camille asked. Despite not being a fan of Crowley's politics, she didn't think he deserved to have his personal life splashed all over the news.

"What did the senator do to me?" Cat asked. "Well, let's see. You may not know this, but I got my start as a journalist in D.C. I worked my ass off and found out some interesting information about the senator. Found out his side chick was none other than a young woman named Shana who just happened to be a high-end escort. I confronted him, asked him if he wanted to offer a response for the article. He did not. Two hours later, the story was killed, my notes confiscated, and I was fired and blackballed as a reporter. Turned out my editor at the paper just so happened to be a good friend of Senator Crowley's." Cat raised her eyebrows at Camille. "So yes, I have a bit of a grudge against the senator."

Camille looked at Fern, who stood there, mouth agape, as if seeing her boss for the first time. She still couldn't believe Fern was innocent in all of this. "But you sent Fern to my office months ago," Camille said. "Had her claim to have knowledge of a series of crimes, of wrongdoings. You're not that clever, Cat. I figured that out two challenges ago."

"That wasn't me," Fern said quietly from her corner. "I told you, that wasn't me."

"Again, Fern is not that smart," Cat said, as if talking to a small child. "She had no idea what I was doing."

Camille was stunned. She was certain that Fern was Nan. How could she be so wrong?

"But the hummingbird tattoo," Camille said weakly.

"I don't have a hummingbird tattoo," Fern said. "It's a fairy. I told you I've never been to your office."

"But what about Nan?" Camille asked.

"Just another unfortunate client of yours," Cat said.

"I'd like to leave now," Camille said, getting to her feet and inching toward the exit. "I want no more part of this."

But Cat wasn't done yet. "You didn't just betray me though, did you, Doctor?" Cat leaned forward, elbows on her desk. "These people came to you for help, and you made them feel like you could help them. Like you were the only one who could. But when you grew bored, or when they ran out of money, you left them high and dry."

"You don't know what you're talking about," Camille said. How could Cat possibly know about the cash, about the tax evasion?

Cat read the question in Camille's expression. "Your receptionist has been very helpful." Cat leaned back in her chair and smirked. "You really should pay her more."

Geraldine? Camille thought. *Reliable, discreet Geraldine?* Camille couldn't believe it. Geraldine would know about the Alftan painting, would know about the clients who paid under the table, the tax evasion, would have known about Travis Wingo.

"Don't try to deny it, Camille," Cat said, opening a drawer, pulling out a file folder and dropping it on the desk in front of her. At the top of the folder was a tab that read "Wingo, Travis."

Camille's heart thumped. Somehow Cat knew about Wingo, but how much? Did she know how he had formed an unhealthy attachment to her? Did she know that he had broken into her house, and that her lies about him had gotten him killed? Did she know that he paid her off the books so Camille could pocket the cash?

Camille lowered herself back into her chair, her legs unable to hold her any longer. Geraldine. Her receptionist. Cat must have paid her handsomely to dig up dirt on Camille, and there was plenty of it.

It was over. Her career. She would never practice again. Cat had gotten the final word. Just like she always did.

FORTY

THE BEST FRIEND

Maire couldn't stand by silently any longer. "Cat? That's what you call yourself now?" It was Lina. Catalina, her best friend and Samuel's girlfriend.

Cat turned her eyes to Maire, then to Samuel. "*Traditore. Uccisore.* Betrayer. Killer."

She knew. Somehow, she knew what had happened on the road that night. "It wasn't like that," Maire said. "It was an accident."

Cat gave a hard little laugh. "An accident you caused."

"We would have helped him if we could," Maire said, the tears she had been holding back finally falling. "He was dead. There was nothing we could do."

Cat pursed her lips together. "I'm afraid that man's family wouldn't quite view it the same way. You let him lay there in the snow like garbage."

"It wasn't like that..." Maire began but faltered. What could she possibly say?

"Damon told you," Samuel said. "He was the only other person who knew what happened."

Cat nodded. "Though I'm a little pissed that it took him

nearly twenty years to tell me. He was in town for a work thing, and we got together, had a few drinks. Turns out Damon hasn't changed much since college. Still can't keep his mouth shut when he's drunk."

Maire shouldn't have been surprised that Damon didn't keep his promise. Yes, she and Samuel saved Damon from drowning, but it was a big secret to keep.

"I thought Damon couldn't tell me anything worse than that, but he had more," Cat said wistfully. For the first time during this odd reunion, Maire thought Cat looked sad.

"I needed you, Maire," Cat said. "After the night at the lake Samuel dumped me with no explanation, and you were just… gone. I was devastated. It took me years to get over you, both of you. Maire, you were my best friend and, Samuel, you were my first love. After Damon told me that he saw the two of you together, it made more sense. You killed a man and then sealed it with a sweet kiss."

"No," Maire protested. "It wasn't like that. Please, Lina. I have daughters. They need me."

"She doesn't care," Samuel said, still holding on to Maire's arm. "She's not going to listen." He set his dark eyes on Cat. "So what are you going to do?"

"Well, I had planned to release the truth as each one of you were voted off the show." Cat shook her head sadly at Maire. "But the game is obviously over, so we can't go out with the big bang I had originally planned. But this might be even better. I can still hit Send on the emails." Cat lifted the lid on her laptop. "A few clicks and the world will know exactly the truly awful people that you are. Finally, you are all going to get what you deserve."

Maire looked at Samuel. *Do something!* she wanted to scream. *Don't let this happen.* She had Dani and Keely to think about. She didn't care about the money anymore. She just wanted to get home to her girls.

Samuel seemed to read her thoughts and lunged for the laptop, but Cat was faster. She slammed the lid shut, held it to her chest, and got to her feet. "Now if you'll excuse me, I think we're done here," Cat said.

"You can't just blow our lives up like this and walk away," Maire cried, trying to block the exit. "Please, Lina, we can talk this through."

"The time for talking is long over," Cat said. "Now step aside, Maire."

Maire turned to Fern. "You can't be okay with this. It's emotional blackmail."

"I think Fern is just fine with things," Ned snapped. "She's complicit in every single sick moment of this so-called game."

"Sick?" Fern whispered. "After what you did to me, you're calling *me* sick?"

"Yeah," Ned said. "That's exactly what I'm saying." He held out his hand to Cat. "Now give me the fucking laptop."

"You'll have to catch me first," Cat said, ducking around Ned and running from the room.

FORTY-ONE

FiggyPudding13 stared at her phone, willing the cameras to come back on. She received the update that no one was hurt in the mishap on set and that the tech team was working on getting the show back on air ASAP, but she could barely stand the suspense. She wanted more Spin, Speak, Shoot. It was brutal in all the best ways. And it didn't hurt that she knew the Boyfriend and the Best Friend. They had gone to college together and Figgy wasn't a big fan of either of them. They were in the same friend group—she and Maire were even close at one point—but everything had fallen apart after Damon nearly drowned at the lake. She hadn't talked to Samuel or Maire since that night.

Figgy couldn't wait to find out who was going to be voted off next. Her bet was on Maire but she figured she would end up quitting before she got voted out. Maire was good at quitting. Besides, she couldn't stand it if Maire went home with all that money.

Already, social media was buzzing with rumors about the Executive. Dozens of women were coming forward claiming that Ned Bennett had sexually assaulted them in the exact same way Fern had described. He had gotten them alone in his office, forced them against a wall, pulled out a letter opener... It was awful, but Figgy wanted more. Did that make her a bad person? Probably.

Finally, the livestream started. Figgy practically squealed in excitement. At first, nothing was happening. The camera kept switching from empty room to empty room. The library, a corridor, the great hall, the kitchen, a sliver of the veranda where there was still a mess of broken glass and spilled wine.

Where is everyone? Figgy typed into the comments.

I think the Executive shot them all

Not funny

Oh, wait, I think something's happening

Figgy peered at her phone. They were right. Something was happening. The camera was pointed down the length of a corridor and a door had opened. Out stepped a woman. Her head was down, and she was rushing down the hallway, something tucked beneath her arm.

Who is that?

What's she carrying?

A book, maybe?

Why would she be carrying a book?

Following close behind the woman were the others. The Executive, Fern, the Boyfriend, the Best Friend, the Confidante. Figgy tried to get a better look at the new woman. She was slightly built and had blond hair cut into a sharp-edged bob. She was wearing all white, but it appeared to be smudged with dirt.

Who is that???

Then it dawned on Figgy. It was Cat James, or rather it was Lina, her old friend. Lina from Tanglefoot, whom she had lost contact with after college. Lina who used to date Samuel and was Maire's best friend. Lina who went on to become the famous Catalina James. But why would Lina be on the set of *One Lucky Winner*?

OMG! That's Catalina James, someone typed. I watch her makeup tutorials!

For some reason they were all scurrying after Lina. The camera flipped to another hallway and followed the group as they rushed to the great hall. Lina hesitated, as if trying to decide which direction to go.

It is her! It is. OMG, this show is the best!

Are they chasing her? Why?

Figgy watched as Lina feinted left, then right, and then moved toward the grand staircase, taking two steps at a time. The Executive wasn't far behind. Fern tried to snag the Executive's arm and hold him back, but he shook her off, nearly sending her down the marble steps. Figgy cringed.

Lina reached the top of the staircase breathing heavily, still clutching the thin silver object in her hands. She grasped the wrought iron railing and it wobbled beneath her fingers.

I think she's holding a laptop.

Yes! You're right.

The Executive slowly stepped closer to Lina, and Fern, once again, tried to pull him away. He wheeled around and shoved her, sending Fern tumbling to the ground.

I don't think this is part of the game.

No shit, Sherlock. Now's the time to call the police.

Don't you dare. I want to see what happens.

Seeing Ned push Fern to the floor seemed to incense Lina, and with her free hand, she struck out at the Executive, punching him in the jaw. His head reeled back but it didn't slow him down. He reached for the laptop and Lina slapped his hand away.

Samuel stepped in and roughly pulled the Executive away from Lina. "Back off, man," he said. His voice was muffled, making it difficult to understand him. Figgy strained to hear.

"Samuel, look," Maire said, nodding over the railing. Samuel abruptly dropped the Executive's arm. At the bottom of the steps, two cameramen appeared, along with a handful of others. They lifted the cameras to their shoulders and suddenly, the livestream zoomed in on the action and the audio became clearer.

"Let's go back in the office and talk about this," Maire urged. "Please."

"Talking's over," the Executive said, creeping forward. Maire tried to step in front of him, but he elbowed her aside. "Get out of my way," he snarled.

"Is this what you want?" Lina taunted. "Come and get it." She leaned against the balustrade and dangled the laptop over the edge.

Figgy held her breath. What was on that laptop?

"Cat, watch out!" Fern cried.

Figgy held her breath as a section of railing dipped backward, then snapped from its base, opening up like a garden gate. Lina was going to fall, but she grabbed on to the Executive and after one precarious moment, it looked like they were both going to go over the edge. Somehow, they regained their balance and remained atop the landing, holding on to one another, the laptop wedged between them. Figgy released a breath, her heart thundering in her chest. Lina was okay. Everyone was okay.

The camera zeroed in on Lina's face. Curiously, there was no relief, no fear in her expression. She was smiling, a soft, self-satisfied uptick of her mouth. Then, without warning, Lina stepped backward off the balcony, pulling the Executive along with her. Together, the two fell to the marble floor below.

FORTY-TWO

THE ASSISTANT

Fern ran down the steps and stood over Cat's unmoving body, crumpled beneath Ned's. They were both dead. The laptop was in pieces, scattered across the great hall. This couldn't be real. Around her she heard screams. Someone yelled, "Cut the cameras," while someone else shouted, "Keep rolling."

Above Fern, Maire, Samuel, and Camille looked down from the balcony, standing close to one another, frozen in disbelief.

Cat had fallen from the balcony and had taken Ned down with her. Live on air. Had *One Lucky Winner* been an act of revenge from the very beginning? Cat knew each and every one of the contestants. Intimately. She knew their darkest secrets and was determined to reveal them to the world in the most public and damning ways. Why?

In the distance, there were sirens. Someone had called for help. Fern moved past Alfonso and the others to the front entrance. She typed in the code that would open the gates.

Soon, the villa was filled with paramedics, police officers, and detectives. Fern saw the contestants whisked away. She was taken to the library and sat in one of the leather chairs for what felt like hours. Finally, a man who identified himself as a homicide detective sat down next to Fern.

"Homicide?" Fern asked in alarm. "But they weren't murdered. They fell."

"Whenever there's an unnatural death, we're called in to check things out, but I don't imagine our investigation will take all that long. It's not often we get the entire event on video. We've already talked to the other witnesses, and I would like to hear what happened from you."

Dazed, Fern explained how Ned Bennett and Cat fell from the balcony in a struggle over a laptop that held damning information about Ned. The video from *One Lucky Winner* would back that up.

Fern lied and said that while she had worked for Ned Bennett briefly ten years ago, she had no real interaction with him, that it was Cat who was a victim of his workplace abuse and wanted to bring him down.

"We've taken the laptop into evidence. What's left of it anyway," he said.

"And we'll need access to Ned Bennett's things. The accident scene and the room he was staying in will be off-limits until our investigation is complete. Do you have somewhere you can stay for a few days?"

Fern nodded numbly. "Yes, I have an apartment not far from here."

"Okay, then. Is there anyone in Ms. James's family who needs to be notified? Any next of kin?"

Fern shook her head. "There's no one." The detective lifted his eyebrows in surprise. "But I can take care of funeral arrangements and let her friends know."

"Alright, then," the detective said, getting to his feet. "We'll also need you to come down to the station for follow-up questions, but I anticipate we'll be able to wrap things up in the next few days."

"Tonight?" Fern asked. She was so tired she couldn't think straight.

"I'm afraid so," the detective said, and Fern rose from her chair reluctantly.

Together they moved through the villa and Fern's mind churned with what the formal interview at the police department might bring. What if they found out about how Fern locked Cat in the cellar? What if she was held liable for the accidental shooting during the competition or the dozens of other things that had gone wrong?

Fern joined Camille, Maire, and Samuel at the top of the stone steps. Together they watched as the coroner vehicles carrying Cat and Ned drove away. No emergency lights or sirens were needed. An officer led each of them to a different car that would take them to the police station for further questioning. No one said goodbye to Fern. She understood.

In the car on the way, Fern thought of all the things she needed to do if she managed to walk out of the police station a free woman. She needed to call the funeral home and Cat's attorney. And then there was the show. Fern knew she needed to make a statement of some sort. By now, the entire world knew that Cat James had died, that she died in a fall at the estate and that she was the mastermind behind *One Lucky Winner*. Fern didn't want to find out what people were saying about her but imagined it wouldn't be too kind. They never finished the game. There was no winner.

Three days later, Fern was back in the villa. It seemed so much larger now without Cat here. So empty. Despite the millions of times Fern fantasized that her boss would go down in a plane crash or choke on a chicken bone, she never actually wished her dead. Not really. But now Cat was gone, and Fern didn't know what to do.

She decided to start by purging the villa of any trace of the remaining contestants' wrongdoings. Fern knew that Cat didn't keep her most sensitive files in her office. Instead, she kept them squirreled away in the most secure spot in the estate. The wine cellar. She made her way down the stone steps, dreading having to spend time in the place where she'd kept Cat prisoner. Fern was so ashamed. Using her key card, she opened the door and propped it open using the wooden box that Cat had sat upon during her confinement. The files were hidden away in a secret storage space camouflaged to blend into the stone walls.

Destroying evidence wasn't as difficult as she thought it would be. Fern gathered all of the hard-copy files on Camille, Maire, and Samuel. She had also retrieved Cat's phone and deleted any email drafts pertaining to the remaining contestants. And there was damning evidence against them. Maire and Samuel had caused a man to die while playing a stupid, childish game and Camille had bilked the IRS out of hundreds of thousands of dollars.

It wasn't that Fern didn't think they should pay for their crimes and transgressions; she did, but hadn't they paid enough already? Maybe they deserved a second chance. Didn't everyone?

If the police came back and decided to comb through the rest of the house, they would find more evidence on Ned, as well as an interesting file on Crowley. Fern felt a little bit bad about that, but the cat was already out of the bag regarding the senator's extracurricular activities—his affair, his secret son, the illegal use of campaign funds. If the authorities chose to do a forensic search on Cat's phone, they might find more, but Fern didn't think they would. The fall had been ruled an accident caused by a damaged railing. Perhaps if Ned had survived, he would have been charged with assault or manslaughter, but he hadn't, so the case was closed.

Exhausted, Fern looked through the remaining files. Per usual, Cat was organized. Each file was clearly labeled and in alphabetical order. *Automobiles, Bella Luce, Credit Cards, Insurance, Medical.*

Fern paused at the file labeled *Medical.* It was unusually thick.

She had always thought Cat was exceptionally healthy—she exercised and ate well. Fern had never heard her mention needing to go to the doctor, but from what she saw here, Cat was being seen often by a doctor at a clinic in San Francisco. Fern flipped through the pages. There were lots of tests—MRIs, CTs, PET scans, and others.

Fern's fingers stopped at another sheet of paper. This one was a printout from Mayoclinic.org with the heading *Huntington's Disease*. She scanned the paper. *Inherited, mental decline, loss of speech, loss of motor capabilities*. And there was so much more, ultimately ending in death.

Did Cat have Huntington's? "Why didn't you tell me?" Fern whispered, and a new wave of sympathy for Cat washed over her. No one deserved that kind of pain and anguish, nor should have had to carry it all alone.

"No," Fern said firmly to the empty room. She brushed away her tears. She would not feel sorry for Cat. The more Fern thought about it, the more it was clear that Cat had used her as just another pawn in her game of revenge and retribution. Now, that would have been a great name for the show—*Revenge & Retribution*.

When she thought of the last ten years, all Fern could summon were the brutal hours, the constant berating, the awful pay. Her family barely spoke to her, and she had no friends, no social life, no hobbies. Her one and only purpose in life had been pleasing Cat James. And she had failed. Miserably. And what was she left with?

There were no winners here, certainly no one lucky winner. Ned and Cat were dead. Camille, Maire, and Samuel had to go back to their own lives with the knowledge that someone knew their deepest secrets. And to make it worse, there was no money. No big windfall. The one she felt the worst for was Maire. Obviously, Maire was no innocent—none of them were—but her daughter was still very sick, and Maire had to return to Calico with empty pockets.

Maybe that was Maire's cosmic punishment. She took a life and now she ultimately had to watch her own daughter suffer. Fern shook the thought away. That wasn't how it worked. But still, she hoped that Maire and her daughters would be okay. She wished the same for Camille and Samuel too.

Fern returned the medical file to its proper spot in the cabinet and continued looking. There was nothing until Fern's fingers landed on the final file tucked into the very back of the crowded cabinet. It was out of order. It should have been filed with the Fs. With difficulty, she pulled out the slim folder with her name on the tab.

She opened the file, and began to read. Inside were a just a few sheets of paper. The first was a handwritten letter addressed to her and dated just a few days ago, right before *One Lucky Winner* began.

Oct. 13
Dear Fern,

If you are reading this letter, I'm sure you have many questions about the events of the last several days and more than likely, I am dead. I hope my exit was spectacular! You know how I like to leave an impression.

My plan was to walk into the lake ala Virginia Woolf—except for stones in my pockets, I would be carrying my laptop and a stomach full of Ambien. But as long as the cameras were rolling, I don't really care how it all unfolded. Did we get a bazillion views?

By now, you have probably figured out that I am sick. Huntington's Disease. Not pretty. And you know how much I like things to be pretty. Anyway, I have it, and no matter how much money I have, or how big of a following I've amassed, there is no cure. If things progress as expected, one day I will die an awful death, all alone.

Instead, I have to go out in my own way, on my own terms. You must think me a bitter woman, seeking revenge in such a public, merciless way. But why shouldn't people pay for what they've done? Why should people like Maire, Samuel, Camille, Ned, and the senator be able to go through life with zero consequences? It isn't right. Sure, I could have just given the pertinent information to the police and to the people impacted, but this was so much more fun, don't you think?

I wasn't always this way. Once I was just as doe-eyed and loyal and ambitious as you are. I was just a girl who fell in love with a boy and wanted to be a journalist. We all know how that turned out.

I know I've worked you too hard, was too critical, too demanding, but you've always risen to the occasion. Well done. Now that I'm gone, I want you to go on and start thinking about your own dreams, your own hopes for the future. Whatever you decide to do, be true to yourself, be bold, and don't back down. It's always served me well. I've left a little something for you, to get you started. Use it wisely.

Sincerely,
Cat

Fern set the letter aside. Catalina had a terminal illness and planned the entire *One Lucky Winner* fiasco as her final swan song. It was unbelievable, but also so like Cat. Fern swiped away the tears and lifted the second sheet of paper from the folder.

I, Catalina James, being of full age and sound mind and memory, do make, publish, and declare this to be my Last Will and Testament, herby revoking and annulling any and all Last Will and Testaments or Codicils at any time heretofore made by me.

It was Cat's will. Fern recognized the executor as Cat's personal attorney, who would have been charged with seeing to all the details.

> *I direct that all my just debts, secured and unsecured, be paid as soon as reasonable after my death… All the rest and residue of my property, real, and personal, of every kind and description and whatsoever situate, which I may own or have the right to dispose of at the time of my death, I give, devise, and bequeath in total to my hardworking, loyal assistant…*

Fern's heart skipped a beat.

Fernanda Elizabeth Espa

She must have read it wrong. She started at the beginning, slowing down, taking in each word and phrase. Fern's name was the only beneficiary listed. It was Cat's signature at the bottom of the document and it had been signed and dated by two witnesses several days ago. It was official.

Cat had left her everything—the house and its contents, the cars, the businesses, the money. Everything.

After all of Cat's debts were settled, taxes paid, her net worth was approximately ten million dollars. Fern sat back, stunned. She had no idea that Cat had valued her in this way. She had no idea that her boss had thought of her as hardworking and loyal. Fern's eyes blurred with tears. Ten million dollars. In the end she was the one, the last one standing.

Fern was the one lucky winner.

FORTY-THREE

THE BEST FRIEND

Six Months Later

Maire quietly closed the door to Dani's room and stepped into the bright lights of the hospital corridor where her ex-mother-in-law was waiting. It had been a rough night, but Dani was sleeping peacefully, the infection that was ravaging her lungs under control for the moment.

"I got Keely off to school and brought you your mail," Shar said, handing her a cup of coffee and a small stack of letters. "I'll drive back this afternoon so I'm there when she gets home."

Maire nodded and looked at the mail in her hands. *More bills*, Maire thought, her stomach twisting.

"Go take a break," Shar said. "I'll go sit with Dani."

Maire leaned in to give her ex-mother-in-law a hug, then moved through the hospital corridors, taking an elevator up to the top floor. She walked through a set of doors to an outdoor garden, a quiet spot for families to find a little respite from the doctors, the nurses, the weight of watching a loved one suffer. The children's hospital was a few hours away from Calico, but it was equipped with the best care for pediatric cystic fibrosis patients.

Maire took a seat and set the stack of mail on the small café table in front of her. The morning April air was cool, but the sun was shining with the promise of a rare warm spring day.

Shar had been a godsend since Maire had come home from *One Lucky Winner*, helping with the girls, never asking what really happened on the show, giving Maire time to recover physically and mentally. Her cuts and bruises faded, her shoulder healed, but the nightmares remained. Maire lived in fear that her secret would be revealed, that a police officer would show up at her door to talk about a suspicious car accident that occurred twenty years before.

Though Maire resisted the urge, she couldn't help but look up the others online. Camille seemed to come out the other side relatively unscathed. Her podcast, *Your Best Life with Camille*, was bigger than ever and a book deal was in the works. There was a small article in the *San Francisco Chronicle* about some tax issues that Camille was having, but her lawyers assured everyone that it was a clerical oversight and was being remedied appropriately.

Samuel was back in Atlanta in his job as a district attorney but was in the process of setting up a nonprofit foundation called the Center for Prosecutorial Integrity. Many times, Maire had considered reaching out to him, for what she wasn't sure. To talk about Tanglefoot Lake, about *One Lucky Winner*? No, some things were better left alone.

After Ned's death, scores of women came forward with the same harrowing story. Ned Bennett was a predator, an abuser, a rapist. They had suffered alone for so long, but now had found a sisterhood and were working together to fight workplace abuse.

As for the senator, his wife of fifty years was in the process of divorcing him, and any hope of a run at the White House was gone. There was also plenty of tabloid coverage about the senator's mistress, who begged the media to leave her alone, to leave her son alone. They didn't.

More than anyone, the public wanted to know more about

Fern Espa, the face of *One Lucky Winner*. Cameras showed up wherever Fern did: at Cat's funeral, at her apartment, at the grocery store. After a respectful amount of time, Fern did the talk show circuit, appearing on all the major network morning shows. The second season of *One Lucky Winner* was in the works. There were missteps, Fern admitted, but in the new iteration, contestant safety would be paramount.

Maire had poured herself a big glass of wine after hearing that news. The press even hounded Maire and the girls for a short time. Camera crews showing up in tiny Calico was a big deal, but she and her family stayed behind locked doors, refusing interviews until the frenzy died down. All she wanted to do was return to her normal, everyday life, with her girls.

Maire went back to making her jewelry. Her Etsy store was getting a boost from the show's publicity. But it wasn't enough. Thankfully, Shar sold her small home and moved in with Maire and the girls to help make payments. They had a reprieve, but it was short-lived. Dani had a relapse and was in and out of the hospital all winter long.

Maire took a sip of her coffee and looked at the pile of mail in front of her. The bills were still piling up. She would lose the house; it was inevitable. With a sigh, she began to sort through the envelopes. An electric bill, a water bill, a vet bill, and, of course, medical bills. The final letter was different. The envelope was expensive, made from fine cream-colored linen paper, but it was the name on the return address that caused Maire to sit up. *Fern Espa.*

A letter from Fern? Why? Maire opened the envelope, holding her breath as she pulled out the folded card inside. The note card was made from the same expensive paper as the envelope and was embossed with the initials *F.E.* What could Fern possibly have to say to her? There had been no communication between them since that last day at the villa. Fern was probably afraid that the contestants were going to sue the show, or sue Cat's estate. Maire's mind spun as she opened the note card and another piece of paper fluttered to the ground.

With shaking fingers, Maire bent over to pick it up. It was a check. A check signed by Fern in the amount of one million dollars. Maire counted the zeros to be sure. Fern had given her one million dollars.

Tears filled Maire's eyes as she read the words that Fern had written on the note card in loopy cursive.

You would have won.
F.E.

★ ★ ★ ★ ★

ACKNOWLEDGMENTS

What a journey writing this book has been! *Everyone Is Watching* is quite different from anything I've ever written before. The idea for the story was big and ambitious, as were each of the larger-than-life characters I was able to spend the last few years trying to wrangle. It was also the first time I took a big step out of my beloved state of Iowa and set a novel almost entirely in another location. This story was written and rewritten several times, and its final iteration is nearly unrecognizable from the first cringe-inducing draft. Yes, I was a bit out of my comfort zone as I worked on this puzzle of a book, and yes, I loved nearly every moment of it.

Thank you to my ever-patient, ever-enthusiastic, and ever-supportive editor, Erika Imranyi, for never giving up on me. Thanks also to Nicole Luongo, whose insights and suggestions were spot-on. Much gratitude goes to everyone at Park Row, HarperCollins, and Harlequin, including the marketing, sales, art, and production teams, and to my wonderful publicist, Emer Flounders.

My agent and friend, Marianne Merola, has been with me since the beginning. Ten books in and we're still going strong.

I'm so grateful for her wise words, her friendship and for always believing in me.

Thank you to Amy Feld, an early reader who provided invaluable feedback, and to Nina Petrelli, who was kind enough to share her experiences with cystic fibrosis. She is a true fighter. This is one of the first novels that I didn't have the privilege of collaborating with former police chief Mark Dalsing. Mark passed away during the writing of this book, and I will greatly miss his knowledge, kindness, and sense of humor. I have so many friends near and far to thank. Nora and Sara—I treasure you both. Kimberly Belle and Kaira Rouda—the Killer Author Club—have been so much fun and the fact that I get to hang out with you and talk all things killing (of the fictional variety, of course) makes it all the better.

Every single day I am grateful for my family. Endless thanks go to Scott, Alex, Annie & RJ, Gracie, my brothers and sisters, and my dear mother. Sadly, my sweet father passed away as I was coming to the end of writing *Everyone Is Watching*. I was so lucky to be able to call this dear, gentle soul my dad and know he will forever be watching over me.